Flowers in December Trilogy

Flowers in December

Coming Home

SECOND chance

Books by Jane Suen

Children of the Future
Murder Creek

FLOWERS IN DECEMBER TRILOGY
Flowers in December
Coming Home
Second Chance

ALTERATIONS TRILOGY
Alterations
Game Changer
Primal Will

SHORT STORIES
Beginnings and Endings: A Selection of Short Stories

Flowers in December Trilogy

Flowers in December

Coming Home

Second Chance

JANE SUEN

FLOWERS IN DECEMBER TRILOGY: Flowers in December, Coming Home, Second Chance

FLOWERS IN DECEMBER
Copyright © 2016 by Jane Suen

COMING HOME: The Sequel to *Flowers in December*
Copyright © 2019 by Jane Suen

SECOND CHANCE: The Conclusion of the *Flowers in December* Trilogy
Copyright © 2019 by Jane Suen

www.janesuen.com

Printed in the United States of America

First Printing: February 2020

Library of Congress Control Number: 2020901129

Paperback ISBN: 978-1-951002-08-4
Ebook ISBN: 978-1-951002-07-7
Audiobook ISBN: 978-1-951002-09-1

In loving memory of my beloved mother.

Always and forever.

Contents

Flowers
IN
DECEMBER

JANE SUEN

Chapter 1

CONNOR CLOSED THE door behind him. He had been dreading this moment. He stood, immobilized. He saw her coffin…across the room, yet he couldn't move. After a long time, he finally took his first step. Reaching her open casket, his throat tightened as he gazed upon her face. He searched, in vain, for familiarity and warmth, but he found only the harshness of rigidity and coldness. His eyes misted, blurring his view. He stepped back as tears welled up and streamed down his face. A droplet fell, and then another as his tears turned into a torrent. No longer caring who would hear him, he released his sobs and wailed into the silent walls as if they could comfort him.

Connor knelt in front of the coffin and whispered her name. First he spoke softly and gently, between sobs racked with pain. Then he shouted her name, over and over, as if he could bring her back. He lost track of the time. Eventually, his sobs subsided.

Chapter 2

CONNOR LAY CRUMPLED next to her coffin, not willing to get up just yet, not ready to leave. He let his mind wander, thinking about his mother, himself as a little boy. This was the one time, the one trip Connor had never wanted to take.

It was a long drive across the state—he had traveled for miles and miles without seeing a gas station, without seeing a mile marker. As the city faded behind him and he drove further and further away, Connor felt a new sense of freedom. He opened his sunroof, basked in the warm rays of the sun, felt the rush of the wind, smelled the fresh air, and tuned into nature. His worries and burdens were swept away with the wind. The further away he got from the city, the better he felt. The vastness of this land, the beauty of it, stirred something deep inside of him. He had escaped the four solid walls of his office with his coveted window, the office he had worked so hard to attain…and that he was now imprisoned in. Long hours, day after day, with little time for fun.

When Connor had first received the call about his mother, he felt a twinge of guilt, knowing that he hadn't visited as often as he should have. Her death was sudden and unexpected. The last time he went home was over the holidays, last year. His family was small, just the three of them: him, his mom and dad. He didn't have kids, wasn't married. His parents had long stopped asking that question. His father had passed first. Now it was his mother. He was the only one left.

Images from long ago appeared, unbidden yet not unwelcome. The time she had surprised him with a birthday party and a pony ride. He had pestered her for this, but she had been cautious. He wanted what every little boy wanted, and he thought that a pony ride was just the thing. As a little boy, he had been fearless; he did crazy things just to see if he could. "Do first and ask later" was his motto. When his parents had found out, he got plenty of whippings for his mischief. He had grown up in the small town. He knew his parents were disappointed that he didn't stay, that he left like so many of the kids before him, packing up his bags as soon as he graduated high school and heading to the big, shining city. He got a little scholarship at the community college and worked hard to get established with solid academics. After two years, he transferred to the state college.

Connor had immersed himself in his studies. The thought of crawling back to his hometown and admitting failure drove him harder each time things got tough. During a particularly rough semester, he seriously thought about throwing in the towel—he even told himself he was meant to live out his life in the little town of Rocky Flats, doing what every generation of the Nortons had done. Maybe he was meant to inherit his family's little hardware store and live out his life there.

No! He was determined to get away.

Now, twenty years later, he was going home at age thirty-eight. He had achieved success and climbed the corporate ladder.

He remembered his mom on his last visit, straightening his shirt collar. "Connor, you know you have more clothes at home. You can come and get them anytime."

"Mom…I know you want me to wear them, but they are out of style. I have to buy new shirts and suits every year." He paused. "I rotate my shirts and suits and take them to the donation center. I have to dress a certain way."

"The styles will come back. They always do, you know."

"Yes, Mom. I know."

"You're my pride and joy, always remember this." She kissed him on the cheek and tugged lovingly at the corner of his shirt collar.

That was the last time he saw her.

Chapter 3

CONNOR STRAIGHTENED HIS clothes and steadied himself as he got up from the floor. Dale was waiting in a fancy red chair in the parlor when Connor walked out, and he immediately stood up.

"Mr. Williams, first I want to thank you. I don't know what I would've done at a time like this," Connor said.

"No worries. That is what we do here." He paused. "Do you have any questions or concerns?"

"As a matter of fact, I do," Connor said. "My mother…I have a beautiful new dress for her and her favorite pearls to go with it." He wanted her to look her best…one last time.

"Is that what you want for her viewing tomorrow?"

"Yes, I'd like for her to wear this dress and the pearls for her viewing and the burial." He turned toward the door. "I have it in my car now. I'll bring it in."

"Of course."

Connor went to the car and came back with the shopping bag. "I can't tell you how much I appreciate this."

"I do want to mention a detail about the flowers," Dale

said. "We ordered a mixed flower arrangement, but we've found out that one of the flowers is in short supply." He stopped, then continued. "The florist has offered to upgrade to another arrangement. Perhaps you can select something that suits your mother and pick out her favorite colors for flowers?"

"I'd like that."

"Good. The flower shop is across the street. You won't miss it."

"Thank you. I'll see you tomorrow."

Chapter 4

CONNOR REMEMBERED SEEING the flower shop when he drove into town. As a kid, he used to save his money to buy candy at the store next to it. He had no need to buy flowers until now.

He pressed his nose against the window and peered in, imagining that he could smell the flowers. A pleasant chime sounded when Connor opened the door. The aroma of fresh flowers and the splash of bright colors greeted him. Glancing around, he didn't immediately see anyone in the shop. Every space in the small store was smartly utilized in an attractive and efficient layout.

"Hello?" a faint voice called from back of the store. "I'll be with you in a minute."

"Take your time. I'll just be looking."

A petite brunette walked out a few minutes later. "Hi. I'm Mary Ann. Can I help you?"

She was short, reaching only to the top of his shoulders. He smiled at her. "Yes, I'm Connor Norton."

"You're Connor Norton!" she said. "I was just about to

call the funeral home to discuss some alternatives for your mother's arrangements. Your timing is perfect."

"I just came from there. Dale told me…there was a shortage with the flowers? I'm here to discuss other options with you."

"I'm glad you came. Please follow me, and I'll show you what we have."

She took him to the back of the store and showed him the arrangements she was working on.

"My mother's favorite color is white," Connor said. "I'd like to see what flowers you have in that color."

"Dale wasn't sure what colors to use, so I'd extra-ordered several varieties of seasonal white flowers. Here's what may work…" Mary Ann reached in the floral refrigerator and picked a selection of white flowers. She paused. "I don't have any lilies. I'm cautious about using them ever since a customer's cat almost died from lily poisoning. It doesn't take much to be potentially fatal…small ingestions of any part of the lily plant or pollen, even drinking the water from the vase."

"I didn't know lilies are so deadly. I've heard certain plants and foods are toxic to cats."

She made a new arrangement and tied it together with blue and white lace ribbons. "What do you think?"

Connor studied the arrangement. He nodded. "I think she would be very pleased."

"That's wonderful." Mary Ann's face lit up. She was eager to get back to work. "I'll add these flowers to the other arrangement, the wreath, and the table centerpiece." She looked up at him. "Would you like to come back later to look at them?"

Connor pulled out his cell phone to check the time. "I've got a few more stops to make. But I can come back later…maybe when you close?"

"That's fine. We close at five but I'm usually still here in the back till six or seven. I'll keep an eye out for you," Mary Ann said. "I'll put the CLOSED sign on the door, but I won't lock it. You can come in. I'll listen for the bell."

"Great. I'll stop by later."

Chapter 5

CONNOR WALKED OUT and closed the door, then headed for Mr. Monroe's office. Rocky Flats was a one-lawyer town, and Mr. Monroe did legal business for everybody. His office was prominently located in the middle of town, right next to the bank. Connor always thought Mr. Monroe situated his office there so he wouldn't have far to walk each time he deposited the money he collected from his clients in town.

He opened the door. A woman in her fifties sat behind the desk, dressed in a severe business suit. Black-rimmed glasses perched on her nose. A slight lifting of her right eyebrow was the only sign of welcome. "Yes?"

"Hi, I'm Connor Norton. I have an appointment to see Mr. Monroe."

"Oh yes, Mr. Monroe is expecting you," she said as she reached for her desk phone. "I'll tell him you're here."

"Thank you."

A minute later the door opened and Mr. Monroe himself came out. The lawyer had known the Norton family for many years and done business with Connor's father. He shook Connor's hand with enthusiasm. "Good to see you. Please come in."

He ushered Connor into his office, nodding to his secretary.

"I've been expecting you," he said.

"Hello, Mr. Monroe. I just got back in town."

"I'm very sorry to hear about your mom. My deepest condolences."

"Thank you."

"I know this has come all of a sudden. We have some business to attend to, papers to sign," said Mr. Monroe as he pulled a folder of documents from a drawer in his desk.

"You have my full attention," said Connor, sitting straight up in the brown leather chair. He felt the unforgiving stiffness of the chair and squirmed, wishing he could sink into a soft, cushioned seat before getting to business. The discomfort of the chair was nothing compared to what he was feeling inside. He wasn't ready to sign off on any big decisions now, even if Mr. Monroe insisted.

An hour later, Connor was back out and walking in the street. He turned toward the church. It was always open—a sanctuary welcoming all.

"Pastor Maller?" he called as he went into the church.

"Oh, Connor," said the pastor warmly. "How are you?"

"I'm fine," said Connor. "I'm sorry to trouble you, but I wonder if you'd say a prayer with me…for my mother."

"Of course. Please come in."

"I just left the funeral home and the flower shop. Is there

anything else we need to discuss before the service?"

"Well…there is the matter of the music. Does your mother have a favorite song?"

"Oh, that's easy. 'Climb Ev'ry Mountain' was my mother's favorite."

"I happen to have that music," the pastor said with a twinkle in his eyes. "I can ask my daughter to sing this song if you'd like."

"Oh, that'll be wonderful. Please ask her."

"I'm sure she'll do it. She's sang this with your mom and knows the song well."

"My mother would absolutely love that!" Connor breathed a sigh of relief. He had not thought of the music for the funeral service and was glad the pastor had brought it up. "Could we pray together for my mother now? I'd like that."

The pastor nodded as he started the prayer.

Chapter 6

WALKING BACK OUTSIDE into the brightness of the day, Connor welcomed the afternoon sun. He raised his head, wanting the rays to penetrate deep down, awakening the parts of him dwelling in the darkness. The day so far had been somber and filled with sorrow. He needed to grieve, and he knew there would be days and days ahead when he would mourn his mother. For now, he closed his eyes and turned his face toward the sun, basking in the sunshine. He thought he felt the gentle touch of God for a moment.

Connor checked the time on his cell phone. It was 4:30. He had another stop to make at the hardware store.

"Hey, Ron," Connor called to the guy loading bags of mulch into the back of a customer's pickup. He had known Ron since Rocky Flats Elementary School.

Ron turned and, recognizing Connor, shouted, "Hey man, you're back!"

Connor reached his friend quickly with long strides and patted him on the back. "Glad to see you out here working so hard."

"Shucks, man, you should have seen the last load," he said with a chuckle. "You just got in?"

"Yep. I'll be staying at the house to get things in order."

"So how long are you planning on staying?"

"About three weeks. If I get done earlier, I may go back earlier."

"Stay for a bit if you can. We haven't seen much of you," Ron said with a grin, adding, "Even if you get done earlier."

"We'll see about that. I've got a lot of work to do back at the office."

"See you around, then," said Ron. Then he turned serious. "You know we are closing the store tomorrow…out of respect for your mother."

"Thanks, man. This means a lot…you can't imagine how much it means to me."

"Your parents were kind to me. Your dad sold me the business after I'd worked for him for over ten years."

"Yes, I know."

"I thought I could do it all, but I didn't know how much was involved in a business." He shook his head. "Don't get me wrong. I love the work, but it's a little more than I can handle."

"So what are you thinking of doing?"

"Well, I've been thinking about getting a partner, and then expanding your father's old hardware business."

"Expanding?"

"Yup. Adding an outdoor section with lawn mowers, furniture, and chain saws; a garden center with plants and more; maybe some guns and ammo. I'm also thinking about expanding the kitchen wares and adding more appliances."

"Sounds interesting. My mom would have liked the kitchen gadgets and appliances. But guns and ammo? I really don't see the need in this peaceful town."

Ron cleared his throat. "We can talk about it. I know you just got in town, but let me put it out to you now. I want to make this offer to you first, partners 50/50. It feels like it's the right thing to do."

"I appreciate this. I'd like to think it over. When do you need my answer?"

"I'll need to know by the end of the year, so don't take too long."

Connor nodded. "Thanks."

He dashed across the street to the flower shop. It felt good to be home. He didn't have to drive around town looking for everyone. People moved in a slower pace here than in the city, or so it seemed. But maybe it was just that people were more relaxed, and things felt more natural. The stress of city life seemed like a lifetime removed. Connor was determined not to think of work and just be here.

Chapter 7

"HEY, I'M BACK!" shouted Connor as he opened the door to the little flower shop and the bell dinged. Connor made a mental note to ask Mary Ann what the bell was made of, what metal made such an enchanting sound.

Mary Ann came from the back of the store, gesturing for him to follow her. "Here, I'd like to show you my new arrangements. Come on back."

Connor walked back, not knowing what to expect. When he got there, his eyes opened wide. "What…you did all this?"

Mary Ann had made good use of her time and her skills. The arrangements were beautiful and elegant. She had saved special blue ribbons and exquisite white lace for a time like this. *This is fit for a queen!* thought Connor.

"Well, do you like it?"

"Like it? I LOVE it!"

"I had a little creative inspiration and added tiny blue flowers in the background, and it was absolutely the right touch to accentuate the table arrangement."

"This is so lovely. Thank you!" gushed Connor as he admired her handiwork. "My mother…this is a lovely tribute…more than I expected."

"I'm glad," said Mary Ann, blushing a bit.

"Well, how can I thank you enough?" said Connor.

"You already have," said Mary Ann. "I'll have these delivered to the funeral home in the morning."

Chapter 8

CONNOR WALKED BACK to his SUV. He felt hungry and decided to stop at the grocery store on his way back to the house. It hadn't changed much. He quickly grabbed a few things for breakfast and dinner, plus a can of coffee and sugar. He would come back later.

Pulling up in the driveway of his family home, he couldn't help feeling sad at the way it looked, a bit neglected. The house needed a fresh coat of paint, and the yard needed work. His dad had taken care of a lot of this when he was alive. Connor parked his car, taking out his luggage and the grocery bags.

Opening the door, Connor smelled the faint odor of musk. He put his suitcase in his old bedroom and quickly ran around, opening the windows and curtains to bring in the light and fresh air. The house was orderly and neat as always. His mom had taken great care to keep it that way.

Soon Connor was heating food for his dinner, and the coffee was brewing. Connor felt exhausted and gratefully sought out the couch. He turned on the TV, but not much was on. The usual stuff...somebody got an award, the weather, upcoming activities. Not much crime here. They did announcements of birth, weddings, and deaths. Connor saw a notice come up about his mother's funeral, along with the lovely photo of her. He looked at the picture and remembered one more thing. Glancing at the clock, he hesitated, wondering if it was too late to call. He picked up the phone.

"Hello, Mr. Williams? This is Connor Norton again." He paused. "I hope it's not too late, but I just thought of something."

"No problem. How can I help you?"

"Well...you know the picture of my mother...the one that was in the paper?"

"Yes."

He nodded. "That's the one...do you have that picture for the service tomorrow?"

"I do."

"Oh, good. What size do you have?"

"Five by seven."

"Do you think it's possible to have a larger size blown up and framed for the funeral?"

"I'll see what I can do."

"Great. Oh, by the way I was at the flower shop. They will be delivering the arrangements tomorrow morning. They are very lovely," Connor added.

"Excellent. Will that be all?"

"Yes...that's all...see you tomorrow." He finished the call.

At some point after Connor ate his dinner, he dozed off on the couch. He was so tired that he didn't even make it to his room.

Chapter 9

THE GRATING NOISE of the garbage truck rudely awoke him the next morning. Connor jolted, realizing that he had forgotten to put out the garbage. It was pointless to run out now, so he lay back for a moment, listening to the birds chirping. It looked like another beautiful and bright day. Sunny. No sign of rain.

Connor jumped into the shower, cleaned up, and dressed in a t-shirt and jeans. Before the afternoon service, he planned to come back to freshen up and put on his new suit—his best suit. He fixed a plate of scrambled eggs and toast. It was a light breakfast but enough for him to get started. He brewed a fresh pot of coffee, planning to drink it black. He took the paper and his cup of coffee outside to sit on the porch. Glancing through the paper, he quickly got caught up with the goings-on in the town. It was a small paper, but full of local news, events, and activities. There was a section for national and international news also, as well as comics, ads, and a crossword puzzle.

Connor smiled, recalling how many times he watched his

dad grab the crossword puzzle page first. His mom would try to get his dad's attention whenever he took too long doing the puzzle. She had gotten irritated more than once at how *slow* he was. She didn't quite get it…that it was relaxing for him, that he took his time thinking about the words. Honestly, it was possible that his dad even took a little longer than necessary to do the crossword puzzle on occasion, especially if she was bugging him. Little things like not putting the toilet lid down or leaving dirty socks around bothered a lot of married folks, but with his mom and dad, he recalled them mostly arguing about the crossword puzzles.

His mom, if truth be told, felt left out whenever his dad did his crosswords. Truly, she felt he had closed a door on her. When he was doing a crossword, she'd lean over his shoulder, peer at what he'd put down on the puzzle, and sometimes she'd shout out a word or two before he could think it. But he didn't like that either. He didn't want her doing that, and he certainly didn't want her to shout out a word before he could put it down. No, no, no! That he didn't like. Connor could see this scenario playing out now…and smiled. He had watched this so many times; it was always the same thing over and over. As many times as he had seen them, they always acted as if they've never had the conversation before. It was amusing to him, but they were serious about it, utterly serious. This was a habit, a routine they did week after week, for years, as long as he could remember.

Chapter 10

IT WAS ALMOST lunchtime. Connor wasn't feeling hungry. Really, he was too nervous to eat. He got out his new suit and dressed slowly before driving to the funeral home. The door to the funeral home was open already. Inside, a table was laid out with brochures about his mom's service, with the eye-catching flower arrangement in the middle and the sign-in book next to it.

Entering the sanctuary, he went straight to see his mother. She was wearing the new dress and the pearls, looking beautiful at rest. A spectacular large flower arrangement was placed next to her. The enlarged eight by ten framed picture, his favorite photo of his mom, was propped on a stand, framed by the gorgeous wreath of white flowers. Everything was perfect.

Connor greeted the pastor, then sat down and waited for the service to start. People came in quietly and filled the room. Somewhere he heard the soft sounds of notes played on a flute! It was calming and echoed in the room as it floated on air. He was lost in the music, surrounded by the beauty and fragrance of the flowers. As he gazed at her picture, the happy memories flooded back. He saw his mother dancing in the field, arms out and twirling, happy and laughing. He smiled. It was as if she was singing and dancing in the meadow and in the hills. Then he heard the most pleasing sound…a voice that started low and then soared higher and higher singing, "The hills are alive with the sound of music…"

He looked around and saw the girl singing—well, she sounded like a girl, but she was a woman singing. The passion and beauty of her voice captivated him. Her face lit up like an angel singing to his mother. He imagined that his mom could hear this music and was singing along with the song she knew so well and had sung to him so many times before. He was really touched. He composed himself and fell into a trance for the rest of the song, forgetting everything else except for this special tribute to his mother.

This was the moment when he realized the beauty of it all. At that moment, he put aside the sorrow. For he was here, among all these people, in this sacred place, surrounded by beauty, music, and love…there would be no sorrow. No sorrow would be sent to her along the way where she must go now. They would send music, happiness, and love. For where she was going, there would never be any pain or sadness; there would be only eternal joy. And there, he firmly believed, she would forever rest in peace. The thought of his mother in eternal peace calmed and comforted him. She would be there waiting for him when it was his time, and she would join her ancestors. That he also believed. So he was really happy at the moment, as he should be, in this, her moment. This was the celebration of her life! A person only got to do this once. This was her moment. The world was a better place for her having lived in it. And she left her mark behind, forever, in this world.

No matter if you were a good person or a bad person, Connor truly believed that when a person leaves this world, they would have a place to go to that would either give them peace or would put them in torment for eternity because of what they did in their lifetime. Or maybe, just maybe, there was a third place, another place between the two, where they would get another chance if they really wanted to be a better person—there would be another way to get a second chance…not in this life, but in the next life, in the middle place…in-between the other two places. Maybe.

But Connor had to believe in something, in the balance of the world or how it all worked. Maybe the good, bad, beautiful, and ugly all had to be balanced. The world wasn't all good or all bad, and it wasn't all beautiful or all ugly. Maybe in the next place there would still be all of this; maybe there would be a chance to have another life that turned the bad into the good or the ugly into the beautiful. Because if everything was the same, then all would be the same. There would be no souls to save if all souls were good. There would be no ugliness if all were beautiful. Would we get tired of it if everyone and everything was good and beautiful? Would we appreciate what each person had if we didn't have anything else? Would anyone know what it was like to be bad or ugly? Would we feel the angst of those who yearned to be, even for one day, good and beautiful? Who would yearn to be bad and ugly? Maybe there would be people who would yearn for that? That and everything in between. Connor's thoughts rambled on and on.

Was there an afterlife? Could he know for sure that she'd never feel the cold? Or the pain? Would he meet her again one day when he was also gone from this world? He wouldn't know the answers until he took the journey, whatever path he would be on. Who knew the path and where it would take him? He would have to see.

The music had stopped. The pastor was speaking, Connor quickly realized. At first he didn't catch the words, but he felt them. The way the pastor was talking, the feeling he was expressing, was so eloquent, so beautiful. Connor didn't have to listen to the words to catch the meaning. It was obvious that it was a tribute to someone dear. The dearly departed mother that Connor so loved. She would have liked it if she could have heard. She would have enjoyed hearing his stories and what he shared.

Connor had chosen not to speak at her service. He wanted to pay his respects quietly and privately. He couldn't imagine getting up in front of all these people, what he would say. He felt a twinge of guilt. He had left twenty years ago and only came back infrequently, staying a few days at a time. Most visits were during the holidays, the obligatory times. A few times he came home for important events like birthdays, anniversaries, or whenever he could make it home. It wasn't like he even knew everybody anymore. He felt like a stranger. Then again, he had changed over the years, and folks who remembered Connor as a child no longer recognized him. His guilt was mixed with regret, with remorse that he hadn't come back as often or stayed as long as he should have. He had become more distant from his dad. Initially, he had pulled back to work out some of his issues. Over the years, the resentment kept him at bay, and he barely spoke to his dad when he came home. His dad was a man of few words anyway, but even so it was noticeable that they hardly talked. There was no meanness between them, just a thin veil of ice that could not be warmed over. His mother pleaded with him, but Connor was stubborn. There were times he looked in his mother's eyes and saw her love. He knew she wanted to see more of him, that she missed him; she didn't even have to say it. He knew that no matter what, no matter how far away he was, she loved him. He loved her too, but he didn't really say it as he should have. It was something he would have to live with. There was nothing he could do about it now.

Connor went through the rest of the service, his memories wandering in and out, not quite sure what he had heard but lost in his thoughts, thinking things that he wanted to say to his mother if she were here. He heard quiet sniffles. Here and there a muffled sob could be heard. Others had tears on their faces and dabbed with tissues or handkerchiefs. He watched as more people expressed their grief. He came out of his grief to join the rest of the congregation in their collective grief, all the while rejoicing her life.

The service was coming to an end and he could hear the

music once again. The flute played; this time it was joined by a violin, and together the notes became a melodious symphony of joyous sounds. The music uplifted and calmed, it flowed and soothed, until his heart was salved, this passage was taken, this tribute done, and her life was honored.

He stood as the service ended. People came up to talk to him, and he went through the motions, greeting each and hearing their words of comfort. The words blended together. Sounding alike and yet distinct. He was polite and thanked everyone for coming. He didn't attempt to smile except for the few times when he returned a smile. Connor stood by her as people came to pay their last respects. It was quiet, orderly, and people even whispered so as not to disturb her rest.

He had a choice of burial or cremation. It wasn't something they had talked about, but he remembered one conversation where he had overheard his mother talking at another funeral, telling someone she was glad there would be a burial. There was something so physically final about totally letting go, scattering ashes to the wind, to the earth, or to the sea. Yes, it was something he had thought about. But a part of him also didn't want to do that. Burial was a time-honored way to go.

He knew she would be buried here, next to his father, in her best new dress and the pearls. He would have a place to come visit her. He could touch the ground, touch her headstone, and know that she was safe in her resting place. He had already purchased a plot next to his mom to prepare for his own journey. He knew that each day he had in the world was one less day that he would have to live, and that each day he lived took him closer to where he was going. He didn't know when or how or where it would happen. But he knew it was inevitable. As life was inevitable, so surely was death. He would be her child forever. She would be his mother forever. Nothing would ever change that. Ever.

Chapter 11

CONNOR SLEPT IN the next morning. He didn't have appointments or activities scheduled. He was going to let the day unfold, see how it went, and not plan anything. He still had three weeks minus two days at home.

One of the things Connor knew he had to do was to go over their belongings. His parents didn't have a lot of things, or it didn't seem like it. But looking over the house, he realized they had more than he had thought. There were several filing cabinets and boxes of stuff in the attic as well.

He stretched his legs and got out of bed. He took his time making breakfast. While the coffee was brewing, he went out on the porch and got the paper. He absentmindedly checked the classified section. He did this in the city, checking out jobs whenever he could, just to see what was out there and see what skills were in demand. He was really on top of his game, some people would say.

But there wasn't a large classified section in this paper, just a few postings. He hadn't expected to see a lot. A few handyman ads, some yard work, odds and ends. There was an ad for a part-time assistant to help with bookkeeping and paperwork. It didn't give the name of the business, just a number to call. He looked at the next section and saw some items for sale. That seemed like a good idea for the stuff he would have to sell. As a matter of fact, he hadn't even thought about what he would do about the house either. Yes, the house.

He made a mental list of the things he had to do; the list was getting longer and longer. The three weeks were suddenly shrinking—so much to do and so little time! *No, don't worry*, he thought. This was his forte! Doing things in so little time. He could do this. There might be other things he hadn't thought of. He would have to factor that in as well. The thought of rest and relaxation vanished into thin air. *Oh, this is not happening!* He should have asked for four weeks off at the onset instead of three. He quickly rolled up his shirt sleeves. He was not wasting any more time.

First, Connor decided to take inventory and see what could be discarded, sold, or kept. If things were old, he would throw them away. As for some of the other things, better yet, he'd rather donate than sell them; that would also save a lot of time. Besides, it would be more personally satisfying than making money from his parents' belongings. Donating to someone who could use the things, who needed the things, was the way to go. Connor grabbed a sheet of paper and jotted down his plan. He got another sheet and started making a list of everything he had to do, putting a big star next to the more important items. He reviewed the list and revised it until he was satisfied.

List in hand, he walked around the house, taking another quick inventory before getting started. The plan should be workable, if he kept to the schedule. He was determined to make use of all his time here and get everything done. He hoped to make the right decisions and honor his parents while he was at it.

Connor took another sheet of paper and made a shopping list of needed items. He had to get boxes, tape, and trash bags for the things he was going to donate, keep, or throw out. He also added a note to check everything in the attic. The walk up stairs to the attic made it easier to bring things down. There were a few pieces of furniture up there, but he wasn't worried about that. He would get those later; they would probably be the last things he'd handle from the attic. A fair number of boxes were stored up there. Some were labeled and some were not. He had no idea what was up there; he would have to find out by opening the boxes one by one. The thought of doing that didn't strike his fancy, but he was determined to plow through as best as he could. He wanted to honor his parents and pay his respects. The thought of hiring some stranger to haul all their possessions away, without even looking at anything, seemed brutally cold and disrespectful.

Chapter 12

ABSORBED IN THOUGHT, Connor didn't hear the knock at the door the first time. It sounded again. He rushed to the door.

"Oh, hi Connor…sorry to disturb you. I'm your mother's next door neighbor," said a grey-haired woman. Her hair was pulled up in a bun and a cat was nestled in her arms.

"Oh, hi Mrs. Rainer. Please…do come in."

"I'm just dropping by," she said almost apologetically. "When this happened, I took little Tom in. I thought I'd keep him for a few days…you know…until things settled." She shifted her foot then reached out to hand Tom over to Connor. "Here…"

It took Connor a minute to figure out what she meant. He had quite forgotten about Tom. Up until now, he hadn't even thought about Tom or where he was or what happened to him.

"Hmm…Mrs. Rainer," he stumbled. "I'm quite thankful that you kept Tom for a few days." He reached out to take the cat. Tom jumped out of her arms and onto the floor, acting as if he owned the place before leaping on the couch and curling up. *Well…this is his home!* Connor reminded himself with a smile. Now that Tom was here, Connor could sure use the company. He knew how much his mom had loved Tom and pampered him. There were only so many times he could listen to her rave about how special the cat was. But now he was happy to see him. "Thank you, Mrs. Rainer."

"I'm right next door. If you have any questions, just come by." She took a step closer and whispered, "I miss her too…"

"I know."

Mrs. Rainer turned around and, as she walked out, picked up a bag of cat food she had placed next to the door. "Here, you'll need this. This is Tom's favorite food."

Connor grabbed the bag. "Thanks, ma'am."

"Oh, Connor…one more thing…"

"Yes, ma'am?"

"Just call me Dorothy…better yet, Dottie for short."

"You bet…ahem…Dottie."

She nodded in approval and left.

Chapter 13

CONNOR TOOK THE cat food into the kitchen. As he passed Tom, he rattled the bag. "Hey, fella, are ya hungry?"

Tom didn't pay him any mind, not even to perk up his ears at the sound of the food. Obviously he had just been fed. Otherwise, he would have come running. Connor knew this much about Tom. The thought of Tom keeping him company for the next three weeks cheered him up. He had grown up with cats because of his mother's love for them.

At one point his dad had insisted on his right to have a dog, so, briefly amid all the cats there was a single dog—a yellow furball that was lovable and so cute as a puppy. Well, that didn't last long, as the puppy quickly grew up to be a good size, a medium-sized dog in the fifty-pound range. Connor loved that dog. He played with him, and they ran in the meadow together. In a small town, folks let their dogs run in the fields. Connor couldn't recall ever seeing dogs tied up in the country like he saw in the city. The dog—*his dog,* was how he thought of him—was named Olive. He was the sweetest dog and a wonderful companion. Perfect for a little boy.

Olive loved to chase, not just Connor but almost any moving thing. One day, when Connor came home from school, he could not find Olive. He looked everywhere but didn't see him. Olive would usually come running to greet him. Connor wanted to tell Olive when he left that morning that he wished he could take him to school. He wanted to explain that the school wouldn't allow that, so Olive had to stay behind. Olive looked so sad sometimes when Connor left. Connor couldn't wait to come home to see Olive. So that day, when Olive didn't come to meet him, Connor knew something was very wrong.

No one said anything to him for a while, until Connor couldn't take it anymore. Then his dad put him gently on his lap and said, "I'm sorry. So very sorry."

Connor knew, and his heart sank. He started crying; he was scared; he didn't want to hear; he didn't want anything to have happened to Olive.

"I want to tell you that it was quick," his dad said. He was a man of few words, but that day he said more than Connor had ever heard him say. "Olive had run outside to go across the street to play with a child. A pickup truck whipped around the corner and came charging up the street, going faster than he had a *goddamn* right to." Connor's dad paused to control his anger. Then he whispered, "Olive never saw it coming."

Connor cried for his dog, demanding over and over again, "I want Olive. I want my Olive!" He thought if he asked for him so many times, the universe would give him what he wanted. He cried, "I want Olive!" until his voice turned hoarse.

From that day on, Connor never asked for another dog.

They buried Olive and said a prayer. His parents never spoke of Olive again. And that was it.

Chapter 14

CONNOR SAT DOWN next to Tom on the couch. "How are you, old man? You must be, what, about four years old now?" he said as he playfully stroked Tom's back. "I know, you're not exactly an old man, but I'm calling you an old man just to bug ya!"

Tom turned over on his back and offered his soft underbelly. Connor tickled and stroked the cat's belly just the way he liked. In no time at all, he had Tom *purrrring*. If Tom could smile, he would have a huge smile plastered on his face. For extra, Connor threw in the ears…stroking behind each ear. He was giving Tom the royal treatment. This was what he had to offer: a really fine homecoming. He couldn't resist picking Tom up and holding him close to his chest, feeling the warmth of his little body and the soft hairs touching his cheek and tickling his nose. "Oh Tom, I'm so glad you're home," he cried out softly before giving Tom a quick rub on the cheeks for good measure.

Tom returned the favor and put his paws out, first stretching and then touching Connor's nose. Connor wiggled his nose and shook Tom's paws playfully, knowing that Tom would never hurt him. He loved Tom. It was so good to have Tom home. He made a mental note to be sure to thank Mrs. Rainer—Dottie—again as he gently put Tom back on the couch, where he curled up and settled in a nook. Yes, Tom was home and he was going to stay.

Tom was mostly an indoor cat, but he had his moments when he wanted out to chase butterflies or go after a mouse. Connor remembered the time he came home and saw a dead mouse on the doormat outside the house. He almost had a fright. But it turned out that it was Tom who had carried the dead mouse in his mouth and laid it on the front door mat for all to see. That was Tom's gift. It was what he had to offer and what he gave them.

Connor's mom had taken care of it. She even made a big fuss over Tom, telling him how wonderful he was to give them this gift. She thanked Tom by giving him special treats. She went overboard with it, Connor thought at the time. But he kept his thoughts to himself. Later, he saw his mom wrap the dead mouse in newspaper and take it out to the trash can. So much for Tom's gift.

Tom was truly a beautiful cat. He was a tabby, all stripes and orange with huge green eyes and long whiskers. Tom had a thing that he liked to do, putting his paws on door knobs to open doors. Connor had never seen any other cat do this, and he was convinced of Tom's superior intellect. Other cats never made the connection between the knobs and opening doors.

Watching Tom lick his paws one by one amused

Connor. He liked that cats were self-cleaning and fastidious. But for the life of him, he couldn't figure out why they would have anything to do with dirty little rats or mice. Maybe cats didn't get the message that those critters…no, scratch that…those *rodents* carried disease and germs. Tom would have to be pretty quick to catch them, with his wits and legs primed for the chase. Connor had never seen Tom in action, but he knew that he was good…so very good. Fifteen times, if you're counting.

Chapter 15

CONNOR ADDED A few things to his shopping list, including a special welcome-home treat for Tom. He added a few toys as well. There was no reason why he shouldn't pamper him a bit; after all, he was special. "Hey Tom, I'm going shopping…you hold the fort now." It was silly, but he felt good saying it. Talking to Tom like he was family…well, they were a family, living together. He loved it.

On the way to the store, Connor felt really good. He decided that the rest of the day was going to be his and Tom's alone. They would enjoy each other's company, catch up on old times, and just relax. That sounded terrific, and he was looking forward to it. Tomorrow would come soon enough, with all the work, the worries, and the stress of tackling his to-do list. Money was no problem, as he had plenty. He knew his parents' house was paid off, so he didn't have to think about a mortgage. As for Tom, that was a no-brainer. He would take Tom wherever he went. He had already decided he would take Tom with him when he went back to the city. For Tom was all the family Connor had now. He would miss Tom if he left without him. As for his condo, having cats was no problem. There were several cats in the complex already. Tom would even have other cats to play with, although he wasn't sure Tom would like that. He might like to have the place to himself. He had grown up in the house by himself.

So Tom was like an only child, except he was an only cat. Connor would keep Tom and not add other cats to the household. One was enough for now. Tom would probably be all he could handle anyway. He'd just have to get used to living indoors in the smaller quarters of the condo. That would be an adjustment for Tom; he'd have to accommodate to a bit of downsizing when he went to Connor's home. Connor would make sure there was a perch on the window for Tom to look out and watch his comings and goings. He'd make sure the window was up a crack so Tom could feel the breeze come in through the window screen. The upstairs bedroom window would work for that. Connor was busy making plans for Tom to stay with him. He was going to keep him safe and take care of him, for as long as he lived. That was a promise.

Chapter 16

SATURDAY MORNING, CONNOR went shopping. He was so absorbed in his thoughts and focused on finding the cat food aisle that he bumped into another cart. "Oh, I'm so sorry!" said a startled Connor as he looked up from the cart. Recognizing Mary Ann, he asked, "Are you okay?"

She laughed. "I'm fine. You look like you're in a hurry," she said. "Need some help?"

"I'm…uh…I'm just picking up some cat food and treats for my cat."

"You have a cat…you just got here?"

"It's my mother's cat. His name is Tom."

"That's a cute name. I have a cat too. Her name is Isabella."

"Oh, maybe Isabella would like to meet Tom sometime?"

"Ha," she said. "That could be arranged." She looked at him. "You can call me."

"Yeah, let's do that. I gotta run…Tom is waiting for me at home."

Chapter 17

WHEN CONNOR GOT home, Tom was exactly where he had left him. As Connor put away his groceries, he wistfully thought that was what he wanted to do: sleep the day away. But he knew better. With a sigh, he started to tackle the stuff in the first room. He had bought tags to label furniture to be donated and boxes to be thrown out or kept. After a while, he had a system. Soon Connor was absorbed in the process, throwing stuff in different piles: donate, discard, or keep. This would be his first sweep. After he got the easy stuff out of the way, he'd take time to go through the to-keep pile. Connor made steady progress and worked at a fast clip. By suppertime, he had already gone through one room. Satisfied, he stopped to eat and rest.

Hearing the shaking of the cat food bag, Tom flew into the kitchen and *meowed*. He zoomed right to the cat dish and got a few treats, along with the dinner Connor had put out. The water bowl was clean and full, but Tom paid no attention to it. Connor started humming and really felt good about this day. Monday he would call the donation place to arrange for the first pick-up; he would have to do that a few times to get the furniture and other stuff moved out. That would free up more space for him to work. He had already stacked up several boxes of paper and files in the to-save pile. It would take a while to go through them. It wasn't his favorite thing to do. He was saving that for last. He was relieved to have these few days to himself. He really needed this break, and there was no one else that could, and should, be doing this.

His mother…he hadn't thought of her while he was working, which took his mind off his grief. He was thankful for this distraction, for this work, and plunged into it. He had promised his mother that he wouldn't just toss out everything. He knew that would upset her. One of the neighbors, an old man who lived alone, had died. He didn't have any close relatives. Afterward, they came into his house and took everything out. They discarded most of the stuff, and there wasn't much of anything left. Then they bulldozed the house until not a scrap of wood or a sliver of windowpane was left. Nothing…just a flattened lot, a vacant and empty space where his house had once stood. There was no service or funeral. Later there was an impromptu memorial held on his lawn. People brought food and drinks, and a grill was started for burgers and hot dogs. Although many people said kind words…Connor knew that some of them had said mean words when the old man was alive. But, in the end, they honored him by coming to his memorial.

Connor wondered what a person would be like and be doing in the next world. Perhaps they would be looking down on us and seeing everything. Maybe where they went, everyone would be the same. Nobody would be rich or poor. They wouldn't use money; there would be no need. Everyone would arrive empty-handed. So what they would use or not use was a mystery. Or maybe everyone would have no needs or wants. They would just be.

Connor wondered if they existed as some kind of ghost or apparition. Or what if there was no form, just energy? Or perhaps the entity was just a spirit that had no form, that just was…and didn't take on any physical presence? Would they be spirits or something else? Connor believed something had to be there to tell the universe you had existed. People couldn't just exist in this world and that was it. If you had no place to go after this, then you had to do everything you wanted to do here, in this world.

Connor shook his head; he didn't know the answers, and he didn't know anyone else who would know the answers. The only ones who absolutely knew were those who had left this world. They would be able to tell whether this world was it, if their life, their existence, was wholly within this world. If they had another existence or another world after this, what would that be?

Connor was not some famous academic who had spent decades studying this or pouring over ancient books and researching ancient lands. He was just Connor, an ordinary man with ordinary questions about life and death. He remembered his mother saying, "Live each day well." He liked that. But he couldn't live each day to the fullest in that sense of the word when he spent his days…well, his long days and evenings with his work. That wouldn't be called living each day well, not by any stretch of the imagination.

Connor was alone in this world. He let that thought sink in. He had not wanted to face this before. He always had a home to come to. He had never wanted to think about the inevitable, that some day they wouldn't be here, and there would be no one to come home to. Or, that there would be no home at all. An empty house was not a home. It was not even close. Grappling with his thoughts, he focused on what he had to do now. Grief was pushed aside momentarily as he threw himself back into work.

Chapter 18

THE NEXT FEW days passed quickly. Connor moved methodically from one room to the next. The donation truck came by several times to pick up furniture, clothes, books, and other items. The garbage can was loaded and surrounded by piles of trash bags, which all got picked up. Connor made quick work going through the big stuff while putting all the to-save piles together in one room. He would have to go through them and decide if anything was worth keeping.

His mom kept a lot of his stuff: his first tooth, his first school paper, his first A on an exam, his drawings, and all his birthday and Happy Mother's Day cards. It was so nice to have it all there. She didn't place them in a scrapbook, but she had kept everything together. He would take that with him. Then there was other stuff: financial papers, mortgage, insurance, taxes, and other documents. He would make another appointment with the attorney to take care of some of this. The house was paid for. He was proud of his parents. They weren't frivolous folks. There was little discretionary money for fun or fancy items, furniture, or clothes. But he never felt poor growing up. He had a roof over his head, clothes, shoes, and enough to eat. His mom made delicious home-cooked meals and packed his lunch at the same time. His lunch wasn't leftovers technically because his lunch wasn't left over from what was cooked at dinner. She packed his lunch first, and then they had dinner. She always made enough and made sure there was extra food for his lunch. She didn't believe in sandwiches. She thought they were boring. How many variations of a sandwich could you make when you knew each time it would be two slices of bread with lunchmeat and cheese in the middle?

She tried to make healthy food for him. She would go to the farmer's market or make delicious meals out of vegetables from their garden. He made it a point to always eat the lunch his mother made for him.

What Connor looked for, more than any other item in his lunchbox, was her homemade doughnuts. He loved her yummy glazed doughnuts and the ones drizzled with chocolate icing. At certain times in the fall, he'd get pumpkin doughnuts. But the doughnuts decorated with her colorful homemade, animal-shaped gummies were super special. Whenever his mom made these delectable treats, he became quite popular at lunchtime and never lacked for kids who wanted to make a trade with their lunches. When they found out that didn't work, they would bring in other items for trade, like a toy or something he didn't have. The more well-to-do kids even offered money to him. He never took money.

Since he was ahead of schedule, Connor allowed himself a treat, take the rest of the day off. He needed this time to relax, to regroup. Leaving his car in the driveway, he decided to take a walk. The day was beautiful, the clouds were white and fluffy, and there was a slight breeze. He wanted to get out of the house and stretch his legs. Where else could you leave your house and walk with the birds singing overhead, the trees and leaves gently swaying, past the meadows and fields and wildflowers and past the tidy houses with the picket fences? Connor enjoyed every minute of it, taking in the beauty around him, and smelling the fresh air.

Ahhhh…this was heaven on earth.

Chapter 19

AS HE WALKED for the first time in years, he realized twenty years had gone by in a flash. Where had all the time gone? Where was he in those twenty years? With a slight pang of remorse, he calculated how many walks he could have taken: 365 days a year times 20 years was 7,300 days. That was a lot of walks.

"Hey, Connor!"

Connor looked around and saw the neighbor Mrs. Rainer outside working. "Hi, Mrs. Rainer…er, Dottie."

"Come here and talk to me a bit," she said as she waved him over.

"Yeah."

"I've been meaning to clip these bushes and trim them a bit. They grow pretty fast," she said. She moved to one side, eyeing her work. "Tell me, from where you stand, do the bushes look straight?"

Connor studied her work, moving his eyes in an imaginary line across the tops of the bushes. "Let's see…I think a bit of trim at the top there," he said as he pointed.

"That would do it."

She clipped them and stepped back to look. "There, that does look better."

Connor nodded.

"Thanks, Connor."

"No problem. Hey, I want to thank you again for taking care of Tom. I am enjoying spending time with him," said Connor.

"Well, I'm glad to hear that. Tom appeared at your mother's doorstep one day. She took him in." She paused to reflect. "You should have seen him that first day…he was scraggly and thin, shivering from the rain. Real sorry looking."

"I would never know from looking at him now. He's the picture of health and getting a little pudgy, I think," said Connor, laughing.

"Yes, Tom has put on a few pounds and then some, but he's still fit and in his prime."

"Cat years are seven to every human year, right?"

"That's what they say."

"So that makes him…four times seven is twenty-eight years old," Connor calculated. "Why, he's younger than I am…in cat years, I mean."

"That's right."

Pleased with this, Connor grinned from ear to ear. "That makes my day!"

"Glad to hear that…have a good day, Connor."

"You too, Dottie," Connor said as he resumed his walk; this time there was a little lilt to his steps.

Chapter 20

CONNOR HAD JUST gotten home when the phone rang. "Hello?"

"Hi, this is Pastor Maller. How are you doing?"

"I'm good. I've been keeping busy. How are you?"

"I'm fine. Well, I thought you may want to pick up your mother's picture. I still have it."

"Yes, of course. I'd like that. Are you going to be there?"

"I will be for a little while, then I have a home visitation. But I'll leave the picture in my office. The door to the church is open. My daughter will be here if you need help."

"Okay. I'll be by to pick it up. Thanks."

Connor grabbed a bite to eat for lunch, before picking up his car keys and heading out. It was a short drive to the church. He went straight to the pastor's office. The door was open, and he poked his head in. The pastor wasn't there but a woman was sitting in his chair typing on his computer. He knocked. "Hello?"

"Oh, hello." She looked up with a smile. "You must be Connor. My dad said you'd be coming by to pick up your mother's picture."

"Yes, I'm Connor," he said, extending his hand to shake hers.

"I'm Eva."

"I recognize you from the service, your beautiful voice," said Connor. "I was touched. I loved the way you sang mother's favorite songs."

"I learned those songs from your mother. I used to visit her and she'd play the records of her favorite songs. We'd sing them together over and over."

"Oh, I didn't know that."

"I know those songs by heart. When I sing them, I imagine that she's right here with me, and that we're singing them together…like we used to." Her voice broke; she paused and then continued, "I miss her a lot."

"I miss her too. Going over her things, in her house, has brought back a lot of memories."

"I know."

Connor suddenly had a thought. "Listen, would you like to have her records and the phonograph? I couldn't think of a better person."

She flashed a smile. "Why Connor, I'd love to! Thank you."

"I've got another idea. Why don't you and your dad come over for supper tonight…if you are free? I haven't thanked you yet."

"I'm sure Dad would love that. I think we are both free tonight…he was just asking if I needed anything from the grocery store on his way back."

"Well come on over tonight. How does seven sound?"

"Sounds good. We'll be there."

"Great, see you then." Connor waved as he headed out to the market to get things for the dinner.

Chapter 21

ONE THING CONNOR was for sure good about: he was a good cook. All those years of watching his mother prepare dinner and his lunch came to good use. At first he had just watched, and then gradually his mom let him help. By the time he was about nine years old, he was making dinner with her, and sometimes she'd let him make dishes by himself. This had really helped him over the years. He was good at whipping things up from scratch, or creating something new from the leftovers. Even his mother said he was a good cook. Over the years, since he'd left home, he had gotten away from this. Cooking for just himself was not as much fun, and he didn't make anything elaborate. He made simple, quick meals that didn't need a lot of preparation. He cherished those times they cooked together when he came home during Thanksgiving and Christmas holidays. This brought back old memories, good memories. He slid into that role like he had never left it. Happy times definitely centered on food in this house.

Connor stopped by the farmer's market for some fresh

produce. He already had a vision of what to make and picked up what he needed. He had plenty of time. It was something he looked forward to. Today he was going to do something he enjoyed with the nicest people coming over for dinner. He was going to make a home-cooked meal. On his way back, he passed by the flower shop and remembered meeting Mary Ann at the store the other day. He hesitated and then decided to run in. She was finishing up an order with another customer. She acknowledged him with a smile. "It'll just be a moment."

As soon as the customer left, he said, "Hi, I was in the neighborhood…thought I'd drop by and take you up on your offer."

"Oh, that's nice. Let's see…do you mean your offer for Isabella to meet Tom?" she said as she laughed.

"Hmm, you got that right. So…how about it? Would tonight at seven work? I'm making dinner and invited the pastor and his daughter. Would you like to come?"

"I'd love to. Really that's very nice of you to invite me. I'll bring my cat also; she can dine with Tom."

"Okay then, see you at seven."

"Would you like me to bring something or help? I'm a good cook."

"No need to bring anything…I picked up what I needed from the market. I wouldn't think of asking you to help."

"I don't mind. How about I come a little early, say around six since you wouldn't let me bring anything?"

"Well if you insist, then come at six. I wouldn't mind some help." Connor looked at his watch. "It's 3:30, so I'll see you in about two and a half hours."

He had two more stops to make to buy some wine and to invite Mrs. Rainer. He didn't know if anyone drank wine, especially the pastor and his daughter. But he wanted to have some on hand, just in case. He didn't know if Mrs. Rainer would come, but she lived alone, and he definitely wanted to include her.

Chapter 22

HE GOT HOME and quickly went to work, rolling his sleeves up and washing his hands to his elbows. Mrs. Rainer had said she'd come. He did a quick count: there would be five.

"Hey Tom, you're in for a surprise tonight."

Tom was not the least bit interested. He just looked at Connor like, *Huh? What are you talking about?*

"Yes, Tom, you'll have a visitor. I know you aren't used to having other cats around, but Isabella is coming for a visit."

Tom looked bored. He was going back to sleep. Ha!

Connor quickly got started, laying out the ingredients and the cutting board. He didn't know what anyone liked, so he planned to have a variety of dishes and a salad. He got to work chopping and cutting. The time went quickly.

Knock knock knock.

He looked at the clock. It was six already! He wiped his hands and went to open the door. "Come in, Mary Ann. I see you brought—"

"Yes, I brought Isabella. I see Tom is on the couch."

Tom was quite attentive now, his ears perked up and eyes wide open. He surveyed the scene, paying special attention to the little white cat perched on Mary Ann's arms. Watching. *On full alert.* Never taking his eyes off the cat.

"Let me introduce them," she said as she walked toward Tom. Isabella chose that moment to wiggle and struggle, but Mary Ann held on. "Whoa…just wait a minute."

Tom started to move, poised to jump off the couch or make a dash to some other area. He really didn't want to move; this was his couch, his house. But he didn't want to be next to some strange cat either. He sniffed as she got closer.

The other cat had her eyes on Tom. As Isabella struggled to jump out of Mary Ann's arms, she was watching Tom to see what he would do. *The couch looks comfy*, she thought. *Wouldn't mind crashing on that.* She preferred the couch to the floor. Mary Ann brought her a little closer, and then slowly eased away to a safer distance, while both cats watched each other. She gently set her cat down on the other end of the couch. Tom relaxed a bit and curled up in his original position, settling back in his place on the sofa. *He wasn't going to have to move after all.* He sighed with relief. He kept his eyes on the other cat, just in case she made a move toward him, horning in on his territory. *He wasn't going to have any of that! He was going to stay in his spot. Let her leave if she didn't like it. He was just fine where he was.*

"Well, that's settled." Mary Ann said, straightening up. She walked over to the sink and washed up. "I picked up some fruit on the way here."

Connor took the fruit and washed it as he updated her on the menu and the various stages of cooking. The broccoli casserole was in the oven. The potatoes were already peeled. He was getting ready to make the salad and spaghetti when she had arrived.

"Let me do the salad. I'll cut up the apples and add some walnuts."

Connor got out another cutting board and moved over to give her room. "I'm almost done with the potatoes. I'll start the water for the spaghetti."

Mary Ann fit right in. Connor was glad to have her help. It reminded him of the days when he worked with his mom in this kitchen. The warmth of the kitchen, the aroma of food cooking, and the clinking of pots and pans made it so much more fun. He peeked over at the couch to see how Tom and her cat were doing. All was quiet on the couch front. No fights yet. At least they seemed to be getting along for now.

Chapter 23

AT SEVEN, MRS. Rainer came right on time. "Hello, Mrs. Rainer, do come in," Connor greeted her warmly and introduced Mary Ann and Isabella. "I'd like to offer you the couch, but right now the chair is all I have."

She glanced at Tom and Isabella on the couch. "Oh, that's quite all right. I see Tom has made himself quite at home, and he has a visitor."

The pastor and his daughter came right behind her while the door was still open. Connor welcomed them and ushered them in. "You know Mrs. Rainer?"

"Yes, of course, hello," the pastor said.

"And this is Mary Ann."

"From the flower shop?"

"Yes."

"I think we're about ready. So why don't we move to the dining room and have a seat?" Connor said.

Connor sat at the head of the table. The pastor and his daughter sat on one side of the table. Mary Ann and Mrs. Rainer sat on the other side. "The seat on the end is reserved for Tom, should he choose to join us at the table," said Connor. Everyone chuckled, and that broke the ice.

They started with the salad; it was a fresh and tasty blend of mixed greens, dried cranberries, fresh apple slices, walnuts, and blue cheese crumbles with homemade strawberry balsamic vinaigrette dressing.

There was plenty of food. Everything was delicious. Connor turned to Mary Ann next to him. "Thanks for your help today."

"I enjoyed it." She smiled.

"I want to thank each one of you for being a part of my mother's life and what you did in the beautiful funeral service," Connor said to the group. "I can't thank you enough." He paused. "I know I haven't been home much in the last twenty years, but you have been here. You have known my mother and father and been their friends. I am touched by your kindness at the service through your words, music, and flowers. Each of you is special to my mother and me...and Tom, too." He cleared his throat. "I know my mother lives within us and that her memories live in all of us. I'm not much for speeches, so that's all I have to say."

Pastor Maller spoke next. "I've known your mother the longest, and I will truly miss her."

His daughter added, "I cherished the time I spent with her, the music we shared, the songs we sang, and we even danced as we sang." She paused. "Thank you."

"Connor, I never thought your mother would leave this world before me. We had grown close, especially after your father and my husband passed. She was my neighbor and my friend. I think about her and miss her," Mrs. Rainer said softly.

Mary Ann was the last to speak. "Your mother ordered the flowers for your dad's funeral. She made all the arrangements and handled the details for his service. I hadn't been here that long when I first met her. She made me feel especially welcome, and she told all her friends about my flower shop. I'll never forget that."

Connor looked around the table. He was warmed by their presence and love, and for the first time since his mother passed, he felt at home. Lived in. "Thank you for making this a home and for being here today. You don't know how much this means to me." He wiped a tear from the corner of his eye, quickly stood up, and went in the kitchen.

"Now, here's what you've been waiting for…the decadent dessert," Connor said as he reappeared a few minutes later.

"Ahhh…" someone murmured as he brought out a five-layer chocolate cake with whipped butter cream frosting and put it on the table; it was as delectable as it looked.

"I'm putting on a pot of coffee…anyone want a cup?"

Four hands went up.

He put the cream and sugar on the table along with the mugs. The coffee brewed quickly, and Connor poured everyone a cup. "There's more if you want it."

They took their time, relaxing over dessert. The soft murmurs, the subdued clinking of silverware on the plates…it was like music to Connor's ears. He was grateful for the people and the good food. He didn't bring out the wine; he had thought better of it after he got home. As it turned out, he didn't really need it. Everything worked out fine.

He wanted this to go on and on; he didn't want to let this end. After a while, Mrs. Rainer got up. "I'm afraid it's past my bedtime now. You young folks stay and have fun."

Connor stood up. "Let me walk you home, it's past nine and I don't want you out there alone."

"Oh, all right. But you don't have to. This neighborhood is pretty safe." She headed for the door and paused to let Connor to catch up. "Bye Tom, I hope you had fun too," she said with a twinkle in her eyes as she watched Tom chasing the other cat and scurrying under the couch.

"Tom has found a new friend." Connor laughed, delighted to see Tom having fun.

Chapter 24

WHEN CONNOR GOT back, the dishes had been washed and music was playing. Eva had brought out the records. His mom had added to her collection since he had left. Connor had not heard these songs for some time; some of the records were quite old. The music livened up the place.

Eva and Mary Ann were dancing. They looked over at Connor. "Come and join us!" Eva called.

"Oh, I'm not much of a dancer. I really am not," Connor said shyly. "If it's okay with you, I'd rather watch."

"Come on, Connor," said Eva as she danced toward him. "Just try it. You don't have to know any steps. You can just shake your bootie…arm…finger…or whatever you want to shake."

"Come join us," chimed Mary Ann as she kicked up her heels. She had taken her shoes off and was dancing barefoot.

What the heck, Connor thought as he joined them. Maybe a little music was what he needed.

After a few songs, he really got into it. Connor got lost in the music and the energy of the dance. He couldn't remember the last time he had danced. He loosened up his body and relaxed his mind and just let go. It was exhilarating, liberating, and so much fun. It made tonight even more special, and he wished—no, he *knew* that his mother would be watching them with a pleased smile. This was how she would have wanted him to live. To dance, to dream, to live!

The dancing went on for quite a while. Connor was the first to stop. He was huffing and puffing. Eva and Mary Ann laughed when he shook his head, put his hands up, and backed out. After another song or two, they also flopped on the couch, out of breath. Connor went to the refrigerator and grabbed bottles of flavored water for everyone.

Connor glanced over at the clock and saw that it was now about 10:30 P.M. Pastor Maller was dozing in his chair. Mary Ann caught his eye, yawned, and said, "It's past my bedtime."

Eva woke the pastor and met up with Mary Ann at the door. Connor hugged and thanked them. "I'm so glad you came; this was very special."

"Oh, I almost forgot. I have to get my cat," Mary Ann said as she rushed past him, back into the house.

"I'll help you find her."

Chapter 25

BY THIS TIME the pastor and his daughter had waved good-bye and were out the door. The cats were still playing some game. They weren't in the living room. Connor made a quick pass through the rooms but didn't see them. He even took a look under the bed and under the dressers. Nope, they weren't there. He called out to Mary Ann as he headed toward the attic. "Maybe they're up here."

Running up the stairs, Connor turned on the light in the attic. It was still filled with furniture, miscellaneous stuff, and boxes. He thought there were lots of nooks and crannies, places where the cats could hide. He peeped in corners and behind boxes. "*Yoo hoo!* Come out wherever you are."

Mary Ann joined him and they looked everywhere. "*Hellooo…*where are you? We know you're here."

They looked everywhere, but they didn't see the cats. Stumped, they came back downstairs. The front door was still open and Tom and Isabella loitered by the entrance as if they had taken a leisurely stroll outside.

"Oh, there you are!" Mary Ann shouted with relief.

"You had us worried when we couldn't find you." Apparently the cats had been downstairs and gone out when the door was open. One thing was for sure. The cats weren't fighting; they actually looked friendly. It would be premature to say they were cozy, but they were tolerating each other well. No fights or meowing or any big fuss. That much was good.

"How about a treat before you go?" Connor said as he stretched out his hand with the cat treats in his palm. He waved the treats under Isabella's nose. She sniffed his hand; then she started licking and took the treat. "I think she likes it!"

"Yeah and now that you've spoiled her...she won't like it if I don't give her sweets," pouted May Ann.

"Hey, that's one way to see it. But look at how happy she is," Connor said as he tickled Isabella under the chin. She stretched her neck so he could rub all the way around her neck and down her back. He laughed.

"Meow..." That was Tom. He rubbed Connor's leg to be sure he was going to be noticed. Connor looked down. "Hold on, old man. I've got treats for you, too." He picked the cat up and rubbed his head. "You know I won't forget you. Not ever."

Mary Ann turned to go and waved one hand as she held her cat under the other arm. "I really enjoyed the evening. Bye, thanks for dinner!"

Connor closed the door and leaned against it, still holding Tom. He looked around the home slowly, reliving the moments when the place had returned to being joyful.

The words *"home sweet home"* came to mind. Walking toward the kitchen, he grabbed more treats for Tom before he turned the light off.

Chapter 26

CONNOR WOKE UP to the sound of *pitter-patter* on the roof. This was the first time it had rained since he got home. He stayed in bed, listening to the drops hitting the roof shingles and splashing on the windowpane. When he was a child, he had loved days when it rained. Sometimes there was no school so his friends would come over and hang out. His mother would bake homemade cookies. Ahh…the tantalizing aroma! The minute the kids caught a whiff, they'd make a beeline to the kitchen, especially Mikey and Ron. They had so much fun.

He liked to smell the fresh air when it rained, that indescribable scent. He would suck in as much air as he could, puffing his chest out and filling his lungs. He had always wanted to have a tin roof. Wouldn't that be super cool? Then you would hear the drops splatter and plop on the metal roof. At the moment, Connor was glad that the old roof was solid and built well. No leaks.

Connor's window was slightly open. Tom came into the room and immediately leaped up on the window ledge; he wrinkled his nose at the open window crack, sniffing the rain and feeling the breeze come through the window screen. Connor decided this was a good day to stay home and work on the to-save pile, which was not such a small pile. He was going to take his time with it. He had to focus his thoughts on this home, this place, and what he had come to do. Everything else faded away and seemed like a dream, almost unreal. The reality was in front of him…and Tom, of course. He sank back in bed to watch Tom press his nose into the open window crack. It was almost comical. It was good to be back home.

Everything was still here pretty much as he left it: his toys, his trains, his posters; all his clothes hanging in the closet; his books and papers on the bookshelf; and his collection of toy cars. Each time he came home, it was like he'd never left. He couldn't imagine not being able to come home to his room. That thought frightened him a little. This was the only place he had known growing up. This was where he spent the first eighteen years of his life. He closed his eyes.

He lost track of time. He felt overwhelmed by the memories of his mother and father. The ghosts of his pets flickered by, too. This was depressing, no way around it. He just wanted to lie in bed all day. He felt paralyzed. He had no energy. He rationalized this was a day to stay in bed; he was ahead of schedule, his calendar was clear, and so forth. What was the point of getting up? Why bother? There was nobody, nothing to live for. He didn't want to do anything.

Grief hit him like a sucker punch, right in the soft

underbelly where it hurt the most. He lay down on the bed and let the tears flow, wetting the sheets. Then the sobs came out, great heaving sobs and loud wails rising to a crescendo. Tom was no longer at the window. He had leapt away when he heard the wails. It scared him, and he left the room.

Connor didn't care if Tom stayed or left. He opened up his grief, releasing it in the privacy of his home. He could not hold it back. He could not pretend that everything was okay, that he was all right.

He had to feel the grief, to feel the pain of loss, and the void that could never be filled. There were no words to describe it. It was the way it was, the way it had to be. Nothing he could ever do, no matter how hard he tried, could bring her back. He relived his past, his last moments with her. Each time the video ended with his crying, "Mother, Mother come back!" It would rewind and replay, leaving a bigger void. He felt the loss as he curled into a fetal position on his childhood bed in the room that his mother had painted for him after he had childishly demanded that he must have a room painted blue.

Nothing in this world could fix the pain. It was too much to bear. Now in the silence of his room, he faced the pain. All of it. Alone.

Chapter 27

CONNOR CRIED HIMSELF to sleep, exhausted. Sleep was a blessing. He slept fitfully, deeply, without waking. Outside, the sky turned deep grey; dark clouds gathered, and thunder roared. Still Connor slept.

Connor woke up hours later. The sky had turned black. There were droplets on the window, and the moon hid behind clouds. He finally got up. It occurred to him that he hadn't fed Tom. Poor Tom! He was nowhere in the bedroom. Connor went looking for him and checked his bowls. Tom's water and food bowls were both empty. He brought them to the sink and washed them in soapy water, rinsed them carefully, and dried them. He put fresh water in one. Getting out the bag of cat food, he shook it. No sign of Tom. Again he shook it, louder this time. Tom came darting into the room. Connor filled his bowl and left him to eat in peace.

For once Connor was thankful that the refrigerator was full of leftover food and he didn't have to cook. He pulled out a few containers, dished food onto a plate, piled it high, and heated it. Now would be a good time to drink the wine. Red wine, heavy and robust, aged in wooden barrels. He poured himself a glass and sat down to eat.

He had no idea how hungry he was until he took the first bite. Now his hunger became ravenous, urgent, craving, and needy. He shoveled food in his mouth as fast as he could chew, not bothering to slow down so he could taste the food or feel the texture of each bite. He was not here to enjoy the food; he was just assuaging his hunger as fast as he could. It became mechanical: shove, chew, swallow, shove, chew, swallow. Food was just a means to an end. Filling his body with calories and fuel. Nothing else. He washed it down with gulps of wine. He didn't know and didn't care how much he drank. He used all his energy. When he finished eating, he felt awful. His body was bloated. He put the dishes in the sink, then he walked to the bathroom.

Slowly, he took off all his clothes, layer by layer. Connor stood naked. He stared at himself in the mirror, as if for the first time, as if he were a stranger. He came into the world alone, and would leave the world alone. You couldn't tell someone you wanted to go with them, just like you couldn't tell someone you wanted to be born...or could you? This body, what was it, a bunch of food turned into skin, bones, muscles? It was just flesh. Without nourishment, the flesh would die. How painful would it be for this death to take place? Sometimes people wanted to die. Sometimes people fought to live, clinging to life as long as they could. In the end, how would he go?

He studied the person in the mirror. The spark inside

him, it was still there. He clenched his fist. His eyes blazed as he fought to breathe life back, cell by cell.

Connor stepped into the shower and turned it on full blast, barely feeling the stinging water as it assaulted his skin. He welcomed the hard pinpricks of water. He stood under the shower for a long time, letting the water pummel his hair, his head, and his body. Letting the water wash over him as the rain washed everything outside.

Finally, after a long time, Connor picked up the soap. He soaped his hair, then rinsed it. Then he soaped the rest of his body. He moved over each area, rubbing the soap hard as he moved down his body. It was physical, his fingers touching his skin, gliding over the lather, moving faster and faster, dancing with his fingers over his body. Then he stopped and let the water rinse it all off, watching as the suds gathered at the bottom of the tub, swirling down the drain, until the water became clear.

Chapter 28

MORNING CAME WITH the bright sun. No sign of clouds or rain. Connor woke to the chirping of birds. Tom was back on his perch on the window sill, paws up and swiping at the birds as if they weren't on the other side of the window. He laughed out loud at how ridiculous Tom looked, swiping away. He got up and swooped Tom off the perch, hugging and kissing him at the same time. "Tom, you old fuddy duddy! Do you know how silly you are swatting at the birds?"

Tom just meowed and jumped down. Seemingly miffed, he led the way to his empty food bowl.

"Aww…is that what you want, Tom?"

Connor filled his bowl with cat food. He watched Tom eat. Tom was a dainty eater, and he licked his bowl clean. Connor made himself a pot of coffee and breakfast before he got down to work. Today he would tackle the huge pile of saved papers. He started pulling out the papers and sorting them into two piles. The to-save pile and the to-discard pile. He was going to do this as thoroughly as he could.

The day passed quickly. The papers were tedious, but after a while Connor was able to figure out a system and organize them rather quickly. He didn't even have to read most of them; he'd see the header and put it in one pile or the other. He was making good progress with the piles. He was pleased that the to-discard pile was getting bigger than the to-save pile. Trash day was coming up, and he wanted to fill the bins. Tom had padded back to the couch, and it looked like he was going to stay there. *What a life!* Connor couldn't help chuckling to himself. *Tom, you lucky cat.* He wondered if Tom loved him. Do cats know love the way we do? Could Tom love another cat the way we love another human being? Maybe Tom didn't love him; maybe Connor was only a meal ticket to Tom. Well even so, he was going to act as if Tom loved him back. After all, Tom could go anywhere, but he chose to stay here. There were no chains to bind him. Tom always came back. Tom always came home.

The phone rang. "Hello?"

"Hi, Connor. This is your lawyer, Mr. Monroe. How are things going?"

"Hey, Mr. Monroe. I've been going through the things in the house. There's quite a bit of stuff."

"Good. I just want to touch base with you on a few things. Have you thought about what to do with the house? Do you want to sell it?"

"I…I don't know yet. Right now, I'm just concentrating on what I have to do."

"Listen, if you want to sell the house, I know a realtor. I

can let her know, and you can talk to her. She may be able to discount her commission."

"Look, I appreciate this. But I can't make a decision now. I need time to think."

"Just call me if you want my help. I'll give her a call if you decide to sell."

"Thanks. I just can't think about this right now." Connor was irritated and upset, and he dropped the handset on the phone. He hadn't given much thought to the house. The decision would not be easy. This was his home. If he sold it, he could never come back to it. There was no hurry. He didn't want to be pressured into selling, even for a reduced commission. The house was paid for, and money was not an issue. He would put aside that decision until all the other stuff was done. He went back to tackle the piles on the floor, hoping to make progress after the unwelcome interruption.

By the end of the day, Connor had gone over all the financial papers. He had even set up online bill-pay for utility bills. His parents were thrifty savers and good money managers. He was not surprised they didn't have any debt. He had picked this up from them. He was careful about his finances and didn't incur debt other than the mortgage on his condo. He knew every month what bills he had to pay and how much money he had left to spend.

There were no messy situations, as some of his friends had experienced when their parents passed. He quickly satisfied the outstanding bills and reconciled the charges. He'd been checking the mail and there wasn't anything unexpected. He put all the paid bills in one pile and the unpaid bills in the other. The thin unpaid stack had utilities bills and a co-pay for a doctor's visit. It would be easy to settle all their financial obligations and move on.

He put old pictures, letters, and cards for birthdays and holidays in the to-save pile. He didn't have the heart to throw them out. His mother had kept them all these years. The people who sent them…some were long gone. Connor felt he was holding a piece of history, a piece that once discarded would remain lost and forgotten forever. This would be a special pile, one that he would go over carefully after he got back to the city. Now was not the time.

Feeling productive, Connor gathered up the discards and put them in trash bags. He took the bags out to the garbage can. He felt like he had put in a full day's work. It was tedious. That's why they called it work; otherwise, it would be called fun. He decided to take a walk. His muscles were tight from being crunched in an awkward position for too long. He wanted to stretch his legs and get some fresh air.

Chapter 29

CONNOR WENT BACK to the house, got his keys and wallet, locked up, and headed for town. Maybe he could pick up something on the way home after he'd worked up a good appetite. He picked up his pace. The stores were still open, but it was getting late. He knew there would still be good light for a while. Connor slowed down to look in the windows, just like he had as a kid when he didn't have much money and all he could do was window shop. Imagine someone coming up with a word for that. Like there was a big difference between shopping inside the store and outside the window. He shrugged.

That was fine when he was a kid; he didn't really give a rat's ass what they called it. The holidays were even better, with bright lights, blinking and sparkly, and the decorations in the windows dazzling and delighting the little boy. But he liked the quietness of the off-seasons too. No Santa or candy canes, but other things. Other interesting things. He was aware that, as sure as the seasons changed, the window dressings changed. He could count on that.

The fanciest building in Rocky Flats was the bank with its marble front exterior. That had to cost a good deal of money. Connor missed some of the stores that had gone out of business in the years since he left town. He recognized some of the family-owned businesses. They had passed from fathers to sons or daughters, aunts, uncles, or cousins. But they managed to stay in the family. Those businesses never changed names. They were the same, with the same signs as he remembered. You wouldn't even know by looking if the father had passed and that it was now owned by another member of the family. It was a smooth transition.

Connor still liked to window shop. He passed each store and tried to remember when he had seen it last. He mused as to whether it had changed owners, or if it was still in the family. Perhaps the new owners preferred to keep the same name so people wouldn't get confused. People were used to old habits; keeping the same name sometimes assured the loyalty of customers. As he walked down Main Street, he passed a mixture of old and new stores. He was rather surprised at the number of new businesses with their fancier storefronts and merchandise from the city. He walked leisurely, with no particular aim in mind, just browsing each storefront as he passed. The only difference from his childhood was that he could now afford to go in and buy items. Reaching the end of one row, he crossed the street and turned around to go back down the other side. It was getting late, and more stores had closed. He quickened his pace to see the last few shops. He didn't have anything in mind that he wanted to buy, so he kept an open mind.

Connor didn't recognize many people on the street, and he doubted they recognized him. A few folks smiled or nodded in passing, just to be polite. He returned the greeting and moved on. If he ran into anyone he knew, he would talk with them. Old men occupied the benches along the sidewalks. Some were socializing; others were waiting for their wives. He wondered if one day he would be waiting for a wife or just be out shooting the breeze with a friend on a lovely afternoon. He wondered if Mrs. Rainer liked to shop and looked for her.

Mary Ann caught sight of him passing the flower shop and looking inside. She waved to him to come in. He quickly walked up the steps and opened the door.

"Hi…saw you waving at me."

"Imagine my surprise. I was just thinking about you…and there you were."

"I'm taking a stroll around town. It's changed since I've been away."

"Well, several new stores have opened since I arrived."

"Do you have suggestions of places to see?"

"Yes, I have a few favorites. The ice cream store next door is one. I wish it wasn't so close sometimes, but it's a favorite of mine. The market is another one. And…oh, the new restaurant that opened earlier this year has good food. There's also a new bead store where I love to browse. I don't make jewelry, but I've thought about taking lessons to find out if I have any talent."

"I went to the market the other day, but I haven't gone to the others."

"I'm about to close up…would you like me to show you?"

"If you have time, that would be great."

"Hold on, let me close out the register and lock up." She smiled as she went through the routine. In no time at all they were walking out the door. "So where would you like to go first?"

"I was headed this way. I'd like to see the stores on this end and you can show me your favorites."

"Three of them are on this side, the market, the bead store, and the restaurant." She led the way.

Chapter 30

THE MARKET WAS buzzing with people stopping by on their way home to pick up something for dinner. The freshest vegetables and fruits were on display. A small selection of cooked foods showcased the soup of the day, hot entrees, and vegetables. These were made fresh daily.

Connor was impressed by the selection and quality in this small store. He was not happy with the large markets in the city. They threw out so much food every day; it was a huge waste. He figured the amount of food that was thrown out every day could feed an army—a very large army. This market, with its small inventory, maintained tight control, managed the flow, and kept food fresh and waste minimal. Often produce went into the soup or meals instead of being thrown out. The cook got very creative in turning older produce into attractive offerings the next day.

"Hey, Connor," said Mary Ann as she tugged his sleeve lightly. "There's the bead store. Do you want to see that next?"

"Yeah, sure." He could tell that Mary Ann wanted to go

in the store. Connor hurried after her. There were rows of containers filled with beads. The variety and colors amazed him. Off to the side were a couple of small rooms with tables. Obviously they were set up for small classes or demonstrations. He saw arrays of jewelry, artfully displayed to show off the beads and designs in finished necklaces, bracelets, and earrings. Mary Ann went straight to the finished pieces, admiring the handiwork and the patterns of beads. She inspected some pieces before she picked out a necklace.

"Isn't this pretty…what do you think?"

He looked at the necklace. The beads were interesting and colorful. He thought the hues matched her dress and eye color, and he told her so.

"I'll take it," she said as she moved toward the register to pay. She immediately took the tag off and put it around her neck, then twirled in delight to show off her necklace.

"It doesn't take much to make you happy," Connor said with a wink.

"I am happy!" she said as she did a curtsy.

They were back on the street in no time and nearing the end of that row. There was one more building at the end, set off a bit from the rest of the stores.

Chapter 31

THE SIGN OUTSIDE said "Manini's." She tilted her head toward it. "This is the new restaurant I was talking about."

"Do they have good food?"

"Oh, yeah! I like it. The sauces and pasta are made from scratch every day."

"Let's go in. I'd like to try it."

This was the first time Connor had eaten in one of the town's restaurants in many years. Whenever he came home, they always had home-cooked meals. They rarely ate out. This place was new, and it was popular. It was homey and clean. The tables were covered with checkered tablecloths and simple wooden chairs.

The waitress led them to a quiet table in the corner with a view. She took their drink orders and left. Connor scanned his menu and looked up at Mary Ann. "Hmm…what do you recommend?"

"I like the spaghetti and a salad."

"I still have leftover spaghetti at home," said Connor, laughing. "I'll have the spinach lasagna."

The waitress took their orders. The salad arrived in no time. It was chilled, just the way Connor liked it. The entrées came out as they finished their salads.

"I was in the mood for this tonight," Connor said as he cut through thick layers of lasagna packed with spinach and rich cheese filling. He took a bite. "This is delicious. I'm glad you brought me here."

"The food is excellent, and the prices are reasonable," Mary Ann said, nodding as she twirled her spaghetti. "It's a good place to eat."

"So…tell me about yourself. What brought you here?"

"Sure. I had taken a part-time job at a flower shop when I was in college. I got a liberal arts degree with a minor in art. After I graduated, I couldn't find a full-time job. So I continued to work at the flower shop part-time. Along the way, I took some business classes at night. I saw an ad in the paper one day…this store was available for rent. I drove here and took a look at the space. It was small, but it came with a small price tag. I figured I could turn it into a flower shop without spending too much money for renovations. I added some shelves and got new countertops installed. I bought a used refrigerator for the back room, a new display case, and opened up shop."

"I think you still had quite of bit of work to set it up."

"Yes, it took me about a couple of months to get it ready. I got a loan from the bank and placed my first flower order with the distributer and jumped right in." Mary Ann shook her head and looked at him thoughtfully. "If I knew now what I had to do…well, at the time I didn't know better. I thought I'd make a go of it. I didn't have much to lose…small rent, some inventory, and equipment. So why not?"

"How is business now?"

"I have a thriving business. I've built up my clientele. Between holidays, birthdays, anniversaries, and everything else, I'm busy all year. Business has been increasing. Of course there is a spike on holidays, especially Mother's Day and Valentine's Day."

"Are you happy?"

"A part of me says I've been lucky, really lucky. I get to use my creative, artistic side every day, creating floral arrangements. I also get to see my customers and make them happy." She smiled as her eyes lit up. "I'm happy too. Flowers are a big part of celebrations. Everybody likes beautiful flowers. Voila! The best of both worlds." She laughed, raising her arms in a V to emphasize.

"That's a wonderful story. I'm glad you shared it with me."

"So how about you…what's your story?"

"Well, you know I grew up here, you've seen my home." Connor looked at her and paused. "I left here when I was eighteen, right after high school. I went to the big city. I went to community college, then transferred to the state college and graduated with degrees in business and technology. I've been working ever since in the corporate world."

"Uh-huh," Mary Ann prompted.

"I tell myself I'm too busy to come home, except on

holidays. The years rolled by, and pretty soon I'd been away for twenty years." He looked at her thoughtfully. "I don't know where my life has gone. I'm thirty-eight. I'm successful in the corporate world, but I don't feel it inside. I feel empty. I don't want to work for another twenty or thirty years to know I'll feel the same way, but with more regret. Regret that I would have spent forty or fifty years in this job and regret at not having lived my life well…and to what end? That I've worked sixty hours or more a week for an impersonal corporation, knowing that I could just as easily be laid off? My life has to mean something more than the corporate profit margin." He sighed. "But then I'm digressing. You asked me a simple question, and I got carried away."

"I want to hear this. I'm interested. I'm thirty-two, and my life isn't perfect either. It may sound perfect to others, but I am not fulfilled."

"I get it."

"I spend a lot of time on my business. I keep the shop open six days a week. I have Sundays off, but I rarely take a whole day off. I have a lot of paperwork, inventory, billing, and all the other non-fun stuff that comes with a business."

"You feel overwhelmed sometimes, with not enough time for yourself…"

"You got that right. I've been doing some calculations, and I can afford to bring on an assistant." She frowned. "I have been thinking about it for a while. When the right person and the right time comes, I'll be able to hand over some of this work."

"Sounds like you have it all planned out," Connor said encouragingly.

"At least for the professional part of my life. The personal part is another story…I can't plan that…" Mary Ann looked pensively out the window. "No matter what I want in my personal life, I can't dictate how and when it's going to happen. One day I'd like a family of my own."

"My mother's passing…my parents' passing. That brought a realization that I'm alone in this world. I'm an only child and always thought I'd have my parents and a home to come back to…" He rubbed his eyes and refocused. "I didn't want this day to come, but the hard reality has set in. I've felt more like a child in the last few days than when I was one," Connor confessed as he gripped his fingers on the edge of the table and pushed away from it, leaning back. "I've got to figure this out…and the rest of my life. I got my wake-up call."

Mary Ann reached out to grab his arm, to reassure him. "Connor, it's not too late. You have time. You do what you want to do…you know what it is, deep inside."

Connor took her hand and squeezed her fingers gently. "I know, but I have to get through this first. I have to…before I can move on."

They lingered over coffee and sat in comfortable silence for a while, each lost in their own thoughts and feelings.

"Hey, Connor! Buddy, how are you?"

"Mikey! Good to see you," said Connor as he looked up to see Mikey at his table. "This is Mary Ann, from the flower shop."

"Hi, Mary Ann," said Mikey. He lowered his voice and turned to Connor. "Man, I'm so sorry about your mom. You doing okay?"

"I'm fine. How about you?"

Mikey turned and gestured to his family watching them from the other table. "I'm married to my high school sweetheart…remember Sally? We have two kids now, boys." Mikey beamed proudly as he waved to them. "You married? Kids?"

"No, not yet. My job at the company, sixty-hour weeks don't leave me much time for anything else," said Connor. He tilted his head toward Sally and the two boys. "You have a beautiful family. I always knew you'd end up with Sally."

"Dang! I'm a lucky guy."

"So what are you doing now for work?"

"I'm still in the plumbing business. My old man passed, and my big brother took over managing the business. Me, I don't like the business end of it so he runs it, and I do the actual work. That's the way I like it. I don't mind getting dirty and crawling under houses." He glanced over at his wife. "But she doesn't like it so much. I tell her a man's got to make a living. She understands."

"I thought you'd end up involved with the family business. You seemed to like it when you helped out your dad."

"Yup, that's what I did. Well, I've got to get back to the family. You holler if you need me, okay?"

"Yeah, thanks man!" Connor shook his hand warmly.

The waitress came back and left the bill.

"You ready to go?" Connor asked as he picked up the bill. Mary Ann tried to grab it, but he wouldn't let her have it. "I've got this."

"Hey, thanks for dinner," she said. "The next one's on me."

"Oh yeah? What makes you think there'll be a next one?" Connor teased, then wished he had kept his mouth shut.

Mary Ann looked away, her cheeks flushed.

Chapter 32

CONNOR GOT HOME later than he expected.

"Tom, where are you?" Connor said, worried when he didn't see Tom in his usual place on the couch. Walking to the kitchen, he ran into Tom sitting next to his empty bowl…waiting. "Hey fella, I'm so sorry I'm late," Connor said as he grabbed the bowl and ran to the sink to wash it.

After Tom ate, Connor rubbed Tom's tummy the way he liked it. Tom purred and stretched and kneaded his paws on Connor's lap in exquisite delight.

Connor viewed the last few piles of to-save boxes and files. He figured just a couple more days would do it. He had labeled some of the boxes, including the one with family pictures, cards, letters, and his school stuff. Others were just papers thrown together. His mother was not the best at filing, and she always had a stack of papers she said she would file when she had a chance, when she could get to it. He worked quickly, promising himself that once this was done, he would reward himself with a treat. He was his own boss. Connor stopped briefly to savor that thought. Hmm!

The next day went quickly. Connor worked steadily, going through everything, tossing things onto a growing to-discard pile. He took a quick break to eat and to brew a fresh pot of coffee. He was high on caffeine, but he needed it to keep going. As he worked, thoughts of the market came to mind, nagging him. He knew about nutritious food and what was healthy. He tried to eat regularly, but that was hard when he was immersed in work. Sometimes at the office he'd binge at lunch to make it through the long workday. If he didn't make it to lunch, he'd binge at the vending machine. He knew it wasn't good for his body. The stuff in the plastic wrappers didn't taste or look fresh. It wasn't like real food.

He made a conscious decision to eat better instead of just grabbing fast food or snacks. All calories were not the same, and Connor's body knew it. It was not too late…he was not middle-aged yet. Uh-oh, how did that slip out? Not that word! Did he really think *middle-aged*? That couldn't be…not yet. That word was not to be used. No, sir. *Cross that word off your list, Connor!*

As he worked, Connor thought of enticing new recipes with fresh green vegetables and the most colorful produce. His imagination ran wild with delicious meals from the cooking channels he watched when he had the time. He loved cooking and experimenting with different foods, textures, flavors. Maybe there was a creative side to him that he didn't know about. As a kid, he had started cooking with his mom. Before he became a teenager, he was preparing meals by himself. His mom wouldn't let him do much cooking on the weekdays when he had school, as she wanted him to focus on his homework and study. She kept it to about one day a week, and that day varied depending on what he had going on...a game, practice or some other activity. However, on the weekends he was free to do the cooking. It might be Saturday dinner or Sunday brunch. He would go shopping with her to get what he needed, but it was basic fare. His parents didn't much care for experimentation. He enjoyed shopping for food almost as much as the cooking. He had a particular fondness for avocados, the feel of an avocado, his fingers running over the rough skin, the firmness of it. When he opened one, he marveled at the size of the seed. How different, how smooth, how round it was! He always wanted to try growing an avocado from the seed.

The thought of food made him hungry. He looked at the clock. It was already seven-thirty. Connor decided to call it quits for the day, pleased with his progress. He heated up the frying pan and made a four-egg omelet with veggies. It was fast, and it took the edge off his hunger. He settled down next to Tom on the couch and turned on the TV.

Over the next day and a half, Connor finished the rest of the sorting. He called the donation truck to pick up one last load of furniture from the attic, and he filled the garbage can with trash. He packed up what was left in boxes and neatly labeled them. It was all that remained of the two people who lived here. But he knew that they had left more, so much more, in the lives they had touched, in the good works they did, and in the generosity of their hearts and their actions. They had lived quietly and didn't make a big show of what they did. But the people who spoke at his mother's funeral paid tribute to her goodness, her works, and how she helped others quietly. The heartfelt words of those people touched him deeply. Each tribute added to the others. Connor closed the last box and taped it up.

Chapter 33

CONNOR HAD ONE more day before his time was up and he had to head back to the city. He used the time to get the house cleaned up. He decided to hold off on the decision to sell the house until after the new year. The holidays would be here in four months.

He got a cat carrier for Tom and loaded up his favorite toys and treats. Tom would have to stay indoors in his condo, and if Connor worked long hours, he would be alone. He worried if Tom would adjust, if he'd be bored in the city, stuck inside a condo all day, all week. Well, they would have to see once they got there, one step at a time.

Connor came across the checklist he had made almost three weeks ago, what he had set out to do. The time had gone by quickly, despite his wish. But he had finished what he came to do.

Finally, Connor needed to say farewell to his mom and dad. It was a short drive to the cemetery. He walked the path to their graves. He said a silent prayer at his mother's freshly dug grave, next to his father's. Connor kneeled, tracing with his finger the area on the lawn where new grass had already sprouted. He moved his hand across the new grass and felt the texture of the soft blades, wishing he could communicate with her, as if the movements could reach her and he could send a message to her. *I miss you, Mom*, he silently mouthed. *I love you so much.*

He closed his eyes and meditated. He heard birds chirping in the trees. Memories flooded back from the time when he was small, the look on her face when she held his hand the first time she took him to school. The look on her face when he brought home his first A. The smile she bestowed when he proudly gave her his homemade Mother's Day card, with his childish scrawling and his drawing of a heart next to a rainbow and a smiley face.

He let his thoughts run free. He felt protective of his mother, even now, and stayed with her for a very long time. He placed the white flowers he had picked up from the market in her flower holder, rearranging them to show their beauty. He placed his hands on his father's plot before he left, shaking loose the slight cramps in his legs from staying in the crouched position.

As he walked back to his car, he turned around one last time.

Chapter 34

CONNOR FELT PAWS gently digging in his shoulders, waking him. Opening his eyes, he got a close-up look at Tom, inches away. He smiled and reached out to hug him.

"You and me…how do you like that?" Connor bent closer and whispered in his ear. "We are leaving today, my friend." He buried his face in Tom's soft fur and nuzzled him with his nose. Tom gently purred with contentment. Somehow, Tom knew.

Connor went to the kitchen. He got out Tom's favorite cat food and poured it into his bowl. Then he heated up some breakfast burritos and ate quickly. In no time at all, Connor had finished loading his car. He put Tom in his carrier and placed him on the passenger seat.

It was early Sunday morning. There was barely any traffic. Connor made the trip back to the city at a fast clip. Even though it was still afternoon, he encountered some heavy traffic, probably from weekend travelers returning to the city. The familiar highway signs flashed by, between glimpses of tall buildings and landmarks. The dense concrete structures rising from the ground contrasted sharply with the small town Connor had just left behind, nestled in the green valley below rugged mountains.

Tom slept most of the way, thanks to a little pill Connor had gotten from the vet and slipped into Tom's food. It would last until he arrived at his condo. Connor smiled as he checked on Tom again and watched him sleep.

For once Connor was thankful that his condo was a townhouse, and he could park in a garage instead of a high-rise parking deck. He quickly unloaded his stuff and then laid out Tom's bowls with food and fresh water. He gently carried Tom to the couch. The cat stirred slightly in his sleep, but he didn't wake up. Connor used the time to unpack and get settled. He wanted to be there when Tom awoke, to welcome him to his new home. *Yikes!*

Connor brushed away a twinge of guilt at the way he had hijacked Tom away from the surroundings he was used to, wrenching him away from his home. He made a promise that if Tom did not want to stay, he would take him back.

Chapter 35

Sometime in late November

MONDAY MORNING CAME too soon, again. Connor got ready for work, hugging Tom as he left. He backed his car out of the garage and looked back at the townhouse to catch a glimpse of Tom at the living room window, exactly where he was a few minutes earlier. He had not moved an inch.

Connor's thoughts of Tom evaporated during the day, as he dealt with one issue after another. He bought a sandwich and ate it at his desk. The day whizzed by, and before he knew it, people were leaving. Usually he'd stay and work late. But not today.

Connor stopped by the pet store and got food the manager recommended, a more nutritious brand of cat food. He was worried. Tom was losing weight, and he wasn't his usual self.

Tom was there to greet him when he got home. Connor bent down and picked him up, feeling the softness of his fur and the warmth of his little body. He whispered in his ear, "Tom, fella, I'm glad to see you, too." He breathed a sigh of relief to be home. "I'm so sorry." Connor gently set him down while he washed his bowls and put out the new food. He hoped it would help…but Connor knew it would take more than just food to bring Tom back to his old self.

Connor popped a frozen dinner in the microwave, and minutes later he was having dinner and relaxing on the couch watching the evening news with Tom next to him. He half listened to the dribble on TV. There was nothing newsworthy. At some point he dozed off. He dreamed of the holidays, the town lit up by the decorations, the carolers singing, and snowflakes falling on his face, tickling him…hey! Connor wiped his face to stop the tickling…and woke up to the sight of Tom, his whiskers and fur softly brushing against his skin.

Laughing, Connor grabbed Tom and flicked the tips of his ears affectionately. How he loved the wisps of hair that peered up from his ears.

"Meow!"

"Hey Tom," purred Connor. "How would you like some eggnog? Let's you and I take a trip home for the holidays this December."

Chapter 36

December 23

CONNOR PICKED UP a bouquet of white flowers before he left the city. The florist put the stems in floral water tubes filled with water to keep them fresh. He cursed under his breath at the late start. Coming home this time, he faced decisions about the house, about Ron's offer, about his and Tom's lives. He hadn't been ready before, four months ago. Going back to the city was what he had to do. It gave him time to think.

With a sigh of relief, he made it to the cemetery before it closed. He glanced at Tom still curled up and asleep in his carrier and smiled. "We're home."

Connor parked at the curb. Stepping out of the car, Connor pulled his coat tighter as a cold gust of wind and snow flurries hit his face. He blew steamy breath out and watched as it lingered, then slowly disappeared. It was quiet, and the hour was getting late. Catching the last rays of the light, he walked quickly up the narrow path to his father and mother's resting place, the bouquet in hand.

Approaching the gravesite, he placed the fresh white

flowers in the vase next to her headstone. Connor slipped his hand into his coat pocket and pulled out a sealed envelope. The one with his name on it, written in his mom's familiar handwriting. The one he had found in the box with the cards. He had waited until now to read it, here at her grave. He carefully opened her letter.

Dearest Connor,

If you are reading this then I have passed.

I hope you'll forgive me for not telling you the whole story until now. Many years ago, when I was a young woman, I left to go to the big city. My parents had suddenly passed, and I was alone in this world. I had a boyfriend who adored me. But I thought he wasn't exciting enough and didn't have enough ambition, so I broke up with him. I thought I knew everything.

Once I got to the city, I was able to find a job quickly as a typist. Thanks to my high school typing class, I took the typing test for the job and passed with flying colors. I didn't make much money, but it was enough to live on. I shared an apartment with two other girls in the typist pool. I was giddy with my freedom, my city life. I quickly fell into the wrong crowd. I was naïve…and stupid. I partied with the wrong crowd, didn't know their names. One thing led to another. The rest was a blur. I can't remember the details, but I got pregnant.

I tried to keep working, but I couldn't deal with the morning sickness. I was running out of money and desperate. I finally called my ex-boyfriend back home. It took every bit of courage and I had to swallow my pride. A lot of it. He came immediately to get me. He never spoke of this later. We got married right away. He was a good man, a kind man. I grew to love him, his quiet strength. When I gave birth to you, he was with me at the hospital. Connor, you were the most beautiful baby, the best thing that ever happened to me.

*When you turned 18, I finally told you that your father had adopted you. You took it hard. You were resentful and angry with me, but more so with your father. I am sorry. I hope you'll understand one day and forgive us. He loved you like a father. **More** than a father.*

Love always,

Mom

Connor carefully folded the letter, slid it back inside the envelope, and put it inside his coat pocket. He had avoided coming home, using his work as a convenient excuse. He had lived in a lie for eighteen years and then could not find forgiveness in his heart for the next twenty years. He stood there for a long time in the stillness, seemingly unaware of the snowflakes falling, softly covering his head and clothes and the ground with a delicate layer of white.

Finally, he looked up and glanced at the flowers in her vase. He selected a flower, the one with the longest stem. He turned to the grave beside his mother's and gently placed the daisy over his father's grave.

Chapter 37

December 24

CONNOR SLEPT WELL that night…a deep, satisfying sleep. He woke up feeling refreshed, relishing this peaceful moment in his bed, in the familiar blue walls of his old bedroom. Outside, the crisp fresh snow brightened the morning light. Sunlight streamed in the room, bringing with it a new day. He watched Tom sleep, curled up next to him. "Hey lazy bones, it's time to get up," Connor whispered with a smile. He gave him a gentle nudge before swinging his legs over the bed.

Connor dressed quickly in t-shirt and jeans. He filled Tom's bowls with fresh water and food, then dashed out. He drove straight to the flower shop. The place was packed with last-minute customers. He looked for Mary Ann, but he didn't see any sign of her. The woman at the counter ringing up the flower purchases was not her. He maneuvered carefully to the side where it was less crowded to get a closer look, all the while quietly chiding himself for not calling her after he left, even though he needed the time to deal with his own grief. Truthfully, he hadn't been ready to start a relationship then. He had to sort things out first by himself, without adding the complications of a relationship…and not just any relationship, but a long-distance relationship. Connor had seen established relationships break up when separated by distance.

"Excuse me," said Connor as an elderly lady gave him a piercing glance after someone shoved him in her way.

"Young man, mind your manners."

"I'm sorry, ma'am." He flashed her his most charming and sincere smile.

"Well, you should be!"

"May I be of assistance?"

"You can help me move up without being trampled by someone else." She grabbed his elbow and pushed him toward the counter.

"Umm…the lady at the counter…would you happen to know her name?"

"Oh, that's Norma."

"Norma…hmm…is she new?"

"I don't know what you mean by new." She threw him a questioning look. "She's been here for…now let's see, about three, no…almost four months."

"Ah…I see." Connor tried to hide the disappointment in his voice. He did a quick calculation. According to the old woman's timing, that meant Mary Ann left shortly after he did.

"Young man, what are you doing?" she asked as Connor tried to extricate her hand from the crook of his arm.

"I…I think I need to leave."

"You most certainly can't! Not until you've escorted me to the counter."

Connor couldn't come up with another excuse, so he just nodded. By the time it was their turn, the crowd had thinned out. The old lady exchanged a brief pleasantry with Norma. Apparently she had pre-ordered her holiday flowers and she was there to pick them up. Norma looked up her order and pulled out the paperwork. There were some notes written on it.

She searched the flower display case behind the counter. "Let me check on your order," said Norma as she headed toward the rear of the store. "I'll be right back."

He turned around, leaning against the counter while he talked to the old woman as they waited. Connor had a feeling she was a fussy customer and perhaps a bit difficult to please. She was getting irritated, and he sought to calm her down, to avoid a scene if Norma didn't find the flowers she had ordered.

"Connor? Connor…is that you?"

He heard someone call his name, a familiar voice. He turned, coming face to face with Mary Ann standing on the other side of the counter, holding a large holiday vase of flowers. "Mary Ann…" he stammered, confused for a moment, not expecting to see her. He blurted out, "I…I thought you had left."

She shook her head and grinned. "I'm here, Connor. I never left."

"I'm so happy to see you!" shouted Connor.

"I'm glad to see you too," said Mary Ann.

Elated, Connor turned to the somewhat perplexed old woman next to him and gave her a hug. "She's here! I wrongly assumed from what you said about Norma that May Ann had left. Can you believe it?" He paused to catch his breath. "I came here today to see Mary Ann…I left about four months ago. I thought I'd missed my chance when I saw Norma here today."

"I'd put an ad in the paper. Norma answered the ad and became my assistant," said Mary Ann. She set the vase with flowers down on the counter and gestured towards the festive holiday decorations and elegant white lights, strung with long ends hanging down from the ceiling, like falling snowflakes. "This…I couldn't have done this without Norma."

The old woman impatiently grabbed her vase. "Ring me up, will you?" she said to Norma. The old woman turned, looking first at Connor and then at Mary Ann. "You kids should catch up. No time's better than now."

She gave them a wink, then turned to leave.

Coming Home

THE SEQUEL TO *FLOWERS IN DECEMBER*

JANE SUEN

Chapter 1

December 24

TWENTY-FOUR INCHES. The width of a countertop. Mary Ann stared at Connor across the space. It seemed farther, the distance between them. She pressed against the rigid surface of the counter, a reminder that something separated them. The noise and bustle in the flower shop had diminished, the crowd thinning as they made the last purchases before the store closed for Christmas Eve. Norma's chirpy voice floated in the air, as she cheerfully rang up sales for the old woman.

The white lights twinkled and danced. The light scent of flowers perfumed the air. Left alone at the counter with Connor, Mary Ann couldn't find her voice. Not the one she reserved for customers or the one she had used with Connor when he was more than just a customer and became something else—(or so it had seemed). When Connor left town four months ago, that voice became faint and distant, until something stilled it. It was replaced with questions, laced with uncertainty. She wondered why he hadn't called or contacted her.

Behind the facade of her pleasant smile, a lump caught in her throat. She clutched her hands behind the counter, keeping a grip on her emotions, holding back the anger.

It seemed like an eternity, but probably only a few seconds passed.

There was an awkward silence.

"How've you been?" asked Connor, his voice betraying a hint of anxiety beneath the surface.

Mary Ann nodded. She wanted to give him a piece of her mind. *Why did he wait so long to come back?*

"Your place is lovely—so festive," said Connor. He turned to look around the shop. Seeing the old woman departing, he gave her a smile—the one who had given Mary Ann and Connor a wink, as if she knew.

"It's my dream come true—my own flower shop," said Mary Ann. "I want to cater to every celebration—birth, love, marriage, anniversaries and holidays. For someone in the first bloom of love, the hopeful romantic, those wanting to make affirmations long after the wedding vows. The beginnings of life, the joys, hardships and illnesses that come after, and finally the end."

"You're passionate ... and you've done a great job with it."

"Norma was a blessing. I couldn't have done it without her." Mary Ann gestured to her assistant, behind the cash register, grateful to have something to do with her hands, and for the chit-chat.

"Was this your idea? The holiday decorations?"

"My creative side took over."

"Weren't you an art minor in college?"

"You remembered …" said Mary Ann, surprised he brought up a remark she had made, months ago.

Connor smiled. "So I did." He often admitted to himself how many times he replayed their conversation that night at Manini's restaurant—the things she had shared about her life; her story. He felt relaxed and comfortable with Mary Ann, and they talked easily then, as if they've been friends for a long time. No cautionary bells had rung.

"Mary Ann," said Norma, interrupting. "Would you like me to stay and close up?" Norma's voice was cheerful. Mary Ann looked at her assistant. She was tall and slightly plump, with a touch of matronly grace. Her hair was cut short and streaked with gray. She had a way with customers. No matter what the customer said, she remained calm, courteous, and business-like—at times effortlessly easing into the roles of a best friend, a confidante, a psychologist, a fortune teller, or whatever fit the situation at hand.

A quick glance confirmed the last customers were gone. It was a few minutes after closing time. "No, it won't be necessary," said Mary Ann. She reached under the counter and pulled open a drawer, taking out a box tied with a beautiful bow and a spray of rosemary tucked in it. "Merry Christmas, Norma."

"Oh, thank you," said a delighted Norma. "I'll put it under the tree and open it on Christmas Day." She set it carefully on the counter. Zipping open her purse, Norma took out a small wrapped package and handed it to Mary Ann. "Merry Christmas to you too."

Mary Ann blushed as she whispered her thanks.

"Shall I lock the door?" said Norma, as she walked out.

"No, you go ahead. I'll be right behind you." Mary Ann sprinted toward the door, catching up with Norma to give her a hug. As the chime of the doorbell announced Norma's departure, Mary Ann locked the door and flipped the 'Closed' sign.

Chapter 2

CONNOR WATCHED MARY Ann gather her coat and purse. His hopes of any reconciliation faded as he realized she was about to leave. Before his return, Connor had indulged in visions of their meeting—how she'd be whooping and jumping, then running straight into his arms. She would have a wide, drawn-out smile, her long hair flowing. In his mind, he would repeat the sequence. This time in slow motion. The bounce of her soft curls, eyes shining and bright, mouth slightly parted, with lips the color of red velvet …

"Connor, what's wrong?"

He shook his head as the image quickly faded. Sighing, he exhaled a deep breath. Here was his chance to tell her. It was now or never. "I'm sorry." He raised his eyes, meeting her square-on. "I'm so sorry I didn't call." He paused. "I was in my own funk, dealing with my life—what's left of it."

She remained silent, waiting for him to continue.

"After I went back to the city, I thought of you. I've picked up the phone." He hesitated again. "You have no idea how many times I tried to call you."

She played with the curl in her hair, twirling it as her feelings went into turmoil.

"But it wasn't the right time. I needed time to heal. I had to mourn … I needed to find myself." Connor fidgeted, shifting the weight on his feet.

"Look, I know you had a lot to deal with," said Mary Ann. "Your mother—"

"Going away, I thought it would dampen the pain. But it deepened it."

"I worried about you. Didn't know if you made it back or if you were okay." She stuck her chin out. She omitted the part where she was disappointed that he hadn't called.

"It was wrong of me. I didn't mean to cause you to worry." Connor shook his head.

She fiddled with the metal pull on the zipper of her purse—feeling its smoothness; flipping it back and forth.

"These last four months or so, I needed time for myself," said Connor. "I had no right to bring you into my world. I was barely functioning, as it was. I had days … well, weeks, when I felt I had nothing more to live for."

Mary Ann looked down, intent on hiding the flush of her cheeks, as her anger ebbed.

"I kept to myself," Connor whispered. "I made myself go through the motions of living, barely making it through each day. I failed poor Tom."

The mention of Tom, his orange tabby cat, brought a smile to her lips. "And how is Tom?"

"He's not his usual self. I'm a little worried about him," said Connor, frowning. "I'm afraid something is wrong. I've neglected him. I was so absorbed in my own self."

"I'll give you the name of my vet," said Mary Ann. "That is, if you're still around after the holidays."

"Sure, I'd like that," said Connor. He added, softly. "Tom lost some weight."

"You'll still be here?"

Connor nodded.

Mary Ann reached across the counter for the notepad, scribbling the name and number of her vet. She tore the sheet off, and folded it. "You give him a call."

Connor took the paper. He smiled, as he read it. "Doc Carlson—so he's still around. He was Tom's vet before."

"He's the only vet in town," said Mary Ann.

"My mother took Tom to see him after the cat showed up at her doorstep one day."

"She had a soft spot for animals."

"Mom had a big heart."

"Your mother ... she was kind to me when I first moved here. After I opened my flower shop, she was one of my first customers." Mary Ann gestured, waving her arm across the room. "I didn't know it at the time, but she had spread the word to all her friends, and they came."

"I appreciated the beautiful flower arrangements you made for her funeral."

"It was the least I could do."

Connor reached out to touch her hand. The barest of contact. Perhaps he imagined it—a connection; an exchange of electrons sizzling in the air, bridging the gap.

Had she felt it, the tiny spark? It was like a weight had lifted—a clearing starting to open. Just a little.

Chapter 3

SEEING CONNOR COME home when his mom died had stirred up raw emotions Mary Ann had buried. The fact he grieved so openly. The loss which could never be replaced. How could one ever get over that?

Mary Ann fought back tears for the loneliness of her own life; for the special somebody to love and live her life with, to share her dreams, to comfort her in times of need. Who would grieve her when she died? She yearned to bare her most innermost feelings—her deepest, most soul-wrenching secrets, and desires. But not just to anyone. She would save it for the right somebody.

That day, four months ago, during Mrs. Norton's funeral, she sat in the church, lost in the breathtakingly beautiful music. It flowed in the air, expanding beyond the pews and vaulting to the ceiling of the church, enveloping her in a rapture-like state. Oblivious to anything and anyone else, she stared at Connor while the duet of flute and violin played. The heavenly music swirled, touching her soul. She was unable to tear her eyes away. Caught in the moment when time stood still. She glimpsed it, briefly—not the ethereal beauty of the notes but what *he* felt, deep inside.

How could she explain it? It was more than empathy and compassion. Shivers ran through her then, as they did now. It was as if she *was* part of it, the intersection of life and death before time pulled one into the beyond; before death took someone further and further away. She knew no matter how fast she ran after Death carrying a beloved away, trying to catch them—the speck of vision, their retreating figures, would get smaller and smaller. Eventually, she would run out of breath and collapse on the ground.

The chords of music brought her back. Brought Connor back.

In that instant, she had traveled with him, down the road one day everyone would travel. But it wasn't their time. Not for Connor. Not for Mary Ann.

Chapter 4

MAIN STREET AT Christmas was Connor's favorite time. Standing outside Mary Ann's flower shop, he looked down the street. Where could he go? The thought of seeing Mary Ann had consumed his mind during the drive down here from the city. He had made no plans for afterward.

The night before, Connor had paid his respects to his parents at the cemetery, leaving a bouquet of white flowers he brought from the city. Early this morning, on Christmas Eve, he fed Tom, then got in his car and drove straight to the flower shop to see Mary Ann. His mind had played a warm welcome over and over, like in the movies—smiling, arms flung wide open and hugs so tight you could hardly breathe.

It didn't happen like that. The disappointment was tough to bear. But the welcome he had imagined was of Connor's own making. Connor let out a deep breath. He watched as it blew into the cold—making its presence known—and then disappeared. He looked around the brightly decorated town and the busy street. This was

Christmas Eve. Where was everyone going? They *all* had a place to go.

His eyes took in the red bows, wrapped around the lamp posts, the strung lights, the hustle and bustle of last-minute shoppers scurrying, carrying bags and boxes.

Connor noticed how much the town had changed. Christmas shopping wasn't like this when he was growing up. They could barely afford it. But he never felt poor. When his mother asked him what he wanted for Christmas, he'd name one thing. A teddy bear, when he was small; a toy train when he got older. His parents somehow managed his one present every year. He was never greedy. Even at a young age, he knew if he had asked for a more expensive item, he would set himself up for disappointment. As soon as he was old enough, Connor did odd jobs around town, earning enough to buy a used bicycle. And with it, he got a job delivering newspapers.

Across the street, the coffee shop beckoned as porch lights twinkled and a warm glow inside beamed its welcome. He caught a glimpse of customers enjoying mugs of steaming coffee, laughing and having a good time. Connor gathered his coat about him, feeling the wintry chill. He was drawn toward the light from a window, warm and inviting. Before he could think too much about it, his feet were marching to the coffee shop.

Holiday music played as Connor made his way to the counter to order—a jazzed-up rendition of "Jingle Bells." Colorful paintings lined the walls, accompanied by white square signs with the name of the artist and the price. Bold landscapes, pastel flowers, portraits, a yellow van covered with love and peace signs. The café had a brash, artsy atmosphere.

For sure, it wasn't a chain coffee house. This one had a uniqueness to it—a quirky, small-town flavor. The tables were made of wood and each crafted by hand in a woodworking shop. No cookie-cutter, coated plywood tables here.

He scrutinized the menu on the chalkboard. Somebody with an artistic flair had outdone themselves. White, evergreen, and holly-red cursive lettering announced the featured specials. "Gingerbread latte topped with …" said Connor, squinting his eyes.

"Peppermint," a voice said.

Connor stared at the person in front of him; at the back of their head and the close-cropped hair. A man, he guessed. A short man, at least eight inches shorter than him. But the voice … it was different, not so masculine.

Connor bent down to whisper. "How about reading the dessert menu?"

"You're not that helpless!" The person laughed, turning around to face him.

The face was definitely not masculine. It looked familiar, yet Connor couldn't place it. "I know you …"

She smiled.

"Wait, don't tell me. Let me think," said Connor, snapping his fingers.

"You're Connor, aren't you?"

"Just give me a minute."

"What'll you have?" said the cashier, breaking in. The

line had moved, and they were next.

"I'll have a cup of hot chocolate," said the person in front of him, moving up to the counter. "Oh, and I'd like some mini marshmallows."

"You're Alana!" said Connor, smiling in triumph as he finally put a name to the face.

He caught the attention of the cashier before Alana could pay. "Put it on my bill, please. I'll have your holiday special, the gingerbread latte." Connor pointed at the menu board.

"I do recommend it," she said, giving him an approving look. "For here or to go?"

"For here, please." Connor turned to Alana before she had time to thank him. "Care to join me?" He moved quickly to grab a table that had just emptied.

Noting her nod, Connor pulled out a chair for her, before going back for their drinks.

He sat the steaming mugs on the table.

"I guess I can stay for a few minutes," said Alana.

They shared a moment of silence, interrupted by a spoon clinking as Alana stirred her hot chocolate.

Connor studied her face, carefully. "It's been a long time." He straightened up in his seat and took another sip of his latte. "My neighbor, Mrs. Rainer, had an only child … a daughter."

"You're right. I'm Dottie's daughter, Alana."

"I knew you growing up, but I haven't seen you for years," said Connor.

"I've been away."

"You left home suddenly. I heard something happened,

but I didn't know what. Mrs. Rainer hasn't spoken of you since."

"It's a long story … and I'd rather not go into it now."

Alana was silent, turning to stare out the window.

"How long has it been since you left?"

"It was eight years ago. I'm twenty-five now," said Alana. The man in front of her was no longer the thin, pimply kid he'd once been.

"I'm thirteen years older than you," said Connor.

Alana nodded. So, sitting across from her was a thirty-eight-year-old smooth-shaven, well-groomed and self-assured man. "Before I left, I saw you, what, maybe a couple times a year, when you came back to visit? It seems so long ago."

"Every time I came home, you'd spurted a few inches," said Connor, smiling as he recalled the little girl next door, shooting up like a thin, straight stalk.

"I left when I was seventeen, after Dad died." Alana shrugged, adding, "You know, the rebellious teenager and all the drama of growing up and figuring out who you are, and—"

"You had a lot to deal with."

"I had it rough on my own. I was almost homeless," said Alana. "I toughened up quick. I became a fast learner. I had to survive." She blew on the hot chocolate, pursing her thin lips, before taking another sip. "Tell me about you."

"I left here right after high school at eighteen. Moved to the city, took classes at the community college, then transferred to the state college."

"You graduate?"

"*Cum laude*. Then I got a corporate job working in business and technology."

Alana noted his haircut—precise and perfectly cut. She imagined it was probably like his life, all neat and in order, packaged and tied up in a bow. Was Connor's life safe and predictable? Had he ever taken chances? Was he happy? He had the look of success. Even dressed casually, his sleek-fitting fighter pilot jacket screamed designer label. Where the jacket was unzipped, she could see a black turtleneck sweater underneath. She slid a glance at her outfit: the cheap winter jacket from Wally World, the plain cotton shirt, the thermal underwear under it, and the well-worn pair of jeans. Alana touched her chest, fingers grazing the natural, soft fabric of her shirt.

"So, here you are, back in town, on Christmas Eve," said Connor after a moment of silence. The guilt of his infrequent visits home weighed heavily on his mind, brought back by the conversation with Alana.

"I just got in today. I can't believe how much it's changed in eight years."

"A few new stores have popped up. But at the core, it's still the same place and people."

"I passed the old theater and the marquee advertising 'The Nutcracker'."

"The *same* movie they show every year, I bet."

"My mom took me to see the show when I was in first grade," said Alana. "We went a few times, but when I turned twelve, I refused to go."

"It was a tradition in our house too. Thankfully, I only went twice with my mother," chuckled Connor.

"The dry cleaner is still here. It's as drab-looking as I remembered it." Alana stuck her tongue out and made a funny face.

"They must do good business," said Connor. "I remember they delivered to our house every two weeks, on Tuesday."

"Oh yeah, I know that delivery truck. It had a gigantic picture of a clothes hanger on the side."

Connor smiled. "My mother sent my dad's shirts out to be dry-cleaned. Of course, he fussed at first. He didn't see a need in it. But she was insistent that he looked every bit the owner of his hardware store."

"Did he?"

"She insisted, and in the end, he agreed and let her. Mother was particular about clothes, always checking me and nagging me about mine."

"Even I could tell she had style," said Alana, wishing it was a talent her own mom had.

"Mom managed to look fashionable. She had a knack for matching and mixing outfits. It didn't need to be expensive—she did it with what we had."

It felt good—sitting in the small coffee shop, all toasty and warm, a mug of delicious warm drink at hand, talking to Alana. Connor didn't want to get into anything that would ruin the mood and was relieved Alana didn't seem to, either. As to why she left town, according to rumors, something happened, and it wasn't good. Going over and rehashing past hurts would be upsetting.

Connor sat back in his chair and smiled. "I'm glad you're back in town. Imagine running into you in the coffee shop."

"I dashed in to grab something warm. You're the first familiar face I've seen since I drove into town."

"You haven't seen your mother, yet …?"

"I stopped for gas, then came in here."

Connor twirled his spoon, scooping up a bit of foam on top. He had plenty of room to slosh around, having drunk half of the latte already. "You know my mother died."

She nodded. "Your mother, she was a good person and kind to me." Alana reached across the table to grasp Connor's hand. "I'm so sorry for your loss."

Connor swallowed, feeling the familiar ache that didn't rear its ugly head as often now. It was, but nevertheless, still there, and might never go away. "I miss her terribly. Coming home for the holidays will never be the same."

She squeezed his hand, covering it with her palm.

He looked up at her, his eyes tearing up. "I don't know what happened between you and your mother. Forget it, bury the ill feelings. Make up with her—while you still have her."

Chapter 5

Eight years ago

IT WAS THREE-THIRTY in the morning when she got up from the bed, dressed, and quietly gathered the rest of her clothes and toiletries, stuffing them in the carry-on and backpack. As she stepped into the hall, Alana paused outside her mother's room. It was quiet. In the dim light, she had crept slowly on her sock-covered feet, making her way to the kitchen. She held the envelope in her hands. Enclosed was a brief note:

I'm leaving. Please don't look for me.
Alana

She placed it in the middle of the kitchen counter, where her mom would be sure to see it in the morning.

Alana looked around the living room—the simple furniture, the scuffed-up wooden floor, the round rug under the coffee table with a stain in the corner from fruit juice she spilled when she was a toddler.

This had been home to her for seventeen years. It was the only home she had ever known. It was scary, what she was about to do. She sighed. It wasn't too late. She could still go back to her room and crawl back under the comfy covers.

She shook her head. It had been her decision, and she was going to go through with it. Zipping up her jacket, Alana tiptoed to the front door, turned the knob, opened the door and walked out. This time, she didn't turn around.

⁂

Now, Alana was back on Christmas Eve. The little town had changed a bit, with new stores and businesses. Alana hadn't seen her mother for all that time. Had the years been kind to her? After she left, Alana had refused to call home for help. She was as stubborn as can be. The last thing she'd ever do was admit she had made a mistake.

Why did she come back? Mrs. Norton's death had something to do with it. Alana missed the funeral. By the time she found out, it was too late to change her plans. Pastor Maller had been kind. He was really the only connection she maintained. She trusted him. He didn't blame her or judge her. He never yelled at her or said hurtful words. He was a man of God, and he took that mantle on. She took refuge with his kindness.

Alana had imagined the meeting with her mother— practiced what she'd say, over and over again. She had chosen her words carefully.

She was tired. Tired of the freezing nights she shivered in her little room, not much bigger than a closet. Tired of the cold that a warm bowl of soup could soothe only for a moment. Tired of begging for money. Tired of lying, cheating, doing whatever she had to do to survive. Tired of gagging on the taste of crusted urine and the smell of body odor when she performed oral sex on strange men. Tired of living, sometimes.

Tired of being so tired. And worried. Worried about catching some disease and becoming ill. Worried about dying alone in some forsaken place. Alana plunged to the depths of despair in a harsh world, so different from the one she understood. Yet she kept on living, not giving up. Her stubborn self refused to give up.

One day, she stumbled on a park. The benches were free, and she could sit and get plenty of sunshine. She chose a warm spot with a good view. She could sit there for hours, and nobody would bother her. Old people liked to go there. Alana liked old people, and she liked talking to them. They had stories. In the twilight of their years, they spoke of their lives, of people they loved and lost. Some confessed their secrets, regrets and longings. They told her while they still could—before everything was forgotten; before they had no more stories to tell; before their voices were stilled.

It was on one of those days she felt so moved. The stories stirred up feelings deep inside, and it dawned on her that she should be writing. She couldn't keep them shoved down. She began on the computer in the library. She took a thumb drive with her and saved her words. She blogged about her life—being penniless and her struggles to survive. Each day was a new adventure. The writing fueled her life, and her life fueled her writing.

Writing became her constant companion, a testament to her will to survive. She laid her gritty life bare for all to read. Little by little, her audience grew, as word spread and people sought out her blogs. Her style was distinct. It was edgy and raw.

She grew a following, as more people waited for the next chapter of her life. After several months, she compiled her blogs. It was one of her online followers who suggested she publish it. She was able to barter for services online: an editor, a graphic designer to do her book cover for cheap. Using free software, she formatted and published it. Her followers spread the word and bought her book. It seemed like an overnight success, but it wasn't. She had grown her readership slowly, bit by bit. It hadn't been easy at all.

Chapter 6

Four months ago

CONNOR HAD FIRST met Mary Ann, four months ago, at her flower shop, when he came back in town to discuss arrangements for his mother's funeral. He ran into her again, later, and invited her over for a home-cooked meal with family friends. They dined at Manini's before Connor returned to his home in the city. Connor had thought of calling Mary Ann. Well, it had crossed his mind many a time. He had reached for the phone to call her, he didn't. Deep down, Connor felt ashamed and didn't want to use her as a crutch—something to ease his own misery. He didn't want to burden another human being. Not just anyone, either, but someone who had been kind to him and his mother. And someone who he liked. He wasn't proud of himself. He didn't want her to see him like this. Not Mary Ann.

Four months ago, Connor had gone back to the city. At work, they had given him some slack at first, but how far could it go? Pretty soon, the sympathies ran short, and he wasn't doing his job well. Connor had cashed in on some favors, and there were many, but that ran dry. People distanced themselves from him. Even the ones he thought were his friends avoided him.

Then, sitting behind his desk, looking out the clear glass pane of the window, seeing blue sky on this cloudless day, Connor knew the day would come when he'd have to give up his coveted window office—the one he worked for years to attain. But he was a proud man. He hadn't and wouldn't simply give up. Not without a fight. Not unless it was under his terms.

Before he left the city, Connor had turned in his resignation. He was done with his job. His bosses had wanted him to come back, for a going away party, but he told them 'no'. He thanked them but held firm to his decision. He was adamant about ending his life in the city and beginning the new year in his home town. He'd start with a clean slate. He had enough money saved up, from socking his money away every payday. This money was meant for retirement, but this felt like the right thing to do with it.

He'd interviewed a few real estate agents about putting up his condo for sale. The suggestions they made were minor—cosmetic touches. Connor sold his furniture and put the rest of his stuff in the back of his SUV. He didn't need much. Most of his clothes—the shirts and suits—went to the church donation center, down the street. Little by little, he bundled clothes, shoes, and other items and took them there. Each step he took, he felt lighter, as he shed more stuff. In the end, at his last stop, he celebrated.

Chapter 7

Two months ago

MARY ANN RECALLED the first time she met Ron. He dropped by the flower shop two months ago, during her lunch break. It was mid-week, on a slow day. They struck up a conversation about plants. It was an interest they had in common, as it turned out. Ron was the new owner of the hardware store. He wanted to expand the outdoor section, adding a garden center with plants.

Mary Ann felt his energy and his excitement, and she was flattered when he invited her to visit his store. She chalked it up to a networking opportunity with another small business owner—a chance to bounce ideas back and forth.

The next day, Mary Ann drove to his store while Norma minded the flower shop. It was early afternoon. Pulling into the parking lot, she spotted Ron immediately. He was busy loading concrete blocks and bundles of chopped wood on a customer's flatbed. It was a chilly day, only slightly warmed by the afternoon sun, but he wore a cotton shirt and jeans. She waited, watching him work while she leaned against the side of her car.

Apparently, he had noticed her too. He walked toward her as the loaded truck pulled away.

Mary Ann watched as Ron approached, crossing the parking lot in long, easy strides. He looked relaxed, not dawdling when he was going someplace where he wanted to be. His hair was disheveled. His plaid shirt was unbuttoned at the top. It clung to his body, plastered with sweat. In jeans, his hips and legs were slim. The rolled-up shirt sleeves provided a glimpse of arms with corded muscles that extended down to strong hands and long fingers.

"Hi, Mary Ann," Ron said, wiping his palm on his jeans before reaching out to shake her hand. She kept her eyes on him as he grabbed a cloth sticking up in his back pocket and wiped his forehead.

"Catch you at a bad time?"

"Nah." Ron shook his head, grinning. The breeze ruffled his hair, giving him a slightly wild look.

"Well," she said, stopping to straighten out an imaginary wrinkle on her skirt. "I see you're a hands-on kinda guy."

Ron burst out laughing, lines crinkling on his rugged face. "You're right about that."

She smiled back. As much as she liked working in her flower shop, getting out today had turned into a pleasant distraction. She had found the hardware store easily, having stopped there briefly once before for a quick purchase. She hadn't run into Ron, that time.

Mary Ann needed to get a life. She couldn't help feeling she was playing hooky today, standing in front of a self-assured and masculine man in his element. She was also cursing herself now for not paying attention to some past gossip about Ron. She couldn't recall anything that had been whispered about him. Mary Ann shook her head, dragging herself away from her thoughts and giving him her full attention.

"Would you like a tour of this place?"

"I'd love to see it."

He tilted his head toward the fenced enclosure near the back. "Let's go this way first."

Ron's face was lit with a goofy grin. His enthusiasm bubbled—he could barely contain himself. He gestured, pointing to the east corner. "I'd like to put the saplings here." Waving over to the side, he added, "The perennials could go there, and maybe some hanging flower baskets and a herb garden, or something fun for the kids."

Ron turned around to the other side. "Lawn mowers and weed whackers could go here. And maybe some outdoor furniture, if there's room."

Mary Ann had to walk fast to keep up with him. As Ron moved quickly indoors, she could hear the excitement in his voice. He was like an eager boy, showing off his treasured possessions. From the way he talked and acted, she could tell how proud he was. She could also see that he was someone who wasn't too proud to get his hands dirty—a man who did an honest day's work and felt good about it.

"This is how the store was when I bought it from Connor Norton's father," said Ron, leading the way to his office. "I'll show you the plans drawn for the expansion."

He opened the door and pulled out a chair for her to sit in

front of his desk. He reached on top of the file cabinet for the rolled-up blueprint. He unfurled it, spreading it across the desktop, using rocks, a screwdriver, and a hammer to secure the corners. Gesturing to her to move closer, he pointed.

"See here?" He glanced at her to ensure he had her full attention. "I'm going to build an addition."

Ron pointed to the space behind the office. "On the other side of this wall, I'm going to add a new space, and put in the large appliances. Refrigerator, stove, washer and dryer." He traced the outline and tapped his finger on the blueprint. "Over here, I'm putting in a small appliances section. It'll be mostly kitchen appliances, fans, space heaters, and odds and ends."

"This isn't just a little remodeling. You're talking about a major expansion."

"This place needs it. I've been thinking about it for a long time now," said Ron. He was slightly hunched over the desk.

He turned to Mary Ann and stood up straight. "This is my dream, Mary Ann." He was staring at her now with an intensity that showed his determination.

"You've got the plans … What's there to stop you?"

Mary Ann wondered if it was the right thing to say, as his firmly-pressed lips appeared to weaken with just the barest twitch.

He ran his hands over his hair. *Damn, she'd nailed it on the head.* What *was* stopping him?

Ron had mentioned his plans to Connor, when he came back in town for his mother's funeral. Ron had put it out to him, then—he made the offer to Connor first, to partner fifty-fifty to expand Connor's family's old hardware store.

Connor wanted to think it over. Ron gave him more time and told Connor he wanted an answer within the year.

❧

Twenty years earlier, Connor had left town after high school, much to the disappointment of his parents. Mr. Norton had hoped his son would take over the family business and work at the hardware store, but he couldn't compete with the pull of the big city and the promises it offered to the ambitious young man. In the end, when the elder Mr. Norton could no longer work, he sold the business to Ron, who had worked for him for over ten years.

From the beginning, Ron had absorbed every aspect of the business and hungered for more. He started out mopping floors and cleaning the toilet, or whatever else Mr. Norton wanted him to do. Along the way, he learned, soaking up everything he could. When a customer came in and had a question, if Ron didn't know the answer then he'd find out. Ron never gave a bullshit response. He'd persist until he could give proper advice. Not a flimsy, carelessly-thrown reply, but a serious, thoughtful one. The customer never forgot. It wasn't just the customer who was satisfied, oddly enough; Ron had a feeling of accomplishment and tucked the new knowledge under his hat.

❧

Ron had gone with his gut feeling, asking Mary Ann to come here. What was he thinking of, sharing his dreams of expansion with her? Mary Ann was a businesswoman—gutsy, hard-working and smart. More than that, deep down, he admired what she had done. He decided to trust his instincts.

"For starters, money," said Ron. "I made an offer to someone, to become equal partners."

"Did they take you up on it?" Mary Ann raised an eyebrow, surprised at the generosity of the offer.

Ron shook his head. "I gave him till the end of the year … but I haven't got an answer yet."

"Well, you don't have much time left. Why is he taking so long?"

"You'll have to ask him," said Ron. He had been patient, but waiting until the last minute wasn't a good way to start off a partnership, albeit a very generous one.

"Him? Do I know this person?"

Ron took a hard look at her. *Should he confide in her? Hadn't he told her too much, already?* "You want to know?"

She nodded, not wanting to appear too interested, but she was curious.

"You know Connor Norton?"

Mary Ann gasped. *Connor!*

Ron felt relief, as he shared the information with her. It had been weighing down on him for a good while. He wasn't in his right mind to give Connor this long to decide. Ron did it out of respect for Mrs. Norton, and her son who had been overwhelmed by grief at the loss of his mother.

"He'd better get in touch with me, or the deal is off," said Ron.

"What's this section?" asked Mary Ann, hiding the blush on her face as she bent over the blueprint, pointing to a large corner space.

"The bathrooms."

"I hope you're remodeling a nice big one for the ladies."

He grunted. "Now, *that* I hadn't thought of. Maybe I'll put in some fancy fixtures."

Mary Ann liked that idea.

Chapter 8

December 24

MARY ANN SWUNG into the parking space. Pumping the gas pedal for the uphill climb, the car had spewed flying gravel on the driveway. Ron had texted, asking her to meet him at the hardware store again. His business had stayed open, closing later on Christmas Eve than her flower shop.

Mary Ann grasped the collar of her coat, closing the gap against the wind. It was an unconscious act, out of habit. Her other hand was flung across her waist.

***

A couple of weeks ago, Ron had casually mentioned something about Christmas, telling Mary Ann he was going to head out to his cabin. It was small but quaint—a cozy, rustic place. He had asked Mary Ann if she'd be interested in joining him.

"A day trip, and we'd be back by evening?" said Mary Ann.

"Yes, and if the weather is good, we could do some hiking."

"So, it's not too far."

"About an hour away," said Ron.

Mary Ann had hesitated.

"Now, when's the last time you took some time off?" Ron pressed.

"I have so much to do, to be invested in my work, but—"

"But what? You couldn't get away?"

"Right. I didn't have any help. But now, with Norma as my assistant, it's taken a load off."

"Have you seen much of this place, outside of town?"

Mary Ann shook her head.

"I grew up here. I'll drive you around. We'll stop at the cabin, have lunch, then head on back to town."

Ron waited, then nudged her for a response. "So, how about it? If we end up with a white Christmas, it'll be even prettier."

Mary Ann found herself considering his invite.

"Do you have plans?" Ron kept his voice low-key and casual.

"Norma has invited me over to her place for supper, if I didn't have other plans," said Mary Ann.

"You have a couple of offers, then. Just keep in mind that mine is going to be more fun." Ron winked, flashing the most charming smile he could muster.

"Okay, okay, I accept!" Mary Ann laughed.

<hr>

"You lucked out today. Got the last one," said Ron,

grinning. "And you're my last customer on Christmas Eve."

"I'm sure glad you had this," said the man, as he fumbled in his pants pocket for his wallet.

"Let me ring you up," said Ron. He lifted the tree stand and scanned the bar-coded label, as Mary Ann stepped inside the hardware store.

"My family will have their Christmas after all." The man sighed with relief, thinking of the cut fir in his truck. "Whoever invented this tree stand is a genius. A piece of plastic with screws to hold up the tree. Santa will be leaving presents under this tree tonight."

The man carried the tree stand as he crossed the room, giving a thank-you nod as he went out the front door. He carefully side-stepped the pile of dirt that the high school kid had swept off the floor. The kid chased the debris again, as a gust of wind rushed in and pushed it along the pinewood floor.

"Joey, go home," said Ron, catching sight of his employee's exasperated look.

"Seriously?"

Ron reached in the cash drawer and pulled out an envelope containing Joey's weekly wages. "I want you to enjoy Christmas with your family."

The kid took the envelope and looked inside. "There's an extra hundred in here," he gasped. He looked at Ron, then at the envelope, and then at Mary Ann.

Ron shook his head, gesturing toward the door. "Now, get going before I change my mind."

"Thank you, sir," beamed Joey. He had been brought up

right and proper by his mama. She'd taught him his good manners.

Ron watched Joey walk outside, the top of his head bobbing further away as he weaved down the hill. Something about the kid reminded him of himself, a long time ago.

Ron strode across the room and flipped the door sign to 'Closed.' His steps echoed in the quiet hardware store with just the two of them.

He walked back to Mary Ann.

"Hey, you all right?"

"Just lost in thought," said Mary Ann, as she blinked her eyes.

"A penny for your thoughts?"

"It'll cost you more."

"Ouch," said Ron, pretending to hold on to his wallet.

"Give it up." Mary Ann laughed, playfully tugging his arm.

"Ready for tomorrow's outing?"

"Tell me what I need to bring."

"Just bring yourself and bundle up. Wear a good pair of hiking boots."

"What time are we leaving?"

"I'll pick you up at eight in the morning."

Mary Ann groaned. "It's so early."

"Let's go for 8:30 a.m. and call it a compromise," said Ron, with a tease to his voice.

"Not on Christmas Day!"

"Okay, then—nine."

"That's better."

"We can still hike and work up a good appetite before noon."

Mary Ann couldn't help wondering if Ron had something else in mind, besides hiking.

Chapter 9

NOW, THE HOUSE sat empty on Christmas Eve. It was bare of holiday decorations. It was devoid of all holiday spirit, since Connor's mom died.

Stores were closing early. By two o'clock in the afternoon, the pickings were sparse, but Connor managed to grab some outside lights, a few decorations, and a misshapen, pathetic-looking fir tree, which had been pushed into a corner and overlooked by shoppers. "A tree has to have something under it," his mother always said. Connor picked up some special treats and toys for Tom, along with some wrapping paper.

He stopped by the market and bought milk, eggs, fresh vegetables and fruits, and enough food to stock his refrigerator for a few days.

Coming home … He hadn't given it much thought until he was well on the way. Getting into the holiday spirit had been the last thing on his mind. He just wanted to relax on the couch and be left alone with Tom.

But walking in the festive town, caught up in the hustle

and bustle, checking out the Christmas decorations, lights, music, food and drinks … it all affected Connor. Despite himself, he found a little holiday cheer wrapping around his heart.

In the end, he gave in and embraced it. For himself. And for what his mother would have wanted for him—to go on and join life, rather than retreat from it. To be happy. It would have been easy to withdraw and do nothing. It took energy to do something. All of this—the latte, the talk with Alana, getting caught in the holiday spirit of this small town where he grew up and where his parents were laid to rest— wasn't what he had planned.

He suddenly realized he wasn't ready to give up. He felt charged with a renewed energy and excitement he hadn't felt since he was a child.

The rest of the afternoon passed quickly, as Connor busied himself putting lights outside the house and decorating the inside. The Christmas tree in the living room was the centerpiece. There was a cloth on the floor beneath it, with a few wrapped gifts scattered on top—mainly cat treats and toys for Tom.

He picked up Tom when he finished trimming, taking a walk around the living room to survey his work. Flicking the lights on, he walked outside, giving a satisfied grunt as the blinking holiday lights and glow of colors brightened the unassuming bland exterior of the house.

"See, Tom?" said Connor, as he held the cat's paw and waved it.

Connor was determined to enjoy the holidays together with Tom and family friends, spreading the cheer. Tom had endured a rough time too, and Connor had been selfish. He'd devoted time to his job, while being preoccupied with feeling sorry for himself. Connor wanted to make it up to Tom. Tom was all the family he had left—his mother's orange tabby cat. *His* cat.

In the end, it was family that mattered.

Chapter 10

IN THE EVENING, Connor attended the Christmas Eve candlelight service at the church. It was something he hadn't done by himself since he left home.

Going to the service had been a tradition when he was a child. Every year, he went with his parents.

Returning to the church brought back so many childhood memories of that time. Before the service started, a candle with paper drip guards was passed out to each person. The simple act of lighting the candles filled the congregation with reverence. When he got older, he was allowed his own candle. He cupped his hands around the flickering flame to prevent it from being snuffed by a draft. It was a solemn yet inspiring moment, made more so when the whole congregation did it together—the beauty of candle lights shining in the darkened sanctuary, bringing the message of hope and peace. It stirred up memories of sitting between his parents, and of the wonder he felt as a child.

The Pastor gave his welcome, embracing everyone—even those who only attended services twice a year, at Christmas and Easter. Connor grimaced, putting himself in that category. In the twenty years since he'd been away, Connor had become one of them—ever since his eighteenth birthday, when he learned the truth about his adoption—by the man whom he called "Dad", growing up. The man who was not his biological father, after all. Connor took it hard. Choked with anger and resentment for two decades, he had avoided coming home as much as possible. But now, as he sat back on the familiar pews and listened to the Pastor, he was at peace. He touched his mother's letter, which he put in his coat pocket after opening and reading it the day before. There, on December twenty-third, at the cemetery where she rested next to his adoptive father, Connor learned the truth about the man who married his pregnant mother.

He stayed awhile after the church service, to thank Pastor Maller and greet town folks he knew. It was good to see the Pastor again—and his daughter, Eva. He hadn't seen them since the funeral.

Spotting Mrs. Rainer leaving, Connor rushed after her. He caught up with her on the lawn.

She tapped his arm, affectionately. "Good to see you home."

"How've you been?"

"You know me—the feisty old woman next door isn't going anywhere."

Connor looked around, hoping to see Alana. He hesitated, not wanting to be the one to ask Mrs. Rainer about her daughter. He thought, *She doesn't know yet about Alana.*

"Merry Christmas, Mrs. Rainer."

"You call me Dottie, and you too."

Connor suddenly had an idea. "Dottie, I have some people over tomorrow for an early Christmas supper. It's nothing fancy. A simple meal. You're invited." Connor gave her a warm hug. "Can you come at two?"

Mrs. Rainer visibly brightened, her eyes shining as she smiled. "Thank you for the invitation, Connor. I'd be delighted. It'll be good to see Tom too. How is he?"

"Tom is fine, although I'm a little worried because he's lost some weight."

"Have you taken him to the vet?"

"In the city. I've got the number of the vet to call in town."

She nodded. "Doc Carlson? Your mother went to him, as well."

"Yes, I know Doc Carlson. I'll be taking Tom there."

⁓⊹⁓

As he sat on the couch, with Tom curled next to him, Connor closed his eyes. He remembered how much he used to look forward to his mother's delicious homemade cookies after church, when they arrived back at the house. As a child, he believed these special cookies were for Santa, to be left by the chimney with a glass of milk. Later, he knew better, and by then he felt no remorse, when eating 'Santa's cookies.' The thought of his mother's mouthwatering treats brought out a pang which came from nowhere, stunning him, as he tried to hold back sudden tears.

Milk and cookies. Laughter. Music. Perhaps, if he tried hard enough, he would catch a whiff of aroma from the oven, as cookies baked in the kitchen, or hear the sounds of music from times gone by.

⁂

Connor reached for his cell phone, scrolling down until he found the number.

She picked up on the first ring.

"Alana, this is Connor." He came right to the point. "I went to church tonight. Your mother was there."

"What's wrong?"

"I didn't see you there. You haven't talked to your mother, have you?"

She hesitated. "No, but I'm thinking about going to see her on Christmas Day."

"Have you made a decision about coming over for an early supper? I've invited your mother, and she's coming."

There was a long pause on the other end, before Alana spoke. "Does she know I'm here?"

"I haven't mentioned it yet."

"Do you think that's a good idea? To … surprise her like this?"

"Couldn't hurt, could it? I mean, what would you rather do?"

"I've been waiting for the right time."

"Think about it. Sleep on it overnight."

Connor tapped the screen to end the call. He held the

phone, his finger raised, frozen in space. Should he, or shouldn't he, call Mary Ann? The meeting at the flower shop hadn't played out like his dreams. She wasn't overjoyed to see him … but she wasn't cold, either. Was it too late to call her? To make amends? He sat back on the couch, his head resting on the sidearm, closing his eyes. He'd messed up.

Chapter 11

December 25

CONNOR WOKE UP to the familiar blue walls of his childhood bedroom. He lingered, for a moment, between reality and the land of dreams and memories. His groggy mind hadn't yet grasped where he was—he wasn't fully awake. Any minute now, his mom would be calling him to go down to breakfast. He felt loved and safe at home, in his own bed, the innocence of childhood not yet blemished. He relished the comfort of his bed, amongst the familiarity of the house he grew up in. His mind paused in the dimension where time stood still. In it, he went back thirty years. He held on to this innocence, not wanting to let it go. He willed his consciousness to stay in that realm.

The alarm on his cell phone shattered the silence, abruptly bringing Connor to the present. Reality set in, as he comprehended the moment, roughly snatching away the past he had dwelled in. It felt like there was nothing his mind could cling to—hold on to—as the clarity of the day replaced the dreamy realm he had occupied, moments before.

Connor felt the aches of grief, stabbing and jabbing him. At times, anger reared its head, at the thought of this unfairness—this loss in his life. The past few months had been difficult. For days, all he wanted to do was linger in bed. He felt like giving in to the sadness and letting it take over. The strength seeped out of him. This constant cycle of feelings felt like a worn-out tape, replayed over and over. On days like this, it was hard to get up and go to work. Back in the city, on days like this, he'd call in sick, relieved he had saved up hundreds of hours of sick time in lieu. He had never expected to have to use them in that way—that he'd relinquish the desire to work, exchanging it with the stronger pull to stay in bed.

He picked up the cell phone, glancing at the date displayed. December twenty-fifth.

Tom's whiskers tickled his face. Connor heard the soft sound of Tom's breathing, with its familiar nasal drone, right before he felt the wet spot of a feline nose, and the soft pads of Tom's front paws kneading on his chest.

Here, in the bedroom where he grew up, Tom was nestled on top of the blankets, his little body giving out heat. But what warmed Connor's heart was Tom's unconditional love.

Connor ruffled Tom's soft fur. He crooked his thumb under Tom's ears and scratched, right at his favorite spot. "Do you know what today is, Thomas?" When Connor wanted Tom to pay attention, this is what he'd call him.

"Me-ow," cried Tom. He rolled on his side, stretched his legs, and gave a huge yawn, mouth wide open.

Connor hugged Tom, holding his little body close.

Tom wriggled a bit, his intelligent green eyes wide open and ears perked up. His tongue flickered out to give a soft lick, then he got down to business, vigorously dampening his paws and rubbing his face and behind his ears. He repeated this over and over until his fur was wet, clumps of it sticking together. Finished with the task of washing his face, a well-groomed Tom strutted to the edge of the bed and jumped off.

"Hey, fella, let's go see what Santa has left for you," said Connor, bouncing off the mattress and hurrying after Tom.

Chapter 12

ON CHRISTMAS MORNING, Ron knocked on the door. He was punctual—right on time at nine in the morning. Mary Ann was drinking her coffee. She set her mug down and got up from the kitchen table to open the door.

Ron stood outside, all bundled up. Behind him, she could see his pickup truck.

"Merry Christmas, Ron. Come on in," said Mary Ann. Ron had previously fixed plumbing problems and electrical faults after hours at her flower shop. This was the first time he'd been to her home.

Ron wiped his shoes on the welcome mat and stepped inside. "Merry Christmas." He glanced around, noting the tastefully decorated living room. "Nice place you have here."

"I just made coffee. Would you like a cup?"

"I'll take it black," said Ron.

She poured a full cup and handed it to him, wisps of steam curling up. A white cat came out to investigate, sniffing him. "Oh, that's Isabella," said Mary Ann. "It's her way of saying 'hi'."

Ron reached down and held his hand out for her to smell, then petted her and scratched her back. He wasn't exactly a cat person, preferring the company of dogs. But he had no problem with cats, as long as they didn't scratch him.

Before long, they finished the coffee and were on their way to the cabin. Ron drove, eventually turning off onto a graveled forest road. Mary Ann wasn't used to the bumps and the rattling noise from the pickup, and the way Ron quick-tapped the brake. It reached the point where she felt nauseous. Mary Ann almost yelled for him to stop. If she had to puke by the side of the road, so be it.

Ron cranked up the radio, and it was hard to talk over the sound. This suited Mary Ann just fine. She held one hand over her mouth, in case a lurch flipped her stomach and made her throw up. Okay, it was gross. But feeling queasy like this was not good, either. She peeked at Ron. He was focused on driving and oblivious to her plight. She closed her eyes, signaling a 'Do not disturb' vibe his way. *One potato, two potatoes …* she chanted to herself, as she lulled to sleep, hoping that a quick nap would quiet her stomach and take her mind off the nausea.

Mary Ann felt a sharp poke in her arm—a great way to wake up. It put her in a lousy mood. She sat up, feeling the discomfort of the hard seat. She tried rubbing her neck, to relieve the cramped muscles.

They had stopped. The truck was parked in a gravel driveway. There was a log cabin a short distance away.

"We're here."

Mary Ann turned to Ron.

He was putting on his gloves. "Let's go."

"I can't wait to go inside!"

"Not so fast. We're going to take a walk first. I'll show you around the property and get the cabin heated up while you climb the mountain."

"What?" she practically screamed.

He laughed, tipping his head. "Just kidding. I think you need to climb out and stretch your legs first."

The door creaked loudly, as she pulled the handle to open it. The hinges were unforgiving and stiff.

"Hold on," said Ron, dashing to her side of the truck. He yanked the door handle, pulling the groaning door open. "I see what you mean. Man, I need to get this door fixed." He held out his hand, offering to lift her down.

"Just give me a moment," said Mary Ann. It was a chivalrous act but, being an independent woman, Mary Ann preferred to do it on her own. She was used to it. But she also liked being pampered and treated like a lady. What a delightful dilemma.

Ron stepped back, hands off. He watched as she gathered her stuff and swung her slim legs out. He chuckled to himself. His momma brought him up to be respectful and polite—ever the gentleman, especially where women were concerned. However, she also valued a woman who knew how to take care of herself. If she were alive today, he was sure she'd like Mary Ann.

Chapter 13

CONNOR LOVED THE crunch of carrots. He slipped a few pieces in his mouth—a cook's prerogative—as he sliced and diced tiny pieces for the salad. It had become a habit to have a salad with his meal, at least once a day. He added arugula, a must-have, due to its peppery, tasty flavor. Curious to learn more about this green, Connor found numerous benefits touted on the internet (ranging from weight loss to fighting cancers, as well as improvements in skin, bone, and brain health). He mixed in some romaine and baby kale, adding these greens for the nutritional value and variety.

By the time he'd built the salad, he'd added enough for a small mountain—plenty for the meal. He'd invited Pastor Maller and Eva, after the candlelight Christmas Eve service. With Mrs. Rainer, Alana, and himself, it would be five altogether. That is, it would be if Alana decided to come.

Mary Ann crossed his mind. Connor had texted her. He wondered if she might still follow up. It was down to the wire. The chances of her attending this Christmas dinner were diminishing by the moment, his hopes of seeing her vanishing as disappointment swooped in to take its place.

Chapter 14

NEW SNOW HAD blanketed the ground with a layer of white. Mary Ann paused to take in the untouched beauty. *A white wonderland. A cabin nestled in the woods.* The crisp air turned her nose red. Bundled in layers of warm clothing, she welcomed Christmas Day, as the expelled air from her lungs breathed life into the cold, marking the presence of a living body.

Ron was in no hurry. He stood beside her, remembering the first time his dad had brought him out here. He was just a tyke. It was summertime, the verdant landscape showcasing the full bloom of beautiful wildflowers, tall, waving grass, and forested land.

Ron and Mary Ann stood in the now-wintry landscape, in comfortable silence, each lost in their own thoughts.

"My dad—he built this," said Ron, quietly.

Mary Ann nodded and waited for him to continue.

"The cabin used to be a campsite for hunters, but an accident changed him and ended his hunting days." He paused. "My mom's always loved animals and never went hunting with my dad."

"When did this happen?" said Mary Ann, as she looked at the rustic cabin, trying to picture the man who built it.

"A long time ago, when I was a kid."

"Did he ever talk about that last time?"

"My dad said he had his sights on the deer. He was going to shoot the doe, then he saw her fawns in the background, moving closer to be with their mother. The doe raised her head. She was a beautiful doe with big brown eyes. As he raised his rifle to shoot, they locked eyes."

"And then?"

"He said, in that instant, he felt a change of heart. As he stood up from his crouched position, he lowered his rifle. Turning to walk back to the cabin, he tripped on a tangled branch on the ground, fell, and hurt himself. It was a serious injury."

"Oh, that's horrible."

"That's the last time he hunted."

"You still come up here with him?"

Ron shook his head. "He passed two years ago."

"I'm so sorry," said Mary Ann. He looked so forlorn she wanted to give him a hug. Instead, she reached out and patted his hand.

"They were married forty years." Ron didn't often act sentimental, at least not when he was at work. At the age of thirty-eight, he craved to find the kind of love his parents had. "My mother died six months later. She couldn't live without him."

Chapter 15

CONNOR RUBBED A circle on the kitchen window, clearing the steam from the glass pane. Outside, the yard was blanketed with snow. The bare branches of a tree were a stark contrast to the whiteness below. He missed his mom. For the first time in his thirty-eight years, he was spending Christmas alone, in the kitchen where his mother first taught him to cook; where they spent many happy hours together. She was gone forever. Staring at the dark tree, devoid of green leaves, he wondered for a moment if it was dead or still alive.

He felt something brush against his leg. The loud meow announced the presence of another living being. He was reminded he wasn't alone. Tom was with him. His mother had loved the cat. Now, it was his. Picking Tom up, Connor buried his face in the soft fur. "You old bugger, you know how much you mean to me."

Having Tom in his arms brought comfort and different memories. Happy memories of holiday homecomings—his rosy-cheeked mom in her apron and the smell of herb-roasted potatoes in the oven. He could almost see the flickering flames in the fireplace, and hear soft laughter and music playing.

Connor made his first ornament in the kitchen with his mom. He was still a child and stood on a stepstool to reach over the counter top. Using ingredients in the pantry, they made salt dough baubles, mixing together salt, flour, and water. He cut the first one in the shape of a triangle and punched out a hole at the top. Later, after the dough was baked and dried, Connor painted his Christmas tree in bright colors. His mother had smiled at his handiwork, admiring it and looking pleased, before putting a red ribbon through the hole and tying it. "You get to hang this one, Connor." It became a tradition.

After moving to the city, every year Connor would bring home a new tree decoration to be added to the collection. Each year he'd search high and low for the special ornament—something unique and precious, to add to the tree. His mom would make popcorn and string it, adding the final touch to the decorations.

Connor's job was to bring down the boxes of decorations from the attic and adorn the Christmas tree from top to bottom, with the top spot reserved for the white star and angel. He was also the one to string the living room with lights.

Christmas dinner was usually early, around two in the afternoon. His mother had started inviting Mrs. Rainer after her husband died, the year she had a falling-out with her daughter, and Alana left town. Mother never pried, but she felt so bad for Mrs. Rainer, estranged from her only child.

He wondered what could have torn them apart, and how sad and lonely they must feel, especially during the holidays. Alana had been gone eight years. Life was too short to let hurt or pride stand in the way.

He felt compelled to do what he could to bring some Christmas cheer, to get them back together—if only for one day.

Chapter 16

"I'LL BE IN later." She told Ron, as he dashed inside the cabin with an armload of wood. Mary Ann needed to check her phone outside. The bars were down all the way. Later in the day, when she got back in town, she'd return calls. Connor had texted her a cute gif with a happy holiday wish. He was alone in the world. All alone except for Tom, the tabby cat, by his side. Thinking of Connor, a pang of bitterness swept over her.

Who had she been kidding?

It all made sense now. Ron's offer of partnership was the real reason Connor came back into town! Seeing him on Christmas Eve, she had gotten it all wrong. She choked back a cry.

Mary Ann pulled the scarf tighter around her neck, digging her chin inside the collar of her coat. If the brisk cold air found its way in, it would encounter her throat. She hated sore throats. She made sure to stock the special slippery elm tea in her cupboards during the winter months. But she'd forgotten to bring it to the cabin.

Ron had gone in to get the wood-burning stove going. He stood, now, in the doorway, waving her in. She went inside quickly, to warm her toes.

Ron held the door open as Mary Ann stepped across the wooden threshold. He closed the door, bringing in a swoosh of swirling snow and blast of cold wind. "Let me take your coat."

She took off her gloves first, before stuffing them in her coat pocket. "Thanks."

Mary Ann was glad she had triple-layered. Coming in from the bright snow, it took her eyes a few seconds to adjust to the gloom. The cabin was small and unassuming, furnished with just the basics. There was a wood-hewn bed pushed against a wall, a few shelves, a table, two chairs, and a wood-burning stove.

"Welcome to my humble abode," said Ron.

"I like it, and it has a rough, rugged charm in its own way," said Mary Ann, smiling as she rubbed her hands.

Water was heating on the stove. Ron rummaged in his backpack for coffee and a couple of mugs. It didn't take long before he offered Mary Ann a steaming cup of java.

She closed her eyes to take a sip. It was strong and robust, which was just the way she liked it. She wrapped her hands around the mug, capturing the warmth of it.

Ron had a funny smile pasted on his lips, as he watched her. This was the first time he'd brought a woman here. The cabin was built by his father, and it had served as a fishing and hunting camp. By the time he was old enough to come with his dad, it was only used for fishing.

His dad was a real woodsman and a survivalist. He firmly believed in being ready and prepared for the worst. He taught Ron to live in the wild; to know what to do; how to survive in the outdoors. Young Ron had imagined what it must have been like living there, back in the days when it was all wilderness; when wild animals roamed and ruled the land. Truth be told, he preferred the knowledge and modern technology of the twenty-first century. A person could have it both ways, in this world.

Chapter 17

THIS CHRISTMAS—THE first since her best friend, Connor's mom, had passed—Mrs. Rainer felt more alone than she ever had before. Her own inevitable path toward aging and dying loomed closer. She had blocked it from her mind and refused to think about it before—her own death. She was afraid. Of the unknown, of pain, of death, and of what it would feel like to die. She was frightened of what lay beyond. She feared dying alone. She couldn't stand the thought of leaving this world with no one beside her bed to say goodbye to. *Dearly departed* resonated, with an image of kneeling loved ones.

The death of Connor's mom left a void and reminded her of her own mortality. She could not escape her future. The inevitable stared in her face. It waited for her.

At Mrs. Norton's burial, Mrs. Rainer had cried again when her friend's coffin was lowered into the freshly dug ground. She had proceeded in a line of cars to the open grave. The sheriff's car led the way, with its red and blue lights flashing.

She had shuffled along with the line of mourners, each holding a single stem of a white rose. Whispered goodbyes, soft cries, and sniffles were the only accompaniment to the final act of farewell. Dottie Rainer said a silent prayer and released her flower, watching as it glided downward toward the departed. It landed gently on the coffin lid.

She took solace in knowing her friend would lie there in peace, surrounded by beautiful flowers sent by loved ones—before shovels of dirt filled the space and sunlight would no longer shine.

Mrs. Norton rested in peace, in a little piece of land marked by a headstone. This was the image Mrs. Rainer couldn't get out of her mind. Her time was coming. Her wish was for her passing to be in the spring or summer, long before the ground hardened, the trees wizened, and the birds stopped singing.

Chapter 18

AFTER MRS. NORTON'S funeral, Pastor Maller had listened to Mrs. Rainer. He didn't interrupt until she was done. He spoke soothingly, in soft tones. Mrs. Rainer confided in him about Alana, releasing the story buried inside—the ache she had carried in her heart for years. The words tumbled out and sobs came, too, interrupting and mingling with the sound of her voice until she stopped speaking altogether. She let it all out and cried, opening up the floodgates. She released the sadness welled inside, the regrets that found no relief, and the guilt that haunted her.

She cried for everyone and everything, for Alana, for herself. Mrs. Rainer sought release from the loneliness of this world. It was a world she had created, pushing away the daughter she had born and raised. Pushing her out of the safe home and into the harsh world. Forcing her out of her life.

She had kept it all inside of her: the shame, the guilt, and the cross she had to bear.

Dottie Rainer felt the gentle touch of the Pastor's hand on top of hers. His touch brought her to the present, offering comfort instead of punishment, and bringing a bit of warmth into her life.

"You're not alone."

"Please pray for me—for forgiveness," whispered Dottie, as she bowed her head.

Chapter 19

THE PLEASANT AROMA of cinnamon spice candles greeted Alana, as Connor invited her inside. The living room was decorated with sparkling lights and a tree in the middle of the room. The couch had been pushed along the wall. Tom had staked out his spot on top of it, and he was all snug and relaxed like he owned the place. His ears perked up when she arrived.

Connor took Alana's coat and hung it on the rack, smiling as he hugged her. "You're the first."

She walked to the lit Christmas tree, admiring the regular rows of lights and strings of popcorn. She smiled as she saw the decorations adorning the tree from top to bottom—the white star on top, and the angel beside it, looking down at them all.

Alana stopped by the couch to pat the cat. "How's Tom?"

"Happy to be home, like he never left," said Connor.

"Hey, remember me?" said Alana, softly. She played with Tom, stroking the underside of his chin. As her fingers rubbed his body, his thinness became apparent. "Is he all right?" asked Alana, the alarm in her voice evident. Did the orange tabby miss Connor's mom? Did he *mourn* her passing? Or perhaps Tom missed being *here*—a country cat far from home in the city.

"He's lost weight since Mom died, after I took him with me to the city." Connor paused, the feeling of guilt washed over him.

"You take him to the vet?"

"I didn't know what else to do."

"Did it help some?"

"I want to say 'yes', but who am I kidding?" He choked back a surge of sadness. "Tom is supposed to be in my care. He's my mother's cat. But I was selfish. I was withdrawn, and barely able to take care of myself, let alone another living being."

Alana nodded but didn't interrupt.

"Tom stayed home all day when I went to work, and when I got home, I basically ignored him. I only refilled his bowl and water, sometimes not even bothering to wash his dishes." Connor's voice cracked as he continued. "Poor Tom. He must have been starved for attention and affection. But I withheld it. I didn't pet him. Because I didn't touch him, it took a while before I realized he was losing weight."

Connor sat on the couch as Alana continued to pet Tom. "I've called the vet here and got an appointment tomorrow."

"Doc Carlson?"

"He's been taking care of Tom since my mother got him. Whatever the reason, Tom isn't his old self anymore."

"I heard about Tom showing up at your mom's doorstep

one rainy day." Alana scratched behind Tom's ear and massaged his back. "Poor little guy. He was a sorry sight— soaking wet, scraggly and thin."

His heart heavy with remorse, Connor bent over to Tom's level and whispered, "I'm so sorry. Can you forgive me, fella?" *What if Tom was sick?* He had been so consumed with his own grief, he had failed at the only thing he was responsible for—the only living connection to his mother. *Oh, God, please don't let anything happen to Tom! He's innocent.* He wished tomorrow was here already, so he could see the vet right away.

The alarm on the oven sounded, summoning Connor back to the kitchen. "Come and keep me company while I finish."

Alana ruffled Tom's fur and gave him a pat. She rose, catching a delicious aroma as Connor opened the oven door. It reminded her how much she missed holiday meals at home, and pigging out on the Christmas feasts. Nothing compared to enjoying the holidays, with a good meal shared with loved ones.

"I'm making ricotta stuffed shells with spinach and tomato, roasted herb potatoes, butternut squash soup, cranberry jello, and salad," said Connor, as he poked a fork in the diced potatoes.

"Yum! What can I do?" said Alana, as she washed her hands in the sink.

"How about setting the table," said Connor, pointing toward the cabinet where the plates were kept, and the drawer for the silverware.

"For how many?"

"Well, I'm expecting your mom, and Pastor Maller and his daughter. So that makes five of us," said Connor. He eyed the chilled jello, which was loaded with cranberries, chopped nuts, celery, and fruits—his mom's recipe. It was one of her favorites. "And we'll need glasses for the spiked eggnog and mugs for the hot cider."

Alana got to work, to ease her nervousness, busy with the task at hand. As she set the table, she couldn't help thinking of her own mother. What Dottie looked like now. Would she still be upset? How would she react, upon seeing Alana? Maybe this was a bad idea.

Connor put on the finishing touches, lighting cinnamon spice-scented candles in the dining room. Everything was perfect. Mama would be proud. He swallowed, overwhelmed with sadness. He yearned for Christmases past. He had taken so much for granted—her presence, the delicious feast she would prepare, and the family around the dinner table. Coming home for the holidays was something he never gave a second thought. He never stopped to imagine that it would end one day. It hit him hard, as reality set in. Being alone—all alone—for the first time in his life. He whispered, "Mama, I hope you're watching over us. I miss you. I love you. I wish you're here." He paused and added, "And you too, Dad."

He felt apprehensive about what the dinner would hold. There hadn't been any deliberate premeditation, before he invited Dottie and Alana. What right did he have to interfere with their family? Was it his own selfishness that made him do it? Or an unselfish desire to unite long-lost loved ones? An emptiness he sought to fill? Or was it the Christmas spirit that guided him in his actions?

He didn't mention that he had staggered the times he'd asked them to come: Alana first, then her mom, and then Pastor Maller and Eva. Was it sneaky of him to spring into action when an opportunity to reunite two lives presented itself? He'd take the blame if it didn't work out. He would find out soon.

Connor said a silent prayer, as the doorbell rang for the second time.

Chapter 20

ONE COULD SAY that Connor was a good actor. As he flung open the front door to welcome Dottie, you'd never know that anything was troubling him.

Dottie gazed around the festive room, her nose detecting delightful scents. At that moment, she felt a nostalgic Christmas cheer.

"Hello, Connor," said Dottie, as she raised her arms to hug him. Crossing the threshold, she almost expected to see his mom. She brought her homemade gingerbread cake, a favorite of Connor and his mom. But it was all different now, this year, and a wave of sadness seized her. Dottie stood in her dear friend's house, where she had been welcomed so many times. A void existed, this year. She blinked, holding back those thoughts and tears. Her friend would want her to have a happy Christmas.

A light touch on her arm brought her back to the present; to an awareness they both had; to a shared thought—a common mourning. Dottie placed her hand gently on Connor's and squeezed. She didn't need to say anything.

When the knock on the door sounded, Alana had retreated to the bathroom. She leaned on the sink, bracing with her hands, grateful for the support. She turned the faucet on and let the water run, listening to the soothing sound. The water flowed out, spattering clear droplets on the smooth surface of the sink. It seemed as if it was alive, while she had frozen, inert with anxiety.

Delaying the face-to-face meeting with her mother for one more minute, Alana turned off the faucet, finding the strength and courage to do that one inconsequential thing, when the important thing felt impossible.

Why did she come back home, after all these years? Was she crazy? When Pastor Maller told her about Connor's mom's passing, it affected her more than she expected. It didn't hit her all at once, but bit by bit. One day, as she was walking, the image of her small-town main street flashed in her mind. In the days that followed, other things triggered her memories too. She couldn't shrug them off. The way she left home, the lingering nastiness, the ill-will. She had disappeared for so long, without contacting her mother. Had she committed an unforgivable sin? Was it too late to ask for forgiveness? The thought refused to go away, showing itself, again and again, until she took action.

Alana gripped the edge of the sink again. She straightened up and stared in the mirror. *Mirror, mirror on the wall.* If only she could ask it a question, and have it answer.

"Connor is right," said Alana. She took a deep breath. "It's time."

She turned around, opened the door of the bathroom and stepped out.

<hr>

"I need to tell you something," Connor said. "Something about today … How can I explain? I'll start at the beginning, I guess. I arrived in town. I drove through downtown, and it was more beautiful than I remembered. It was all decked out with Christmas decorations."

"I do love this time of the year. Main Street is so festive," said Dottie. The memories of happier times surfaced. "Your mom and I; we had fun shopping. One time, she was looking for a present for you. She found this stuffed bunny with a misshapen nose and a flopped ear that covered one eye—and we couldn't stop laughing."

Connor chuckled. "I know I *didn't* get that one."

"She had a knack for picking out the cutest outfits for you … and the little red dress for Alana."

"I remember," said Connor, pausing before he continued. "Yesterday I walked around downtown. I saw the coffee shop and stopped in to get a nice, hot drink." Connor smiled, adding excitement in his voice. "Guess who I ran into?"

Dottie shook her head.

"I don't understand. Who, you mean …?"

"Alana." The words escaped from Connor's lips, bursting

out. "I invited her to Christmas dinner today."

Dottie gasped. "So … you invited her? *Alana?*"

"I didn't plan exactly this, but she had nowhere else to go, and it's Christmas."

"You have some explaining to do, young man," said Dottie, with a hoarse rasp.

"At the coffee shop, I didn't recognize her at first."

Dottie stared at Connor, latching on to each word.

"We talked, for a bit. Then I … well, she didn't … it just popped out. I invited her over." Connor straightened up. "Please do it for me? Let's just enjoy this meal together—on Christmas Day."

The tiny quiver of Dottie's lips betrayed her feelings, long-buried.

"Can't we just eat and be happy, today of all days?"

⚜

Alana could hear the murmur of conversation.

Connor was sitting with Dottie on the couch. He caught the flickering movement as Alana approached.

Dottie followed his gaze, her eyes resting on Alana. As she stared at her long-estranged daughter, emotions wrestled within her.

No longer the gawkish teenager, Alana had become a young woman. She looked thin, but healthy. Her hair was cut short, almost like a boy. Her cotton shirt was tucked neatly in her jeans.

"I don't care what you do tomorrow," said Connor, looking between the two women. "You'll have to eventually choose if you want to work it out between the two of you. But today, while you're here ..." He paused, taking a deep breath. "Please stay. You are my family, today ... I invited you both here."

Connor choked, as the ache in his chest throbbed with every beat of his heart. "Do it for my mother." He stood abruptly and walked down the hallway toward his bedroom, to give them time alone. He turned his back, to hide the tears rolling down his cheeks.

Chapter 21

MARY ANN STUDIED Ron's profile as she drank her coffee. He was bent over, intent on putting more logs in the wood-burning stove, his arms stretched out. *What was she thinking, when she accepted Ron's invite?* Spending Christmas with Norma's family would've reminded Mary Ann of the emptiness in her life, still single in her thirties.

She wasn't desperate, but the ticking clock only moved in one direction. She couldn't rewind it. If someone had to use three words to describe her, it would be successful, attractive, and independent. And loving? Was this part of her description? She was capable of it. But Mary Ann was older and wiser now, not so eager to give away herself, or her heart. How would it be if she had a partner? One who loved her and supported her. Someone who was her equal. Someone who had everything going in their lives—except in the partner department.

Between work and sleep, Mary Ann didn't have much free time. At least, that was true until she hired Norma to make sure things ran smoothly. Now, she'd run out of excuses. She thought of Connor, and the time she spent with him. That had felt … good. Then, he left town abruptly, without contacting her. Now, he was back, and he wanted to pick up where he had left things. Or had he returned for something else?

Two weeks ago, she had zero prospects. Now, she had two.

Here she was, in a cozy cabin with Ron on Christmas Day. Initially, Mary Ann had dismissed the idea of spending the day out of town. She had pictured herself curled up with a good book and a cup of tea, Isabella close by. Norma was the one who had encouraged her to go out and enjoy herself.

Her thoughts wandered. They found themselves at Connor. What was he doing? He had texted. She read his message, but with no cell coverage, she'd have to respond later. She shook her head and set her focus on the present. On Ron.

She looked out the tiny window of the log cabin. The morning flurries had ceased by the time they arrived. The air had been crisp in the freezing temperature, despite the bright sunny day. Even without the wind, it was still a harsh frozen landscape outside with a layer of fresh snow blanketing it in white.

"Mary Ann." Ron's voice broke through her thoughts.

Mary Ann took off her scarf, feeling the rising temperature warming the room. She scooted closer to the wood-burning stove.

"Hungry?"

She nodded, wondering what he had packed for lunch.

Ron reached into the insulated carrying bag. He pulled out two large containers.

Recognizing the stamped fresh market logo, Mary Ann stifled a laugh. *The man had ordered their holiday dinner takeout.* The market sold produce and cooked food to go, using organic vegetables and eggs. Their holiday meal was known to be extraordinary. She had seen the advertisements and been tempted to forgo cooking this year. She had pegged Ron as someone who didn't spend much time in the kitchen, and she was right.

He was smiling, offering the food as if she was his goddess. Okay, it wasn't quite like that, but he did have a boyish grin on his face.

"What do you have, here?" she asked him.

"A meal fit for a princess."

"Let me guess," said Mary Ann, laughing and pointing. "And you cooked it yourself."

He made a silly face, scrunching his features.

She bent over, cracking up.

Seeing her chest heaving with laughter, his lips parted, revealing his strong white teeth, adding to his charm. Ron joined her, adding his deep, hearty laugh.

Chapter 22

RON DROPPED MARY Ann off at her house around nine-thirty at night. It had been a long day. He walked around his pickup to the passenger side and opened her door.

She got out. "I've had a wonderful Christmas," said Mary Ann. She turned, glancing at her front door.

"Day's not over," prodded Ron, angling for an invite inside.

She touched his arm. "Thank you."

Ron tried to hide his disappointment, but Mary Ann caught a glimpse of it in his eyes.

"I'm tired."

"Do I get a hug?" He opened his arms wide, smiling.

She stepped up into his arms. Mary Ann was short, barely reaching up to his chest. Ron bent his head, inhaling the faint scent of her apricot honey conditioner. Her hair was soft. Stray wisps tickled his cheek. He held her, wrapping his arms around her, enveloping her small frame.

Mary Ann relaxed into the hug, feeling the warmth

penetrate her coat and winter clothes. She nestled her face on the thick fabric of his jacket, finding just the spot to bury it in the slight depression of his shoulder. Was this her wish for Christmas? She had not asked for it. She had maintained the exterior of independence. Ron had chipped it, finding a tiny crack. He worked at it, as if he had taken a chisel and gently scraped the old caulk between the cracks. It had been a time-consuming process, for him.

Outside, the air was crisp. The night sky was clear, and the stars twinkled. Mary Ann closed her eyes, feeling his protective arms surround her, wrapping her like a cocoon. Like a newborn wrapped in a blanket. She could stay like this, in his arms. It was a tempting thought.

She gave him a slight push.

He released her slowly until she broke away.

She raised her head and peered into his eyes. She saw earnest adoration.

He saw a hint of promise in her eyes, of how things might be, in the future.

Mary Ann dug into her purse for her house key and walked up to the door. She turned the lock. "Good night … and Merry Christmas, Ron." She smiled at him before she stepped inside.

Isabella came up to her, meowing noisily and making her presence known, as Mary Ann closed the door.

Bending down to pick up her cat, Mary Ann took a moment to pet her before moving to the kitchen. She opened the special cat treats she got for Christmas and watched as Isabella finished them, daintily.

"Yummy?"

A lick on the chops served as an answer.

It was getting late. Mary Ann shed her clothes and jumped in the shower. Her body ached for the warm water to pulse and soothe every inch of her.

She set her mind free, letting her thoughts wander, going back over the day. It had been a rare break for her—a time for self-reflection and inspiration. A glimpse of hope, on Christmas Day. A connection with nature. It was a change of scenery she sorely needed. She was grateful that Ron had brought her to his cabin—a quiet place to relax, to be in touch with her inner self. She had been out of tune. A powerful connection was missing in her life. She had been overwhelmed with the hard work and worries involved with starting a new business, and she had shouldered a heavier burden than she had anticipated.

She had loved hearing the crunch of snow impacted by the weight of her boots, yet she almost hesitated to step on it. Disturbing the pristine white canvas felt wrong. She tried to imagine the cabin in the summertime—trees with thick, green foliage, abundant wildlife, flowers, butterflies, and bees. Being outdoors rejuvenated her, beyond anything else she could do, filling her lungs with fresh air and renewed energy.

The awesomeness of nature was breath-taking. The flowers she sold in her shop were created by it—untouched by human hand until they were cut away and harvested to adorn homes and bring joy or comfort to special occasions. Without knowing how it happened, she had gravitated to nature, to a job where she was surrounded by the most beautiful flowers, every day, in the full bloom of their beauty, some more fragrant than even the most expensive manufactured perfume. She needed to find what inspired her. She had to make sense of her future, of her past; to find the connection with the earth, and feel grounded. This was what she had almost forgotten. This was what was missing— the salve for the aches, the loneliness, and the hardships in life.

The day in the wilderness had touched Mary Ann's heart, stirring it, prodding and searching for life. It had awakened her. It had located the spirit she buried deep inside of her. This was a true gift on Christmas—unexpected and innocent. Stripped away from the commercial frenzy of the season, Mary Ann found peace, solace, and meaning. She felt like one of the animals and bare trees, who braved the harsh winter, waiting for the spring to bring new life.

Chapter 23

DOTTIE COLLAPSED IN tears, overtaken by the surprise and shock of seeing her long-lost daughter.

Alana reached out and grabbed a tissue box.

Dottie sobbed, uncontrollably, her shoulders shaking.

Staring at the stranger sitting on the couch, an image from happier times came to Dottie's mind—a little girl wearing the red dress, the one she got for Christmas one year.

"Do you remember the little red dress … the one you loved to wear?" said Dottie, her voice trembling between sobs.

Alana nodded, her eyes moist.

"I remember, when you wore it … how you twirled around and around." Dottie twisted the wet tissues in her hand. "I was afraid you'd get dizzy and fall."

"I loved the dress," said Alana. "It brings back memories. Good memories. How it used to be, when I was a little girl."

"When you were three years old."

"You loved me, then, *Mama*," said Alana. "Why can't

you love me now?" She thumped her chest, crying out in anguish. "It's me. I'm still Alana." Tears gushed out.

Dottie stared at her. A vision came to her, of the last time she saw her. The words Dottie said then: harsh, cruel words, meant to cut and wound. How could she ever take it back? Did Alana still remember those three words?

As if she read her mind, Alana murmured, mouthing the very words Dottie said then.

Dottie's hopes sank, hearing them. She didn't deserve forgiveness. What she had said was unforgivable. She turned her face, as tears flowed, spilling onto her cheeks. Those words were etched in her soul. She had confessed to the Pastor—asked God for forgiveness for her sins. But she hadn't asked Alana.

"Mama!"

Flashes of the past flickered, like the fast-forward of a silent film: the day Alana was born; the first time she held Alana in her arms; the sweet smell of a newborn; the knit cap on her head, the rest of her body swaddled in a pink baby blanket. Then, the first day Alana crawled, took her first step … the first word out of her mouth.

The years flew by. More memories emerged: Alana spewing green florets and throwing her spoon across the table, when she first tasted broccoli. Alana, the toddler in the white leather shoes and a flash of red dress as she danced and twirled. The preschooler, hesitating before the door on her first day of school, reluctant to leave her mother standing outside. Then, the years afterward showed. What had gone wrong?

"Mama, talk to me."

Dottie's mouth felt dry. The upsetting memories of when her precious little girl grew up and became someone foreign to her. Someone she disapproved of. *What happened to my little girl?* Dottie had become unyielding, hardening her heart. She drove a wedge between herself and her teenaged child. They say that wounds heal, and it's true—a physical wound does. But words cut deep into the spirit; into the heart. What salve is there for these wounds?

Dottie sighed. It would not be easy to swallow her pride and admit she was wrong. It would be harder, still, to ask for forgiveness. To say those other three words: "I am sorry." The apology stuck in her throat. She shook her head and got up, moving toward the kitchen to get a glass of water.

What about Alana? Was she sorry?

Chapter 24

THE KNOCK ON the door announced the arrival of Pastor Maller and his daughter, Eva. Alana yelled to alert Connor.

Outside, it had stopped snowing. The clear, bright day brought a breath of fresh air and sunshine as Connor opened the door, mixing it with the scent of candles. He greeted Pastor Maller and Eva, warmly, and ushered them inside. He hung their coats up and carried Eva's dish of quiche into the kitchen. It was still warm from the oven. "Please, have a seat. How about some warm apple cider?"

A chorus of "Yes, please!" returned to him. Connor smiled as he got four mugs, adding one for himself. For a moment, he thought of Mary Ann. Then, he poured the cider and brought the cups out. He handed one to each person.

It had been a long time since Alana had seen the Pastor and his daughter. They engaged in an animated conversation, getting caught up. Dottie stayed quiet, but she listened intently, not missing a word. Connor interjected, once or twice, to ask Alana questions on things she had brought up. He took care not to pry into anything uncomfortable. The talk was lively, touching on highlights. At times, it was a bit sad, but they quickly moved past the hard emotions and on to the good things. Nobody brought up, or asked about, the night when Alana left.

A pleasant ding of an alarm sounded from the kitchen. "The food is ready," said Connor. "Shall we move to the dining room?" He held the chair for the Pastor, nodding to Eva to sit next to him at the table. Dottie and Alana sat across from them.

Connor brought out the dishes, before he sat at the end of the table.

"The food looks great," said Eva.

"Yeah, it's a feast," added Alana.

"Would you please pray?" said Connor, looking at the Pastor.

Pastor Maller nodded and closed his eyes. He started with the usual blessings. Then, he spoke of things more specific—of Christmas and everyone gathering together. He paused. Then, he said a heartfelt prayer—a prayer within a prayer—for Connor's mom, Mrs. Norton, and their first Christmas without her. He felt Eva's hand touch his. It was a firm grasp.

Eva was grateful for her dad. She had heard his prayers and sermons countless times. His prayers for other people— to give them hope, soothe their pain, lift them up, and bless their happiness. Prayers for babies coming into this world and those departed. Eva said a silent prayer, now, for her father. She thought of the things she wanted to say to him but had never voiced. She composed in her head a blessing for his excellent health. She had noticed his age, becoming slightly stooped as he walked. She saw his fragility, as he forsook himself for God and others.

Connor held back his tears. He wiped the corners of his eyes, grateful they were closed in prayer. He gulped and swallowed. For as long as he lived, in his thirty-eight years, he'd spent Christmas here. In the twenty years since Connor had left home, his visits had become fewer, but he made sure every year he returned for Christmas. It would never be the same again. This year, his mother's chair sat empty. This year, he honored his mom, keeping the tradition. He shared the love she gave him with the people dear to her.

Dottie squeezed her eyes shut. She missed her old friend and had felt a heavy sadness since her death. Dread and despair descended, trapping her. The only way out was through the door to her impending fate in life. Her days were numbered, marching to a clock which would one day stop.

Alana snatched a peek at her mother, opening one eye briefly. The years had not been kind to Dottie. The gray in her hair was much more pronounced than when Alana left. Her face had become more angular. The lines were more prominent. Her slight frame was thinner. But Dottie had lost more than her weight. Something had changed. How many times had Alana thought of picking up the phone and calling her mom, of coming home? Alana was ashamed. She relived the angst of the past. It was a punishment Alana dealt out to herself. The past eight years had been hard on Dottie, and she was the reason. Mrs. Norton's death had been her wake-up call, and Alana returned before it was too late. She teared up at the thought of losing her mother … and prayed for her.

Chapter 25

AFTER DINNER, EVA helped Connor with the dishes. Alana stayed at the table, sitting next to her mother. She handed her a wrapped present.

"Merry Christmas, Mom," said Alana.

Holding the neat oblong package, Dottie looked at the colorful paper and the neatly-tied ribbon. "What's this?"

"Go ahead. Open it."

Dottie slowly peeled back the taped ends, and pulled out her gift. Her eyes opened wide as she caught sight of the book title and the author. "This is *your* book?"

"Yes, it's new, just released in December," said Alana, speaking with excitement and pride.

Dottie turned it over. The back cover had a description and a photo of Alana. "This is your story ... *The Runaway*."

Alana nodded. "Like the photo?"

"It's casual, but it looks professional."

"Look inside," said Alana, flipping the pages to her inscription. "I signed the book."

"I see, and you dated it December twenty-fifth," said Dottie.

"One more thing. Turn the page."

Tears welled up in Dottie's eyes when she saw Alana had dedicated the book to her mother and father.

Alana reached over and grabbed a clean napkin on the table. "Here, use this."

"Thank you."

"Mama, what happened was an accident."

"Which part? You never meant to be caught?" said Dottie, talking between sniffles.

"I never meant for any of it."

"That night …"

"I waited until everyone was asleep before I got up."

"You thought everyone was sleeping."

"I snuck in the kitchen; to the secret place where I knew you kept it."

"Why?"

"I thought I had enough money for Christmas, but something unexpected threw the best-laid plans off."

"So, you stole money."

"Yes, but it wasn't for me, and I planned to replace it before you found out."

"Your dad …"

"I jumped when he came up behind me. He'd gotten up to get a drink of water in the kitchen."

"Caught you in the act."

Alana looked down, her cheeks aflame.

"He was furious, livid with anger … like I've never seen him," said Alana. "He grabbed me. I was still holding on to the money. I wouldn't let go." She wet her lips. "We struggled."

"I woke up to the noise," said Dottie. "I saw him falling to the floor, gripping his chest." She paused. Reliving the moment was difficult. "I rushed to him and called 911."

Alana said nothing. She'd give anything to relive that moment; to give back her father's life. All she could remember was her mother's chilling words, spat out in the heat of the moment, without thinking. Those three accusatory words: "You're killing him."

Chapter 26

December 26

CONNOR PULLED INTO the parking lot of Doc Carlson's office. It was housed in a nondescript building. A solitary, faded sign—which said "Veterinary Care"—hung over the doorway. It was quiet. Low bushes lined the somber gray cement of the walkway. Behind curtains, a soft glow lit up the building.

It was early morning, a few minutes before eight, on the day after Christmas. The lot was empty, except for a dusty pickup, which probably belonged to the vet. Connor had called the Doc and left a message. In the city, he wouldn't have expected to get an appointment over the holidays. Good old Doc Carlson had called him right back and gave him the first available slot. In this small town, the good Doc put his patients first.

During the journey, Tom had been curled up in the pet carrier. He was alert and awake, now. He knew something was going on. And he was pissed. He didn't like to be cramped and locked up in a tiny cell. *Imprisoned like a criminal!* He'd have none of it. His funk had gone from bad to foul. The mood had begun when he was awakened early that morning, at the most inopportune moment—just as he dreamed of catching the mouse. The tip of its tail was flickering in front of Tom's whiskers. His prey was inches from his grasp …

"Hey, guy, yes you," said Connor, adding as much charm as he could muster, when talking to his cat.

Tom didn't even blink an eye.

He bent, putting his face closer to the wire door of the carrier. "I know you're not going to like this." Connor stifled a laugh—no point in rubbing it in.

Connor stopped his humiliating baby talk. By golly, Tom was a full-grown cat! He remembered how Tom was: how he stood and strutted in all his glory. *A ferocious mice hunter!*

"It's okay, fella. I'm going to get you all checked out, ready for the new year," said Connor.

Connor turned the car key, cutting off the engine. He reached for Tom's carrier. "Let's go get this over with." *For you and me both*, he wanted to add.

The bell chimed, when Connor opened the door. The waiting room hadn't changed much from the last time he was here, with his mom. Doc Carlson was a no-frills kind of guy and didn't waste money on interior decoration. The Doc never married. To put it another way, he was married to his work. The loves of his life were his animal patients. In his younger days, he used to do house calls. As the years rolled on, he established an office and did less traveling.

"Doc Carlson?" said Connor, nodding to the man in a

white coat standing behind the counter. He looked older, the patches of white hair having wholly taken over. His lips seemed thinner and sterner. His head was tilted forward a bit, his shoulders slightly rounded. But the blue eyes that stared back at Connor were bright and sharp, like the mind behind them.

"You're Mabel Norton's boy," said the Doc, as he greeted him.

Connor extended his free hand in greeting. "Yes, sir. Connor Norton." He turned the carrier a bit, so the front door would face the vet. "And this is my mama's cat, Tom."

The Doc chuckled. "I sure remember Tom."

Connor gave him his full attention.

"That day, he was a sorry sight, all wet and scrawny-looking, but your mama poured all her love on him, and nursed him back to health." He paused, eyes on the cat. "You'd hardly recognize Tom, after he was cleaned up and recovered. He was gorgeous—all orange stripes, with round, green eyes and long whiskers."

"He sure is a handsome fellow," said Connor. "He was all I had, after my mother passed. I took him back to the city with me."

"Let's take a look at him," said Doc Carlson, leading the way to the examination room down the hall.

Connor put the carrier on the counter in the middle of the room. He opened the hatch. Tom needed no coaxing to come out, extending his legs to stand on firm ground.

"I'm worried about him. He's losing weight."

"How long has this been going on?"

"I'm not sure," said Connor, wracked with guilt over his neglectful behavior.

"You've had him for a few months?"

"About four months."

"Take him to see a vet in the city?"

Connor nodded and reached in his coat pocket. "I have this." He retrieved a few pages of folded papers and handed them to the vet. "They ran some tests. Here are the lab results of blood samples they took."

Doc Carlson glanced at the numbers, dated mid-December. The city vet had done extensive testing, ruling out kidney disease or renal failure, liver disease, hyperthyroidism from excessive amounts of thyroid hormone, diabetes, tumors, digestive disorders, and other conditions. There were no abnormal results. The city vet even did X-rays.

"His kidney and thyroids—"

"Checked out fine. He looks to be in good health."

Connor let out a sigh of relief on hearing the last part: 'in good health'. "But he's losing weight."

Doc Carlson weighed Tom and gave him a physical. "Seven-and-a-half pounds."

Connor tensed, his heart rate sped up.

"Let's try this." He wrote the brand name of a cat food on a piece of paper and handed it to Connor. "Adjust his diet gradually. Be sure the cat food is on a clean plate, especially wet food. Do you give him fresh water daily, in a clean water bowl?"

"I've been too busy at work … I've been forgetting to clean his bowls or change the water." Connor fidgeted, uncomfortable about admitting to his role in Tom's condition.

Doc Carlson's eyes pierced through Connor's flimsy excuse. Mabel would not have neglected her cat, and Tom had been Mabel's constant companion until she died. Could the shock of losing her have affected Tom?

"Have you noticed any changes in Tom, after Mabel died?"

"He's lost interest in food," said Connor. "And he seemed to have less energy and he's sleeping more."

"You took him to the city. What kind of place did you have?"

"I had a two-bedroom condo. It wasn't a high-rise."

"Did you have a yard?"

Connor shook his head. "Not much of one. Space was at a premium, and the designers chose to optimize the square footage of the living area."

"So, Tom stayed indoors while you went to work?" said Doc Carlson.

"Yes."

"How long did you leave him?"

"I leave for work early and get home by dark most days. It would be about ten to twelve hours."

"Those are long hours."

"I'm used to them," said Connor. He attempted a joke, adding, "It's the price you pay for an office with a window." Above him, only the top executives got the corner offices with windows on two sides.

"What did Tom do, while you were gone?"

Connor looked up, his mind switching back to the cat.

Honestly, he didn't know. "He had the whole condo to himself. He was alone."

Doc Carlson didn't have the fancy equipment of the city vets. But he was a skilled diagnostician. His years of experience and his talent earned him the respect of many owners.

"Did you know animals can grieve?" asked Doc Carlson.

Connor stared at the older man, trying to translate this. He hadn't thought of Tom as grieving.

"You mean Tom could be in mourning?"

"From what you've described of Tom's behavior, and the changes he's experienced, I'd have to say 'yes'."

"From losing my mom?"

"Your mom was his constant companion. It was just the two of them, living in the house." Doc Carlson spoke firmly, and steadily. "Not only that, the change in environment when you moved Tom from the small town to the city—from your mom's house to the condo." He paused. "And being alone in a strange environment all day."

Connor digested all this information—all these changes must have affected Tom. *Poor fella.* "I must admit I failed with Tom. I was absorbed in my own world … my grief."

"Tom would have sensed it too—*your* grief."

"Poor Tom." Connor just wanted to beg for his forgiveness and hide. *How could he have done this?* Tom was the only living thing he had left in the world, after his mom died. The cat was her companion to the end.

"Mabel loved this orange boy, dearly," said Doc Carlson. "If it wasn't for Tom, she may not have lived that long."

Doc Carlson's brow furrowed. He opened his mouth to give Connor a piece of his mind, but the remorse on Connor's face stopped him.

"Let's just keep a close eye on Tom. Will you be staying a bit?"

"I've quit my job in the city."

"You'll be here?"

"At least until I figure out what to do with my life."

"There are a few things you can do to help him."

Connor nodded, eagerly, hoping for a chance to do something before it was too late. "Anything."

"Spend more time with Tom. Since you've quit your job, you're not going to leave him alone all day. Touch can be healing, for both of you."

"I can do that."

"Get yourself a cat comb or brush. Pet Tom, brush him, talk and sing to him. Do whatever you can do, to connect."

"I'm afraid singing is out of the question," said Connor.

"Play some music. Pick something your mother liked. Ease him back. Let him go outside."

Connor laughed, pointing his finger. "You should see Tom in action outdoors. He loves to chase butterflies. And he gets in plenty of trouble going after his favorite rodents."

Doc smiled. "Your mom was fond of retelling Tom's feats: how he'd carry his prized mouse in his mouth and laid it on her front door mat."

"But she never scolded him."

"No, she made a big fuss over Tom, and thanked him for his gift by giving him special treats."

Connor glanced at Tom—the smart, beautiful, healthy and muscular cat he was. And now he's just lying there, muscles limp and out of practice. He made a promise to Tom. *We'll have to change things.*

"Bring Tom back in a couple of weeks. We'll see how he's doing," said Doc Carlson.

Connor stopped by the store on his way home, to pick up the new cat food, bowl, and a plate for Tom, along with a comb and a brush. Visual reminders of change. Those were easy gifts: the ones money could buy. What Connor needed to do was to give Tom the gift of time and his love. Gifts from the heart. It was time Connor honored his mother and took proper care of the cat she loved so much.

Chapter 27

AFTER SEEING DOC Carlson, Connor stopped by in town to see Mr. Monroe, the attorney. Going up the steps, he could see a little sign posted on the door. The business was closed for the holidays, until January second. Connor wasn't surprised. He would call and make an appointment to be sure his parents' affairs were settled.

He continued the short walk to the flower shop. Mary Ann had texted him back, a nice thanks and well wishes. He'd figured she'd have holiday plans, and he hadn't expected her to drop everything and spend Christmas with him, when he appeared out of nowhere on Christmas Eve. Connor was curious about who she had spent her day with. The expectations he had of her were all his own making; in his own mind. He hadn't taken any action or kept in touch, for four months. What right did he have to expect anything from her? It was a stretch, but he had a lively imagination. Mary Ann had been the bright spot in his life, after his mother passed. He had kept her in mind. Connor had no right to expect anything from her. Was he a cold-hearted, selfish man? Was he ready for a partner? Connor couldn't even take care of a cat.

He stopped, steps away from her flower shop. Then, he slowly turned around and walked away.

Chapter 28

MARY ANN CARRIED the chalkboard, setting it down behind the counter. It was Norma's idea. It was now a ritual to write on the chalkboard in the morning, and it got her creative juices flowing. She opened her tray of colorful chalks and got started. The flowers changed weekly, and it was seasonal. She drew the flowers, wrote out the name and added a short factoid, about the plant she'd drawn.

If there was a sale or a promotion on, or a holiday around the corner, she'd add the details of that too. Now, she erased the 'Merry Christmas' and replaced it with 'Happy Holidays.' Soon, it would be changed to a New Year greeting.

She thought about the day before, in the cabin with Ron, and the hug they had shared afterward. She'd almost hung mistletoe on her porch but didn't get it done in time. It would have assured a kiss! She wondered what a kiss with Ron would have been like. She had said 'yes', when Ron invited her to his cabin. She was ready for a change in scenery, and it felt good to get away. Ron had called, and let her know he had a good time. She smiled.

"Someone had a nice Christmas," said Norma. She walked in wearing a new coat, carrying her purse in one hand.

Mary Ann blushed.

"C'mon, out with all the juicy details."

"I'd rather admire your new coat."

Norma stopped in front of Mary Ann and unbuttoned it. "Feel how soft it is."

"It suits you," said Mary Ann. Her hand caressed the soft fabric. *It must be a new blend*, she thought. It wasn't scratchy and rough, like wool. "And camel tan is your favorite color. So, how did Stan know exactly what you wanted?"

"I don't pussyfoot around. Not when it comes to what I want." Norma took off her gloves, pulling one finger at a time. She started with the thumb and worked her way down. "I tell him."

Mary Ann watched Norma fold her gloves and stuff them in her pocket.

Norma cleared her throat. "And if that doesn't get the message across, I cut out the picture in the catalog, or print it off the internet, and hand it to Stan."

"That's clear as mud," said Mary Ann. She couldn't resist a little tease.

"Back to where we were. You changed the subject," said Norma. Nothing much got by her. Not when it came to the customers. Not when it came to Mary Ann. "So, you had a good time with Ron?"

"I ... I warmed up to it—the cabin, him, well ... everything."

"You see what you would have missed by not going?"

Mary Ann laughed, then leaned back to admire her handiwork on the chalkboard. "What do you think?"

Norma nodded her approval. "I like it."

"I think I'll leave this up until New Year's Eve," said Mary Ann. "Four more days, then we start over for a new year."

"You got plans?"

"I'll probably be snug in bed." *Or I'll be partying with Ron*, Mary Ann thought.

"Not big on watching fireworks?"

"Maybe I'll watch it on TV, if I'm up. You guys have a celebration?"

"Not a big one. We'll have dinner with the kids."

"Well, good," said Mary Ann. Satisfied with her finished artwork, she set the chalkboard easel display on the sidewalk.

Chapter 29

December 31

CONNOR WOKE UP early on New Year's Eve. He spent a quiet holiday in his mother's home, aside from seeing Mrs. Rainer again when she came by. He had been touched by her kindness; her visit to see how he and Tom were doing.

He had actually considered inviting her to his mom's house, for a New Year's Eve brunch. But she beat him to it. Dottie Rainer had sounded chipper when she called, which had made him feel a bit sad, if he was completely honest. Connor was fighting off a bout of doldrums after Christmas. When Mrs. Rainer extended the invitation, he quickly accepted. It might cheer him up.

He made two dishes to bring: an asparagus mushroom casserole he'd converted from his mom's old recipe, and his own signature salad. Growing up in Rocky Flats, Connor had even foraged for wild mushrooms when they were seasonal, and made this substitution in her recipe. Now, he still enjoyed being creative and experimenting with food.

Connor had been thinking about food a lot lately. He was even considering getting a part-time job at the fresh market, cooking. He had thought long and hard about Ron's offer to be partners at his hardware store. Connor had called him back to thank him for his generosity, but to say he couldn't accept. He apologized for taking so long to respond. It wasn't a decision Connor made lightly. In the end, he went by his inner voice. He knew his heart wasn't in it.

At two o'clock, he walked next door to Dottie's, taking Tom with him. Her place had become drab and neglected, after her husband died and Alana left. When Connor knocked on the door, Dottie flung it open, immediately.

"Well, do come in," said Dottie. She was acting like an excited hostess.

"Oh, Wow!" Connor's face registered surprise upon seeing the pleasing freshly-painted walls.

Before he could set his food down, Alana appeared. "I'll take it to the kitchen."

"You're here!"

"I've been busy working," said Alana, waving her arms across the living room. "Like my paint job?"

"It looks great," said Connor. "You've done wonders for this place." He hadn't seen Alana and had been wondering if she'd left town again. So, this was what had kept her busy.

Before long, Pastor Maller and Eva arrived, too. It was like one happy family again.

During dinner, Dottie told them what happened after she went home on Christmas. She had read Alana's book and cried, long and hard, finally coming to terms with the night Alana left. She had asked her daughter for forgiveness.

One question kept bugging Connor. He turned to Alana. "The night it happened, why did you take the money?"

"I needed it, to help out a friend."

"Couldn't you have just asked your mother?"

Alana shook her head. "No, I promised I wouldn't tell."

"So, you thought you had to steal the money?"

"Yes. I knew it was wrong, but my friend counted on me. She was in trouble and couldn't tell her parents."

"We've forgiven each other," said Dottie. "Alana came home. It's all that matters."

Alana smiled. "I love you, Mom." She turned and gave her mom a hug. She planted a tender kiss on Dottie's cheek, before releasing her.

Dottie looked up at her tall, lovely daughter; the spark back in her eyes. "I love you, Alana."

"I'm home, Mama."

Chapter 30

December 31

HE USED TO love New Year's. After the hustle and bustle of the holidays, it meant one more day of relaxing and having fun. One more day before he went back to work. But it had all changed, this year. He cut the chains that were pulling him back. The coveted office with the window he'd finally reached seemed of little consequence, now. The many years he'd invested in achieving this goal left a taste of bitterness.

Connor looked forward, now. For the first time in many years, he felt a stir of anticipation; of a new adventure—the bloom of new life.

Even Tom had changed. Connor watched the cat's chest rise and fall, with each breath. Connor let him sleep, not disturbing him. Since coming back to his childhood home, Tom had slowly slipped into his old habits, finding his favorite nooks and crannies. He was taking possession of the place, again, like it was his home—which it was. He jumped up on the couch, the bed, or wherever he felt like plopping down. He even explored the snow.

Connor propped up a makeshift window seat in the living room, so Tom could look out the window to his heart's content. It took little to make him happy. Connor could count the ways on his fingers.

He suspected the move from the city had done wonders for Tom. He enjoyed watching him revert to his old self again. Wise Doc Carlson had been right. The little spark had not been extinguished.

Tom had come home. So had Connor.

Chapter 31

Around Midnight, December 31

MARY ANN LED Ron outside her place, a few minutes before the stroke of midnight. "I want to see the stars tonight." Faint popping sounded in the distance.

Ron enjoyed spending time with Mary Ann. Ever since the trip to his cabin on Christmas, they'd been almost inseparable. He liked the things they had in common, her understated sense of humor, and her strengths. Her adventurous side, as well as her reserved side. He was patient, earning her trust bit by bit. As she became more open, and exposed her vulnerabilities, he felt protective. He couldn't deny the strong attraction and a growing fondness—something special he'd never felt before, for any other person.

They stood together under the clear night sky. Side by side. "It's beautiful," said Ron. He wrapped his arm around her shoulder, pulling her closer.

She curled her arm, reaching behind his back and around his waist, and whispered his name.

The moon was visible. The stars twinkled across the vast expanse of space, as far as the eye could see. It was breathtaking. A natural canvas that no human painter could ever recreate.

As midnight approached, Ron turned to face Mary Ann. His fingertips affectionately caressed her cheek. She tilted her face. They stared into each other's eyes; deep into each other's souls.

At the stroke of midnight, their lips met for the first time.

THE CONCLUSION OF THE *FLOWERS IN DECEMBER* TRILOGY

SECOND *chance*

JANE SUEN

Chapter 1

SHE FELT SOFT hairs brush against her leg a moment before Isabella leaped on the couch and joined her.

"Well, Happy New Year to you, too," said Mary Ann, her lips brushing the silky white hairs as she planted a kiss on the cat's head. Mary Ann had settled in for a few minutes of quiet time to write, curled up on the couch, a steaming mug of hot chocolate within easy reach on the table. Putting her pen and notebook aside, Mary Ann gave Isabella some love—rather some extra love—on this special day, as the cat nestled and carved out a snug spot next to her. She petted her cat, feeling the warmth of Isabella's small body and hearing the soft, contented purr.

Mary Ann glanced at the resolutions she had scribbled on the pad. It helped to see it in writing. Made it more real, accountable. She always started with her best intentions, but knew most of them would fall to the wayside long before the year was over. She'd learned a long time ago not to be too hard on herself and to celebrate when she achieved just one thing, even if it was the smallest of goals.

On the notepad, Mary Ann had written one word: love.

Her grandfather had shown her the meaning of love after her father died. Thinking of him brought a familiar ache to her heart. Grandpa Evert had passed almost two years ago. He had been the one person she loved more than anyone, since her father died when she was six and her mother remarried to Steve a few years later. Her stepfather—the thought of him, and that word, stepfather, repulsed her. He had forced Mary Ann to say it, call him *Dad*, and then he'd watch as she choked on it, spitting it out. Her mother never understood why Mary Ann was so stubborn. Why her daughter wouldn't accept *Dad*.

But Grandpa did—he understood and knew Mary Ann better than anyone. He practically raised her. Mary Ann had spent as much time with him as she could. He and Grandma lived in the same neighborhood and within easy walking distance, and Mary Ann would pass by their house on the way to the elementary school. She treasured the memories of those happy days.

After school, Mary Ann would race to their front door, her skinny legs flying. She was always hungry right about this time, and they took care of her. Grandma made sure she had a snack, the homemade kind—not something you'd buy in a plastic wrapper to tear open. More often than not, it'd be a chewy cookie and a glass of milk. Grandma used to say, "Let's not spoil your appetite." When Mary Ann finished and wiped the crumbs off her face, Grandpa would be waiting in his favorite easy chair. They'd sit and chat for a while; he always wanted to know how her day went.

Sometimes Grandma would join them or sit in her chair and knit. Sometimes Mary Ann stayed with them for an entire weekend visit.

Mary Ann didn't mind homework, though they didn't call it "work" for nothing. Grandpa made sure she stayed on top of things and didn't slack off. His motto was "homework first," so he'd make sure she did it. If she had questions, he was more than happy to help. Grandpa didn't lavish praises on Mary Ann when she did well in school. But he'd ask for her report card, taking his time to put on his glasses and look over her grades. The most he ever said was "good." Once Mary Ann overheard Grandpa talk about her, saying she was "smart as a whip," and she felt happy and all warm and wonderful inside.

She smiled, remembering Grandpa. He was a tough old man—both outside and in: wiry and without an ounce of extra fat on his lean frame, and possessing a resilience born of survival through hard times. His parents struggled during the Great Depression—difficult times that almost tore apart the fabric of their family. They were proud folks and refused to take government handouts and avoided the shame of going on welfare. They didn't buy new clothes for a long time. Instead, his mother patched their worn-out clothing.

The family lived mainly on soup and bread. His mother struck up an acquaintance with the butcher and bartered with him, taking in his laundry and doing some sewing in exchange for soup bones and occasional scraps of meat. Nothing was wasted. Old vegetables were never tossed away unless they were rotten. Odds and ends of veggies found their way into the soup. It'd simmer for hours on the stove; the delicious smell wafting in the air as his mother lifted the cover, adding scraps and stirring the mixture, mixing in seasonings and herbs to flavor the broth.

Mary Ann loved to hear Grandpa's stories of the hardships they endured during those Great Depression years, and how they survived and grew closer through the experience. They lived through it, became stronger. She teared up, glancing at his picture, the frame propped on the table against the living room wall. Even in his nineties, Grandpa looked handsome. A head full of shocking white hair, a deeply lined face, and just a trace of a smile below stern, proud eyes.

Chapter 2

THE STARK WINTRY scene was a reminder to dress warmly. Mary Ann pulled on a thermal shirt and tucked it into her jeans. The weather reporter warned of another storm brewing, with a snowfall of likely a foot or more. Walking out her door, she scrunched her face to gaze up at the sky. Dense gray clouds had blocked out the sun. She shivered, zipping up her jacket.

The holidays had almost depleted her food supplies. Mary Ann needed to stock up and refill the pantry. She'd meant to go earlier, but the week had passed. A hankering for a bowl of hot soup and slow-cooked ingredients simmered for hours came to mind. She swallowed in anticipation. She wasn't up to cooking today.

Mary Ann was ready for the winter to be over. The last few weeks had been bitter cold—the kind that cuts through, chilling to the bones. Yet she hadn't minded it too much as long as the sun was out. Now, Mary Ann dreaded the approaching storm and the upheaval it would bring. It was best to reach the market before another stampede cleared the shelves. She should be getting used to the weather by now, living in this small mountain town.

When Mary Ann opened the flower shop in Rocky Flats, she became a member of its business community and the town itself. Connor's mom and the other folks she met had welcomed her warmly. Mary Ann got to know them when they ordered flowers for birthdays, graduations, jobs, marriages, holidays—occasions for celebrations, as well as for get-wells and the passing of life.

This time of year especially—home, family, the meaning of life, and Christmas brought back fond memories for Mary Ann: of her childhood with her father, those years she had with Grandpa Evert and Grandma, the happy days of long ago. Memories tugged at Mary Ann's heart and transported her to a time and place that was magical, so many years ago—to the life she'd had as a child, the joys she'd experienced. This quaint and charming town had brought back those special childhood memories.

Mary Ann stopped by the grocery store for essential staples: coffee, eggs, milk, cheese, bread, and to be sure—something for Isabella. Quickly maneuvering down the familiar aisles, Mary Ann got her shopping done before the rush.

The fresh market was her next stop. Mary Ann occasionally shopped at this place for healthy prepared food and organic produce. Today, she fixated on soup. Pushing her cart to the counter, she eyed the selections: navy bean and vegetarian chili. There was nothing like a nutritious, hearty bowl of soup, and theirs was blue-ribbon quality. A little pricey, but totally worth it. Mary Ann bent down to read the list of ingredients.

"Mary Ann," a masculine voice called out.

She almost jumped. Immersed in her thoughts, she hadn't expected to run into anyone. The voice sounded familiar.

He dashed toward her, crossing the gap in quick strides.

Straightening up, she hid her fluster. "Connor—" she said, blinking and trying not to stare.

"Yours truly," said Connor. He grinned, his hands touching his chest, as though to hide his racing heartbeat. The market logo was displayed across the front of his green apron with monogrammed leaves.

Mary Ann blushed. "You … haven't … left town?" she stuttered, apparently suddenly interested in the apron.

"Still here."

"What about your job in the city … your home there?" It took a moment for Mary Ann to digest this. Connor was still here. She had tried to push him out of sight and out of mind. Yet here he was, beaming at her, in flesh and blood— and looking *too* darn good, as her primal brain kicked in, taking instant notice.

"I quit my job and moved back here."

"But why?" She kept her tone neutral, as she glanced at his face, searching for clues.

"I decided to put the big city life behind me—for good."

Hearing this news, Mary Ann's stomach fluttered. He'd left the city for good? She felt as if she stood at a crossroad, wavering between going straight or turning left or right. Her logical brain took over her thinking. *Remember what happened when you let your guard down? Opened your heart?* Emotions swirled, stirring up the anger, the hurt, and the disappointment. "So … you came back to stay—"

"I'm at my parents' home," said Connor. "With Tom," he added.

The mention of Connor's orange tabby cat brought a slight curl to her lips, and then a bit of a frown as Mary Ann recalled his worries about Tom. Connor had come back from the city, and they had last talked on Christmas Eve about taking Tom to the vet.

"Did you take Tom to see Doc Carlson?" she asked, concern in her voice.

"Doc gave us the first available appointment and saw Tom right away. He puts his animal patients first, even during the holidays," said Connor, taking a deep breath. "He's a skilled diagnostician, sharper than the other vets I took Tom to. You're lucky to have Doc Carlson in this small town. He has his fingers on the pulse and knew what was wrong."

"Is Tom better now?" She didn't have to ask, judging from the cheery grin Connor threw her. This unexpected run-in took her by surprise. Just like the last time she saw him on Christmas Eve, when Connor popped into her flower shop after not hearing from him for four months when he went back to the city after his mother's funeral in town. She pursed her lips, a wisp of anger creeping back.

"Doc told me animals *can* grieve. Tom was my mother's constant companion. Mom loved her orange-striped tomboy dearly." After a moment of silence, Connor brushed a piece of fuzz off the apron, adjusting the strap. "Doc said the cat would have sensed *my* grief, too."

Mary Ann shook her head. This was not the place to give him a piece of her mind. The holidays had calmed her, took some sting out of her seething anger. Besides, Connor had apologized and seemed genuinely sorry. But was she ready to forgive him?

Chapter 3

"MARY ANN—" HIS voice was soft. Seeing her again took Connor back to that day when they had met at the flower shop. The petite brunette who had greeted him was professional and poised, yet compassionate. Mary Ann had made the floral arrangements for his mother's funeral, selecting the white flowers which were his mother's favorite color. That beautiful girl with the radiant smile had warmed Connor's heart in the dark days that followed, and she'd been his strength when he was weak with grief.

"You enjoy working here?" she finally asked.

"It's good. I'm usually in the back, in the kitchen. Not full-time, just a few hours when they need me."

"You're right at home in the kitchen," said Mary Ann. She recalled the time he had invited her, Mrs. Rainer—his mother's dear friend and neighbor—and the pastor and his daughter Eva over for dinner. It was his way of thanking them for being a part of his mother's life, and afterward, the beautiful funeral service. He had even invited Isabella to meet Tom. Mary Ann had never known a man who was so comfortable in the kitchen. Connor had explained he owed it to his mother, who taught him how to cook when he was so small he had to stand on a stepstool to watch her.

"I'm the soup cook, preparing vegetables from what we have in the market, picking those that are older and using them up first." He ventured a smile. "They make tasty broths, and I make them just like my mother did."

She stepped up to the counter and scrutinized the day's soup offerings. "Which one do you recommend?" Mary Ann held a sturdy paper to-go container in her hand.

He leaned in, squinting at the labels. Connor had put them on himself. It was an excuse to move closer to Mary Ann. "What are you in the mood for?"

"Something hearty and fulfilling."

He resisted the urge to tell her he could hold her, warm her up, right here and now, in the middle of the store. "Do you like red or white?"

Mary Ann laughed. "We're talking about soups, not wine, right?"

Connor loved to see her like that. The way Mary Ann's beautiful brown eyes lit up, the tiny crinkles at the edges. The way her perfect lips parted, the cute dimples appearing on her cheeks. He'd never tire of looking at her—her face, her smiles, her laughter.

He picked up the ladle and stirred the bean soup, hoping she wouldn't notice the shaking in his hand.

She studied the bean soup before she answered, watching the contents swirl, dispersing the navy beans that had settled to the bottom. "Tonight, I have a hankering for a rich, red soup."

Connor pointed to the vegetarian chili. "This fits the bill. It's tasty and thick, in a tomato base packed with red beans, onions, celery, bell peppers, and meatless crumbles."

"Not too spicy or hot?"

"Green chilies hot enough?" teased Connor.

Mary Ann's eyes widened.

"Just kidding."

Mary Ann glanced at the chili, then smiled. "Okay, I'll try this."

"You'll like the chili," said Connor with a wink, reaching for the container in her hand. He filled it and popped on a lid. As he handed her the soup, his fingers brushed hers lightly. Their eyes met and locked in a gaze. Her touch. Her eyes. Her blush. He was smitten all over again.

She felt a zing. A definite redness colored her cheeks.

She nodded, noticing how Connor looked different now. Gone was the designer suit and expensive tie; instead, he wore a soft cotton shirt and jeans. But it wasn't just his attire that had changed. There was something else about Connor. She couldn't quite spell it out, but he sported a relaxed posture, appearing content and more at ease. Even his gaze was softer … and a sparkle was in his eyes.

"How'd you end up here?" said Mary Ann.

Connor chuckled. "I like shopping here for fresh organic fruits and vegetables. I bumped into the owner one day, and well … she remembered me." He paused. "I didn't know she was the owner here when she and I first met at your flower shop, the day I went to see you on Christmas Eve. It was crowded, and people were pushing and shoving. She was the old woman that I escorted to the front counter." He grunted, shaking his head. "You should have seen how she beamed when she saw me again, here in this market. She mentioned that business had picked up. They didn't advertise for a position, and they didn't really have one with enough hours to qualify for full-time, but they needed someone part-time in the kitchen."

"And that suited you—"

"That's right." Connor nodded. "I love to cook, and this interested me. Besides, I don't need the money from working full-time. Where else can I get paid to do what I enjoy?"

This brought a curve to Mary Ann's lips. This Connor was different. The other Connor, well … he wasn't in a good frame of mind. He'd even admitted that much.

"Welcome back," said Mary Ann, blurting out the words as a gesture of goodwill, despite the trace of bitterness that lingered. When he'd invited her to supper on Christmas Day, she didn't accept, and she didn't respond right away until it was too late. Her pride, her ego, whatever it was, had held her back. Connor had apologized, but it hadn't been enough. Was she bent on exacting revenge, making him suffer for the pain he caused? She had another option on Christmas Day: an earlier invitation from Ron, the owner of the hardware store. She couldn't very well cancel on Ron at the last moment—on Christmas of all days. She had guessed that Ron was interested in her that time at his store, when he shared his dreams of expansion, and so his invite wasn't unexpected.

Mary Ann had first met Connor on the day he arrived in town and talked to her about the flower arrangements for his mother's funeral. He was in town for three more weeks to take care of things. During that period, he had invited Mary Ann over for dinner, and they'd spent more time together, dining at Manini's restaurant before his departure. But Connor had left abruptly and without saying goodbye. When he came back to town again a few days ago, his apology on Christmas Eve was small consolation for the bitter disappointment she had experienced. Mary Ann had sworn not to fall into that trap again.

Connor looked like he was working up the nerve to say something. Perhaps another apology? Whatever it was, Mary Ann suddenly decided she wasn't interested in hearing it. Not now.

"I need to run and do all my shopping before the storm hits," said Mary Ann, her voice terse as she set the soup container on the counter, freeing her hands to reposition the contents of her overflowing reusable grocery bag, moving celery stalks and a bag of oranges about to spill over the brim. She hastily turned toward the checkout lane. "I still have to stop by the flower shop to put up a sign and close early."

"Norma minding the store?"

"Yes." Mary Ann adjusted the straps of her full bag, redistributing the weight digging into her shoulder.

"Old man winter is still kicking. I'm afraid it'll be another bad one."

"Well, the florist business has slowed down after the holidays. I'll keep the shop closed for a few days, with this storm brewing." Mary Ann moved away, joining the growing line in front of the register. "I need to get going."

He nodded, watching her as she reached the cashier, paid, and walked out of the market, carrying her shopping bag. The curls in her long hair bounced with each step, soft and free-flowing. He remembered the way she'd looked the first time he saw her in the flower shop. She had tied her curls back in a ponytail. He liked seeing her hair down. There was a lump in his throat as he stared at Mary Ann's retreating figure.

Even as she moved out of earshot, Connor still blurted out, "Come back again." The words fell on empty air, lost as she opened the door.

Chapter 4

CONNOR HAD AN urge to run after Mary Ann as she walked out of the market, before her trim, petite frame disappeared from view. He'd missed his chance to tell her how he felt. He missed her already. He longed to gaze into her lovely eyes framed by soft long lashes, to hear her voice, to be with her. He wanted to draw her closer to him. So close that she'd feel the thump of his beating heart.

Seeing Mary Ann brought her back into his mind, squarely in front. He had tried not to think of her these last few days, to leave things as they were, to come to terms with the fact she hadn't accepted his invite to spend Christmas with him. Had he lost her?

In his heart of hearts, she had never left. He had held on to the connection in his mind, as he suffered and grieved his loss, struggling through those days, weeks, and months after his mother died. But he'd never told Mary Ann how he felt. How could he then? He could barely hold on to himself.

Connor had experienced the darkest period of his life in those four months when he went back to the city. He lost his zest for life. His ambition to climb the corporate ladder no longer fueled his drive. With no one to share his success, he felt an emptiness, a void. He had pulled back into himself, withdrawn away from Tom, who he'd inherited from his mom. A part of him deep down knew he had nothing to give Mary Ann. If he had reached out, he'd be leaning on her, a burden to her. Many a time he'd thought of calling her, but he'd resisted. Instead, he replayed the times they had spent together, keeping Mary Ann alive in his mind and, in this way, she stayed with Connor during his darkest moments.

He fell into a bleak existence, absent of the comfort of good food, not even making simple quick meals. He forgot to feed Tom on more than one occasion, leaving his bowl empty. When he did, it was the cheap cat food from the grocery store. Connor himself skipped meals. It became a task, a mundane shuffling of cardboard-tasting food from vending machines, frozen dinners, and the occasional late-night drive-thru to squelch his hunger with greasy fried food. In between, he stockpiled snacks from the stores that sold items for a dollar, amazed to find selections that changed from week to week.

Sometime in late November, he made a stop at the pet store to buy more nutritious cat food. The night before, Connor had flinched, jerking his hand away, when his fingers felt the cat's thin, bony body under the fur. The realization had sunk in—Tom had lost weight—and with it, Connor's shame and dread. A heavy ache stuck in his throat.

He had sunk to the floor and held Tom in his arms, sobbing as he rocked back and forth.

He knew then it would take more than food to bring Tom back to his old self—and himself, too.

On Christmas Day, up until the last moment after the other guests had arrived for supper, he'd still held hopes she'd walk in the door. He almost went to see Mary Ann at the flower shop afterward. But he nixed the idea, turning around before he set foot in her store. What right did he have to expect she'd come running to him? The distance that had separated them for the four months was of his making. He had pushed her away and hurt her. He should have … well, it was too late to be rethinking this. What was done was done.

Connor had dreaded this holiday, his first Christmas alone, with only Tom by his side. He had run into Alana, his neighbor Dottie Rainer's long-estranged daughter. He had invited them, along with the pastor and his daughter, for Christmas supper. It had been a sad, but bittersweet Christmas, one without his mother. But she would have approved of her only child and friends gathered together to honor her. Coming home had been the right decision.

He had kept busy, which helped to push away the melancholy and dispel the self-pity.

People made resolutions for the New Year, full of promises and good intentions. Connor had made his— leaving the city, his job, and his condo—coming back to his small hometown to start anew. It was bold, a major decision. A turning point.

Connor hadn't expected to run into Mary Ann today. She looked good, but seemed a bit frazzled. He had wondered how she was doing. Their chance meeting, the brief conversation fanned the tiny flame in his heart—injected it with a breath of fresh oxygen. This time, he wanted to make another effort, try again. He would go slow, to do whatever it took.

He had climbed the corporate ladder. He had fixed his eyes on the goal, and the office with the window was a special perk along the way. After his mother died, it had all changed. He searched his inner self and knew his heart wasn't in it. What if he rose higher and made it to the expansive executive corner office? They'd only want more of him, more than the sixty-plus hours a week he'd already given. What other price did he have to pay to gain entry to the top level?

Connor had left and never looked back. Now he'd settled into the slower pace of life with Tom; a life he'd lost so long ago, one that didn't suck the life out of him.

Mary Ann. He remembered the times they spent together. They were like precious gems. They were scenes he'd played and replayed to remind him of the good times. Connor couldn't help grinning, feeling the quickening of his heart as his face lit up, his hopes raised. Mary Ann—he wanted to cry out her name, dance with her, take her in his arms. Oh, *stop* … she wasn't his.

The things that held him back raised their heads. The doubts. A voice of caution. Remember the disappointment?

A chill chased the butterflies in Connor's stomach at the

thought. Was there someone else in her life now? He had so much he wanted to say to Mary Ann. Things he wanted to ask her in person. But Connor hadn't brought it up today, hadn't wanted to break the cheerful mood. He didn't want to risk her answer or her rejection.

Chapter 5

NORMA LOOKED OUT the window. The heavy clouds heralded the oncoming storm. She had to stay at work, but called her husband, Stan, to pick up food and supplies. Occasionally the weatherman was wrong, but something told Norma he was right about this one. The last customer had just left when she heard a ping on her cell phone, Mary Ann texting she was on her way.

In a few minutes, the door opened and Mary Ann breezed through. She was rushing, panting. "We can close early," said Mary Ann, tossing her head toward the darkened sky and threatening clouds outside.

Norma nodded. "I called Stan. It looks like a bad one's coming."

"I'll put up a sign while you close up," hollered Mary Ann, disappearing into the back room.

Norma brought the chalkboard easel display on the sidewalk inside the shop and closed out the cash register.

"How's this?" said Mary Ann as she came back, holding up the hastily written sign, "Closed due to inclement weather."

"It works," said Norma.

Mary Ann scurried to prop it on the storefront window, then flipped the sign on the front door.

"How long will we be closed?" said Norma.

"Tomorrow is Friday, and we have the weekend coming up. Let's see how the storm goes. I'd like to open by Monday."

Norma nodded. "Are you all set for the storm?"

"I've got enough food to last me and Isabella for a few days."

"We're used to this." said Norma with a reassuring nod. "You'll figure it out and learn how things are around here."

"I'm really liking it here."

"You wouldn't be talking about a certain young man, would you?" teased Norma.

"Now, why would you say that?" said Mary Ann with a throaty giggle. She still hadn't told Norma what happened with her and Ron on New Year's Eve. And she didn't mention seeing Connor a few minutes ago.

Chapter 6

MARY ANN HAD wondered what it would be like to kiss Ron at the stroke of midnight on New Year's Eve. She had built up the moment after their "date" at his cabin on Christmas Day. In her heart of hearts, Mary Ann was a romantic. Although, she hid it behind her no-nonsense business exterior.

She had imagined it would be like this: like the soft petals of a flower glistening with dew, her lips parted. She felt his warm breath as their lips met in this first kiss. The touch was magical, sending little waves of pleasure through her body. Her eyes remained closed. Mary Ann opened into the kiss and the embrace as the man wrapped his arms around her. She reached up to clasp the back of his neck, pulling him closer while her fingers intertwined in his thick hair, tugging it playfully, but not yanking it.

She lost track of the time as she kissed and didn't care. Keeping her eyes closed, she explored the new senses: the lingering smell of his cologne, the scratchy tickle of his stubble on her smooth skin, the warmth of his arms around her, the taste of his lips. Mary Ann murmured involuntarily, lost in the moment.

When they broke away, Mary Ann would notice the shy gaze of adoration on his face. The heart-thumping, utter devotion of a man in love. It was sweetness, joy, all wrapped up. His eyes were fixed on her. As he gazed, the grin never left his face.

His warm eyes spoke to her without a single word. She returned it with a slight curve of her lips and another tender kiss.

STOP. Rewind.

But it *didn't* happen like this. *Not with Ron.*

Mary Ann was not the touchy-feely type of person to begin with. After her father died, her mother was quick to marry the first man who showed an interest in her and who held a steady-paying job. She wasn't cut out for the "single mother struggling with child" role. Her mother was shrewd and calculating, and she knew her value as a woman, a commodity with her clock ticking. Men looking for younger women to date or women who didn't have a child, didn't look her way once they found out she came as a package of two.

Her mother knew the older she got, the slimmer the pickings. So, when her stepfather-to-be came along, a middle-aged salesman past his prime, she overlooked his thinning hair and the patch of baldness, his expanding girth, and his penchant for cheap food and sloppy eating. He was a sloth. Yet somehow, when he displayed the crooked grin that accentuated the dent in his chin, dialed up the charm and sweetened his glib tongue, he talked his way into many a sale, especially among women customers … as he did her mother.

He didn't really care for kids and told her mother at the onset. Then, he reconsidered as more bright-eyed, younger men came along to join the sales force. He decided a ready-made family with a kid offered him something they didn't have—respectability and social acceptance at another level. So he became a family man, husband and father. To the outside world, he became a responsible member of the community. To Mary Ann, he became her nightmare.

The heavy hand of her stepfather made her wary of men and slow to trust. At first, he was nice, opening car doors for her and her mother, helping them to carry groceries, being a real gentleman. A month into the marriage, his behavior visibly changed with Mary Ann, the kid. He spoke to her gruffly and said hurtful things when they were alone. He was careful not to leave marks or bruises, but he was physically abusive—grabbing her hard, pulling her hair, pushing her, and frightening her. Who knew what he did behind closed doors in the bedroom? Mary Ann wasn't close to her mom and certainly her relationship didn't rise to the level of a confidant. Sometimes at night she heard loud noises, thumping, and shouting.

Mary Ann would concentrate on something else, think of her real father, who died when she was a child. But there

When she was about four and a half, Mary Ann's father took her to the Christmas tree farm to pick out a live tree. It was cold, the tips of her ears and nose reddened despite the scarf wrapped around her face. Her tiny, mittened hand felt warm and secure, enveloped in the extra-large, gloved hand of her gangly father.

Cheerful Christmas music blared from the wood cabin where they were heading. It was lit with bright, blinking lights and decorated with ornaments hung from the ceiling and fresh wreaths and garlands. The enterprising owner's son, a teenage pimply boy, sold steaming cups of apple cider and hot cocoa from his stand. The mood was festive, with shrieks of laughter, the fresh smell of fir and pine trees, and chirpy notes of holiday tunes floating in the air as Mary Ann happily sipped her hot drink, the warm liquid trickling down her throat.

They would take their time to pick the most beautiful tree. Not the biggest, nor a sapling, but one that was just right. At night, they headed to the fire pit. Mary Ann loved to watch the bonfire, the flames flickering and dancing in the dark. Sitting with her father, she'd stretch her hands toward the fire to warm them. He'd get her a bag of popcorn and ask if she'd want to toast marshmallows. She'd squeal in delight. That was their tradition. He'd put his arms around her shoulders, and she'd snuggle against him. It was perfect, the happiest she'd ever been.

Mary Ann looked up to her father. This was their adventure. Her favorite time of the year. The magical season of Christmas—a special time with him, just the two of them.

She would have one more year like that. Then it would stop. His life was cut tragically short. Nothing was the same after that. A part of her died with him, but she held on to their good memories together.

Chapter 7

WHAT HAD SHE been thinking? It was the holidays. Caught up in the festivities and excitement of the season, but with no one to share it with, Mary Ann was acutely aware of her loneliness. It was at Norma's urging that she had accepted Ron's invite for Christmas. To be fair, he had checked off most of the boxes as she ran down her list quickly in her mind. The list she had memorized. Ron was tall and handsome. A striking and masculine man. Check. Ron was self-sufficient, the owner of the hardware store. Check. He was intelligent. Check. He was single. Check. He was available. Check. He was interested in her. Check. He was friendly. Check. He liked Isabella. *Wait* … that didn't get a check. Okay, so Ron wasn't a cat person. He preferred dogs. That wasn't a deal breaker … or was it?

Mary Ann didn't want to be alone for Christmas—or New Year's Eve. Did she use Ron to ease her loneliness? Did she encourage him and lead him on by accepting his invite? Yes, she was selfish. But she'd felt more alone than ever. So much so she couldn't bear to be by herself. So, she went on a date and spent time with Ron. Mary Ann made no promises. They had a good time together, as friends … until the stroke of midnight on New Year's Eve when they kissed.

But it was leading up to that and bound to happen. She'd almost expected it, a wrapping up at the end of the year.

But there were hints along the way, things that sounded alarm bells. Deep within, Mary Ann knew—and her actions betrayed what was in her heart.

She hadn't hung mistletoe on her porch or over her doorway.

She remembered Ron had pressed to come inside her home after their Christmas date, but she didn't invite him in.

There was something else too … something she didn't like. The way Ron poked her in the arm—sharp and hard. The harsh insistence she saw in his eyes instead, when she looked for the warm tenderness of love.

She had brushed aside the warnings that seeped through at first, determined to have a nice holiday with him. What was troubling her … the bits and pieces finally came together, sending chills through her body. Mary Ann suddenly felt weak in her legs and knees, gripping the shower curtain as her body trembled under the warm spray of the morning shower. It was like the wrapping came off—and she saw it clearly for the first time—what was inside, unmistaken in the light of day. She knew the signs so well—her stepfather had taught her.

All along, she felt a guiding hand working behind the

scenes. Maybe it was her father watching out for her? Whatever it was, Mary Ann knew that she wasn't falling in love with Ron—and never would.

Chapter 8

THE NEW YEAR had started with a bang at the flower shop, and then it slowed down. There would be a lull before business started picking up again for Valentine's Day. People who spent too much at Christmas suffered buyers' remorse in the weeks after the holiday rush and gift-buying season passed and things settled down. In the harsh light of the cold wintery days, everything seemed clearer.

After Christmas Eve, Mary Ann had plenty of time to think and replay her conversations with Connor. She convinced herself that in hindsight it was better this way, not to see him again. Otherwise, she sure would give him a piece of her mind, a big piece at that. His invitation for Christmas dinner was a feeble attempt at an apology on his part.

Mary Ann had put Connor out of her mind again, thinking he had gone back to the city after the holidays. The last thing she'd expected was to see Connor in an apron at the market. He was beaming and practically bouncing when he saw her. The excitement was palpable and real.

Intelligent and successful, Connor was also wholesome

and good-looking, though not in a rugged way but more urbane. In the competitive corporate environment, he had relied on his wits, grit, and determination. Luck played a part too—bestowed on this well-dressed, keen young man— in his rise to the coveted office. If anyone added up all of Connor's qualities and talents, it would be impressive.

Maybe it was time she settled down and raised a family? Her clock was ticking, but she had a few more years of eggs ovulating. Still, it was her logical self, thinking.

Should she settle and risk going to her grave with regrets?

Was Mary Ann's heart beating for a certain someone?

Someone who brought out the flush on her cheeks, the fluttering in her belly, the song in her heart, the catch in her throat?

Someone who made her pulse quicken, her steps lighter, and brought a twinkle to her eye?

Dare she hope for more in life, for the grand love of her life—for the person truly worthy of Mary Ann and all she had to offer?

Chapter 9

CONNOR'S GLANCE LINGERED until Mary Ann's figure disappeared. He took a step back, bumping into the rigid surface of the counter. "Ouch," said Connor, putting his hands on his lower back to rub it.

He felt a nudge on his arm.

"You really need to talk to her."

Connor turned, seeing the market's owner. "I tried to, Mrs. Steele."

"When?"

"At the flower shop, after you, all the other customers, and Norma left. We were alone. So … how are you?"

"Young man, when you ask old folks how they are, prepare for a long answer. But I won't bore you with that. I'm as good as I can be," said Mrs. Steele, with a lift in her voice and a firmness that spelled out a no-nonsense and take-charge attitude. She sniffed and shrugged. "You're changing the subject. Did you have a *good* talk back then?"

"Ah, back to that," said Connor. "I apologized to her. Told her how things were after I went back to the city, dealing with my life, my pain. How I went through the motions of living, barely making it through each day."

"Have you told Mary Ann how you felt about her?"

He hesitated. "I told her I've thought of her, picked up the phone and tried to call her." He shook his head and sighed. "But she knows the call never came."

She stared at him. "And then?"

Connor had a feeling that little got by Mrs. Steele. He liked her, despite her quirkiness which he'd glimpsed the first time they had met. But, who was he to judge? People had quirks, all kinds of different ones, and that was one of the things that made everyone different and unique. He liked interesting characters, especially a person who spoke their mind, and she certainly did that. He coughed to clear his throat. Darn, she had a good memory too. He said, "I told Mary Ann I failed poor Tom, too, and I worried about him."

"What did she say?"

"Told me to call Doc Carlson."

"What about today … did you tell her?" she asked quietly.

Connor made no excuses. He straightened and stretched himself to stand tall, chin up.

She focused her sharp blue eyes on him. "You kids *really* need to catch up."

Chapter 10

CONNOR WASN'T USED to such direct questions. He had enough sense to know she demanded a direct answer. No beating around the bush. Maybe she commanded respect because of her age? Or maybe she was always like that, and the trait became more pronounced as she got older. His silence betrayed him, the pause before he answered.

"No, the best intentions can go astray," said Connor.

She frowned. "Well, what went wrong?"

Connor shook his head. "Long story, I'm sure you don't want to hear it."

"Young man, time is what I've got. I'm all ears."

He sighed, thinking about where to begin. She'd probably heard snippets over the years, but not directly from him. He started his story. "I grew up here and left home at eighteen, lured by the big city and eager to start a new life. I went to college, studied hard, and got a good job at the company. Stayed there and worked my way up the ladder to the coveted office with a window," said Connor. He paused, glancing at Mrs. Steele.

"Go on," she said impatiently.

"I was a driven young man, so sure of what I wanted. As the years passed, I came back home to visit less frequently. It was down to twice a year, but I always came back for Christmas and stayed to the New Year," said Connor, speaking softly. "Last year, after my mother passed, I was all alone in this world with no one except for Tom, her cat." His voice quaking now, he paused.

Mrs. Steele reached out, giving him a gentle pat on his arm.

"I … I came back for her funeral. And stayed for three weeks to take care of things. Her husband, my stepfather, had passed first." Connor spoke slowly, at first reluctantly, then with a haste to get it all out to this woman who had strength and a kind, understanding heart beneath her tough, sharp exterior. "I met Mary Ann when she made the flower arrangements for my mother's funeral. I tried to communicate what I wanted and envisioned, and failed miserably at that, or so I thought. She got it, and when I came back to see her arrangement, I saw it was beautiful and perfect for my mother."

A slight smile appeared on Mrs. Steele's face, but she didn't interrupt.

"After the funeral, I bumped into Mary Ann at the grocery store while I was picking up some cat food. She found out about my cat, Tom, and told me about her cat, Isabella. I said, 'Maybe Isabella would like to meet Tom sometime?' Later, I invited her to a dinner I was having at my home with the pastor and his daughter, and Mom's friend and neighbor, Mrs.

Rainer. The dinner was my way of thanking them and honoring my mother." Connor's face lit up as he remembered that warm, cozy evening. "I love to cook, and my mother was the best teacher. That night, we ate, danced to Mom's favorite records, and watched the cats play." He paused, reflectively. "I felt Mom was there … and I wasn't all alone."

"She probably was," said Mrs. Steele, her voice soft and kind.

"I spent more time with Mary Ann, and we went out to dinner before I left. We had a delicious Italian meal. We talked and got to know each other better. But my time here was ending—I had used up the three weeks off work I took for the funeral and to put things in order. I left the next day and returned to the city."

Connor ran his fingers through his hair. He pursed his lips. Mad at himself at what he did next, or rather—what he didn't do.

"For the next four months or so, I barely survived, going through the motions at work and neglecting Tom. I didn't call Mary Ann. Didn't want to be a burden to her, or use her as a crutch. But I found out differently when I came back in town, the day before Christmas Eve." Connor stared at the old woman, owning up to it. "I had hurt her by not calling, leaving her like that."

"What are you going to do about it?" said Mrs. Steele.

"Do? I can't force her to give me another chance."

"Do you want to win her back?"

Connor was taken aback by her directness. "*Win …
her—*"

She nodded.

"I messed up, okay?" He gritted his teeth.

"Young man—"

"Yes," sighed Connor, his chin quivering. He withstood her unwavering glance even as she waited. *He wanted Mary Ann. But could he admit that, out loud, to Mrs. Steele—and to himself?*

She said, "You know what to do."

Chapter 11

AFTER MRS. STEELE made her way down the aisle, Connor occupied himself with busy work, cleaning up and wiping a spill on the countertop. At the end of the counter he noticed a carton of soup, sitting where Mary Ann had left it. *Had she forgotten it in her hurry to leave?* He picked it up and popped off the lid to check. It was the chili. *Her chili.* His heart thumped, beating faster. *I could bring it to her,* he thought.

Connor whipped off his apron and dashed back into the kitchen, holding on to her soup. He shouted to the cook, "We closing early man, I'm taking off." He grabbed his jacket and rushed toward the cash register. When it was his turn, he paid for the chili, putting rubber bands around the carton and over the lid to secure it before placing it carefully in doubled-paper bags.

A burst of cold wind blasted his face as he opened the door, whirling flurries of snow greeting him. He headed for the flower shop, farther down on Main Street. The sidewalk was already slick, wet, and covered by a dusting of snow as he arrived in front of Mary Ann's store. A handwritten display in the window confirmed he was too late, and beyond it the darkened interior. Seeing the "Closed" sign on the door, he cursed. He'd just missed her. He stood on the sidewalk as people hastened by, scurrying to rush home, not one person strolling or stopping to talk.

Holding the bag, Connor pondered what to do next. There was only one thing he could do—his pulse raced with excitement and he shuddered with uncertainty. He wanted to see her again, and this could be another opportunity. He could drop off Mary Ann's soup at her home. He'd never been there, but they had exchanged contact information four months ago. Taking out his cell phone, Connor quickly scrolled to her name and found her address.

The drive to her home was short, only a few minutes. As Connor arrived at her place, he recognized her car parked outside. His heart raced as he moved quickly, before he lost his nerve and chickened out. In quick succession, he slid out, locked his SUV, and walked up to her door. He knocked once, then two quick taps. He waited. Counting the seconds, he hesitated, wondering if he'd made the right decision. Would he have time to make it back to his car and drive away before she came to the door? Shuffling his feet, he made a move to step away—just as the door swung open.

"Why Connor," said Mary Ann. Her eyes widened and a flush of red appeared on her cheeks.

"Uh, I—" said Connor, glancing down as Isabella greeted him with a meow, her body rubbing against the legs of his jeans. He chuckled, giving a silent prayer of thanks for this perfectly timed break, and searched for the right words.

"Isabella likes you. She doesn't do this to everybody," said Mary Ann.

A sheepish grin spread slowly across his face. "I like her, and I'm sure Tom does too."

Mary Ann shivered as splats of wet snowflakes landed on her bare arm. "Well, don't just stand there, come in." She giggled, adding, "I won't bite."

Connor stepped across the doorstep. Her home was warm and cheery inside. It was modest. A few attractive pieces of modern furniture, some tasteful decorations, and small glass vases of bright flowers adorned the living room. He wiped his feet on the doormat, stomping to release the snow.

"I just got here a few minutes ago," said Mary Ann, closing the door behind him.

"Here's your soup," said Connor, handing her the paper bag.

"Oh, thanks! I realized I'd left it at the market when I put away the groceries. I'm sorry you had to go to the trouble."

"No trouble at all. I was about to leave and noticed it on the counter. I'm afraid it's gotten cold by now."

"I'll just warm it up," said Mary Ann. She took the package from him and whipped off the paper bags, seeing the round paper carton. She plucked off the rubber bands and headed to the kitchen.

At that moment, Connor's stomach growled. He clasped his chest, as if his lungs had anything to do with his belly.

Mary Ann glanced back, lips twitching as they betrayed a smile.

"Well … uh … I best be going," mumbled Connor as he turned to leave.

Chapter 12

LEAVING SO SOON? Looking at Connor, the ill feelings Mary Ann had harbored in her heart were no longer at the forefront. Empathy crept in, and a flutter of regret. Was he just here to do his job, making sure she got her soup? She turned away as tears pricked her eyes. She quickly put the soup container down and snatched a tissue from a box on the kitchen counter. She prayed he didn't glimpse the wet gleam on her cheeks. She didn't trust herself to speak until she cleared the lump from her throat.

When she'd composed herself, she realized that Connor was still standing by the door. He had an odd look on his face, sort of contorted, like he was trying to hold his stomach in—or something else.

"You're not ill, are you?" Mary Ann walked toward him.

He shook his head. Then his stomach sounded again. No mistaking it, and this time it was a louder, deeper rumble. The funny look on Connor's face was priceless as his arms crossed over his tummy.

"You're sure?" she teased, dragging out the moment.

He mumbled as he spoke, so low she couldn't catch any words.

She saw his eyes, darting around as if to escape, and burst out laughing. Mary Ann released her pent-up anger and negative emotions, expelling them, as the weight lifted.

Chapter 13

MARY ANN WAS holding her hands over her face, gasping before giggles burst out of her lips again.

Relieved and finding the perfect moment to cover his embarrassment, Connor broke out with laughter of his own.

The only one who had a straight face was Isabella. Connor glimpsed the cat, reclining quietly in the corner, observing the two humans making a racket. One of her ears was flicked back at an odd angle. Connor hooted as he pointed at Isabella, urging Mary Ann to look. All the while her cat remained composed, regal, a slight quiver of whiskers betraying her vexed tolerance of the silly humans.

When Mary Ann finally recovered, she straightened and walked back to the kitchen. "I've just made a fresh pot of coffee." She grabbed two mugs. "The least I could do is offer you a cup and a bite to eat, you know … to quell the rumbling."

"Yes," said Connor. His legs carried him across the room in swift strides before she changed her mind.

"Cream and sugar?"

"Black for me, please."

"We can share the soup," said Mary Ann as she popped the cardboard carton in the microwave. She opened the refrigerator and pulled out a block of cheese, quickly slicing it and arranging the pieces on a plate, adding the freshly baked French bread she had just purchased in the market. She placed a cluster of grapes in the middle. Holding the plate in one hand and her coffee mug in the other, she nodded to Connor, tilting her head toward the dining room table.

Connor grabbed two bowls and spoons, the soup carton, and his mug. As he passed Isabella, he gave her a wink.

Chapter 14

AFTER THE LAST drop of coffee was gone, the soup consumed, and the plate of bread and cheese cleaned up, they still sat at the table and talked, getting to know each other again. Tossing shy, flirtatious glances between the laughs and giggles.

Connor didn't want to move, but from where he sat, he could see the fading sunlight and the nonstop flurries outside the window. He yearned for spring to come soon, and with it, the blossoming of flowers and love in the air.

He slowly pushed back his chair and stood up, gathering the empty plate and bowls, and mugs and spoons, taking them to the kitchen.

"Just leave them in the sink," said Mary Ann, hearing the clinking of dishes as he set them down.

"Okay," said Connor. He picked up his jacket, put it on and zipped it closed. Opening the door, he peered outside. A layer of soft snow blanketed the ground. His foot rested on the doorstep. He paused, his fingers jiggling the car keys as he delayed his departure for a few more seconds. He turned to Mary Ann, giving a broad grin. "Listen, I had a great time." He wanted to hug Mary Ann. But all he managed to say as he headed out the door was a "thank you."

Connor had parked his SUV right in front, next to Mary Ann's car. He cleared the snow from the windshield, windows, and hood before he got inside and turned the key. It didn't crank. He tried again. The engine didn't turn over. It was dead. His eyes met Mary Ann through the windshield.

She dashed outside to his car as he rolled down the window. "Got jumper cables?"

"In the trunk," said Connor, getting out. He opened the trunk, grabbed the cables, and popped his hood open.

Mary Ann ran back inside to grab her car keys and returned, clasping her sweater tightly as a blast of cold wind blew, stinging her uncovered face. She popped her hood and waited until Connor connected the cables before she started her car.

"Pump it," yelled Connor.

She pressed her foot on the gas pedal, giving it a few hard taps.

Connor tried again to start his car. Only the still sound of a dead crank met his ears.

Mary Ann rolled down her window. "We can call the guy from the garage. He has a tow truck."

Connor turned off his key and got out of his car. He was ashamed to admit that he had neglected his car in the last few months. He stood there, muttering under his breath, oblivious to the mass of swirling snowflakes landing on his head, melting into his hair.

"Come on, let's go inside and call him," she said as she moved back toward the front door.

Connor shivered as a gust of cold air slammed his face. He followed her to the door, again stomping the snow from his shoes before going inside.

Mary Ann removed the phone book from a kitchen drawer and put it on the counter, flipping it open to the auto repair section.

Pulling out his cell phone, Connor quickly dialed the number for the garage. There was no answer. After four rings, it went to voice mail. He left his name and cell, and her home phone number, with a brief message about the problem. "I'll try again if he doesn't call back soon."

She nodded, setting the phone book back in the drawer.

He started to put away his phone, but changed his mind and dialed another number. It was picked up after one ring. "Mrs. Rainer? This is Connor."

Mary Ann listened as Connor explained what happened. He asked Mrs. Rainer for a favor, to check in on Tom and feed him.

He ended the call, then filled her in on it. "Mrs. Rainer still has the key to Mom's house, and she'll take care of Tom." He let out a long breath, relieved that she'd agreed to help.

"Give me your wet jacket," said Mary Ann in a firm voice. She walked away and hung it on the coat rack to dry. "There's nothing else you can do now."

"I hope the guy calls soon."

"You mean Clay—"

"Yeah, is he reliable?"

"He's helped me out and Norma, too. However, it may be a while since he's busy, especially in this weather."

Chapter 15

IN NO TIME at all, they found themselves back at the dining room table. Connor put his cell phone on the table where he could see it. He almost jumped when the phone buzzed. He put it on speakerphone when the phone number of the tow truck guy flashed. "Hello?"

"Hey, it's Clay calling you back. So, what's wrong with your car?" said the man on the other end. He sounded rushed.

"My car won't start. Can you give me a tow?"

"I'm swamped. I can't come to you anytime soon."

"What's your best estimate?"

"Can't say."

Connor choked. "It's *that* bad out there?"

"Let's put it this way. I may head home myself before the missus gets real mad."

"I don't blame you. Stay safe. Thanks, man," said Connor, ending the call.

Mary Ann threw him a sympathetic glance. "There's nothing you can do till he gets here."

"It sounded like I may be in for a long wait," said

Connor, frowning. He ran his fingers through his hair and massaged the tense muscles in his neck.

"Might as well relax."

"What do you do to relax?"

"Oh, I read books, listen to music, watch a good movie," said Mary Ann, maintaining a calm, soothing voice.

"Got any cards … normal cards with a king, queen, and a joker?"

Mary Ann pushed her chair back and stood up. "I may have one stashed away in the closet. I brought a box of games and stuff when I moved here, and I'm pretty sure there's a deck of cards shoved in there." She left for a few minutes and reappeared with a triumphant grin, holding a box of cards in her raised hand like she won a trophy.

Connor smiled. "So, how about playing some card games?"

She shrugged, raising her eyebrows. "I haven't played in a long while."

Connor took the deck from her, opening the box. His fingers glided over the slippery, waxy texture, loving the feel of new cards. His hands moved like a choreographed dance—a tap on the table, a flick of the wrist—making a quick cut, shuffling, and the ruffling of cards.

Staring at his long fingers, deftly dealing the cards, Mary Ann was mesmerized. Like a child being shown a magic trick, watching every move, not wanting to miss any action.

"Know how to play Old Maid?" asked Connor.

She shook her head.

"Hearts … Rummy?"

"Nope."

"Ever play Go Fish?"

"It's been awhile," said Mary Ann. "I'll need a refresher."

Connor explained the game and Mary Ann nodded, listening.

"Oh, if the card you draw from the stack is the card you asked for, then you get another turn to draw."

"So how do you win?" Her eyes widened, innocent and inquisitive.

Connor liked Mary Ann's childlike curiosity, her willingness to learn new things, to figure it out. "When you get a book of four cards of one kind, you place it on the table, face up. The player with the most books wins. A game ends when all the cards are played and books are displayed on the table." Connor grinned. "See how easy it is?"

They bantered back and forth. She used her novice status to real advantage, asking more and more questions. As the game warmed up, it went faster. Mary Ann squealed in delight when she won anything. It was so silly, and Connor laughed so hard.

He'd never seen this side of her. It jogged his fond memories of his childhood and his parents, so long ago. How much time they'd spent on the crossword puzzles in the newspaper. His dad sitting on the oversized reclining chair in the living room, wearing his short-sleeve cotton shirt, reading glasses hanging low over his nose, the newspaper flipped to the crossword puzzle. His mom propping on the armrest and leaning over his shoulder, her slender finger pointing to a word he'd thoughtfully filled in as she whispered something in his ear, the gray strands of her hair loose, falling over her face, her hand touching his arm affectionately. The adoring glances his dad gave her.

There were playful times too, when his dad was focused on his crossword puzzle, all serious and frowning, and she'd tried to get his attention. Running her finger down his cheek, tugging or tweaking his ear, ruffling his hair, or wiggling the eyeglasses dangling on the edge of his nose. But he wouldn't get mad at her. Connor waited for him to swat her hand away like a mosquito. The first time his mom did it, he clutched her hand, still keeping his eyes on the puzzle. After that, she'd try again. He'd turn his head slightly and kiss her hand, then let it go. Other times, he'd look at her and say, "Mabel, I need to concentrate on this," telling her he didn't want to be interrupted, his voice soft-spoken yet firm, commanding her respect.

Connor sat back and watched Mary Ann, playing like a pro. A real pro. He'd ask if she had a card, just because he was holding one. She'd shake her head. Later, when he almost thought she'd forgotten, she'd come back around and she'd get him, claiming his card. Connor was good-natured and laughed. All Connor wanted to do was relax and have some fun. If he won, that was fine.

But he wasn't focused *just* on winning ... *the cards, that is.*

Chapter 16

HE LOST ALL track of time, but a glance at the darkened sky outside told Connor it was late. His cell phone stayed where it was on the table, untouched since the last call. A yawn escaped as Connor's hand fumbled toward his coffee mug.

Mary Ann raised her eyebrows, glancing up from her cards. "I'm on a roll."

He raised the mug to his lips, catching the last drop. "That's it," said Connor as he slowly set it down.

Mary Ann snatched the last card from the stack and beamed in triumph as she slapped the last four-card book down. She counted out loud. "Eight, I win."

"What?" Connor mumbled. It'd been a long day, and his mind was operating on its last battery.

"Aren't you going to write the score?" She paused, waiting for him to tally it.

He rubbed his face, pulling the skin down over his cheeks, then blinked his weary eyes. It took a moment before it sunk in, what she had asked, before he picked up the pencil and scribbled the number on the pad. He dropped the pencil, and it bounced, making a soft plop as it landed across the table and rolled to a stop. "What time is it?"

"About eleven-thirty."

He yawned, covering his mouth, and stood up to stretch, struggling to keep awake. "Well, I need to get going."

"But … your car."

"Oh, yeah," murmured Connor. He was so tired he'd forgotten about his car. All he wanted to do now was sleep. "Clay … he didn't call."

"He won't come this late," said Mary Ann.

"I should go." Connor fumbled with his shirt, straightening out the sleeves. Checking the buttons. He had fun tonight, hanging out with her, playing the card game. Man, was he wiped out.

From the look on her face, he thought Mary Ann seemed disappointed. Was it because the game ended? Or because he was leaving? But wait—wasn't he stranded? He didn't want to go anywhere, and he couldn't. He was too much of a gentleman to ask her for help, to impose on her anymore. If he had to, he'd sleep on the floor.

"You'd best stay here." Mary Ann stood up and walked to the hall closet, pulling out a thick folded blanket and a pillow. "You can crash on the couch tonight. I doubt Clay will show up at this hour."

"I—I don't know." He mumbled, smiling shyly.

"Here, take it," said Mary Ann.

Connor reached out to grab the plaid blanket and pillow, swaying a bit as weariness descended. His fingers slipped and brushed across her hand. It was small and soft. He felt a zing, a spark of electricity as they touched.

He stared at her. Did she feel it too? He thought so, from the flicker of surprise that flashed across her face.

Connor felt a small surge of adrenaline, a crazy overwhelming desire to wrap Mary Ann inside the blanket as she stood near him. He pictured her in it—the soft cotton of the red plaid framing her lovely face. He could purchase another one for a matching set, but it must be a blue plaid blanket. He smiled to himself as he recalled a day long ago in his bedroom when he threw a fit at his mother, shouting in his childish voice that he must have a room painted blue.

He wrestled with his emotions. He could just casually whip the blanket around her; perhaps make a joke about it, like it's big enough for two. But Connor also wanted to do nothing more than sleep. He was losing it. Tiredness won out. He grabbed the pillow and tossed it on the end of the couch. He kicked off his shoes before he sunk onto the white couch.

"Good night," Connor muttered, glimpsing the red plaid color as he pulled the blanket over him and surrendered to sleep, his eyelids fluttering shut. In his dreams Mrs. Steele poked him, her blue eyes piercing. He could hear her voice chanting, *"Win her back—"*

Chapter 17

MARY ANN CLOSED her bedroom door, took off her clothes, and pulled on her long underwear. She slid between the cool sheets and snuggled under the thick fluffy comforter.

Easing one shoulder and wiggling into a comfortable position to settle in for the night, she took care not to disturb the familiar bump of the small warm body curled next to her. She cocked her head to look at Isabella, already checked out in la-la land.

She thought back to the day's events—running into Connor in the market, forgetting her soup, and rushing to get home before the storm. She hadn't expected Connor to deliver her soup in person—nor his car trouble. She had fun playing card games. Mary Ann saw a side of Connor that she hadn't before—a playful, easygoing, lighthearted side. *Who would have thought he had a sense of humor?* She had responded, giggling like a schoolgirl, flirting innocently with him. She had thoroughly enjoyed it. And, then … the touch of his fingers on the back of her hand.

She fell asleep with a smile on her lips.

Chapter 18

CONNOR WOKE UP to bright light streaming in the window. He didn't expect he'd sleep so soundly, descending into a deep, dream-filled realm. Connor stretched, his mind groggy, taking a second to realize where he was: not the familiar blue walls of his bedroom, but the beige walls of a strange room. He bolted to a sitting position, viewing his surroundings. Then it came back to him … the plaid blanket, the white couch, the cards on the dining room table. He looked down the hallway. The door to Mary's Ann room was closed. It was quiet. He swung his legs off the couch and got up.

During the night, the storm had raged, dropping a ton of snow. He opened the curtains of the living room window and touched the icy cold glass pane; the frost clinging to it. The world had transformed into a white landscape. The wind had retreated, leaving behind a stillness and frigid cold. Connor shivered. He padded to the kitchen in his socks to make coffee, filling fresh water in the coffee maker. He opened the refrigerator door, whistling when he saw the shelves well-stocked with food. Intent on checking out the contents, he didn't hear Mary Ann until she walked up to him in her fluffy slippers.

"Good morning," said Mary Ann, cheerfully. She wore a long-sleeved cotton top and loose pants; her hair was tied up in a ponytail.

"You're perky this early?" He looked at her face, freshly scrubbed and natural.

She nodded. "I slept well. Did you?"

"Your couch wasn't so bad. My back isn't hurting." Connor grinned, pivoting his shoulders and stretching his back.

Isabella chose this moment to approach her food bowl, strutting her way to the kitchen with her tail curled up in the air.

Mary Ann reached down to pet Isabella's back and scratch behind her ears. "And you slept well on my bed." She picked up the cat's empty bowls and washed them before pouring fresh dry food in one bowl and water in the other.

"What can I do?" Connor asked.

"Feed me quick," said Mary Ann, smiling. Making a funny face.

"Scrambled eggs and toast coming right up," said Connor, reaching for the carton of eggs and rummaging in the fridge. "Where's your butter?"

"The soft butter in the tub is on the top shelf to the right. There should also be a couple of sticks in the butter compartment in the refrigerator door."

Connor had the skillet heating on low while he cracked

eggs on the edge of the bowl and beat eggs, milk, salt and pepper with a whisk. A delicious aroma burst out as he slid a generous slab of creamy butter in the frying pan and poured in the egg mixture, making slow scrambled eggs. While it was cooking, he popped two slices of bread in the toaster.

Mary Ann filled two glasses with orange juice and brought them to the dining room table, putting them down next to the steaming cups of coffee.

In no time at all, breakfast was on the table. Sitting across from Mary Ann as the bright sunlight streamed in the windows and cast a pleasant glow on her face, Connor couldn't help but think how much he was enjoying this. After years of being single and eating alone at home, it was nice to just relax and enjoy a meal with someone. He thought he knew what he wanted. But now he wanted more—with Mary Ann—and the joys of having breakfast for two was just the beginning.

Maybe it was the angle of the light, thought Connor, as he looked into her eyes, shining bright—and perhaps there was a glint of affection. His heartbeat quickened at the thought, bringing with it a sliver of hope. Her eyes seemed different this sunny morning, after last night. He wouldn't ask the question that had been eating at him for so long or press her for an answer until she had her breakfast and coffee.

"Have patience", his mother would say when he was a little boy, when he couldn't contain his excitement at Christmas. His eyes had bulged at the sight of the colorful, decked-out fir tree in their living room and the pile of wrapped presents underneath. He would rip off the gift wrap, not caring how it tore. His mother, though, took her time to unwrap each gift. They had a tradition of opening one present at a time, each person taking a turn. He didn't know what was worse, the waiting for his own gifts, or the waiting for her to open hers. But he knew she loved him, for all his faults and foibles, for all the troubles he got into growing up and the pain he caused. His mother never lashed out at him. It took him a long time to understand this and put himself into her shoes. How she put up with him was beyond Connor.

He wanted to be the man he wasn't for his mother. Connor wanted to show Mary Ann he could learn from his mistakes and do it over, and better. His mother would have given him second chances, but she was gone now. He'd like to believe she was still there, in spirit, and watching over him. A tiny flame of love fanned in his heart—a heart that held on to hope.

Connor watched Mary Ann as she ate, the way she held her fork, the dainty bites she took. He knew she must have been famished, but she didn't throw away her manners.

This morning he saw her face, bare and without makeup. Mary Ann looked beautiful, youthful, and vibrant.

Connor raked his fingers through his hair. Was Mary Ann so comfortable around him she didn't bother with makeup? Or did she think of him as just a friend crashing on the couch—nothing more?

He took a long, deep breath, as he watched Mary Ann take the last bite of food on her plate. "Finished?"

She put the fork down on her plate and dabbed her mouth with a napkin, covering the broad grin underneath. "All done."

"Good?"

"Yummy! Oh my gosh, it's *the best* scrambled eggs I've ever had, Connor."

"That is *the best* compliment I've ever gotten," he said, giving her a thumbs-up. He felt like singing, shouting to the world. He wanted to bask in her praise and soak it in, while another part of him flinched, glitzy with excitement. "You can dress it up with cream or cheese, or sprinkle toppings on it," Connor added, keeping his voice calm and steady while his heart raced.

He got up to take her plate and clear the table. "I'll do the dishes." Noticing her near-empty cup of coffee, he made a mental note to bring back a refill before sitting down to have "the talk" with Mary Ann. He could see Mrs. Steele now and hear her stern voice saying, "Do you want to win her back?"

Chapter 19

THE PHONE RANG, but Connor couldn't hear what Mary Ann was saying. The sound of the running water in the sink muffled her words. His thoughts had dwelled on the moment—the big moment he'd been dreaming of, choosing with care the words he'd say to her. He rolled them over in his mind, syllable by syllable, running with it, then reworking it, and rehearsing it. He imagined how she'd respond: perhaps a kiss or the moist glint in her eyes as she teared up when he finally declared the secret in his heart. His love. Connor hastened to finish washing the dishes and cut the water off, catching the last part of her conversation.

"I'm all right," said Mary Ann. She paused. "Yes, quite sure. Clay gave you the address, but he couldn't come, so you're helping?"

Connor could see her shaking her head from side to side.

"So, you thought it was me when you realized where it was … no, it's not my car," said Mary Ann, as she lifted her eyebrow and shot a glance his way across the room. "It's my friend's car."

She dropped her voice and mumbled into the phone, cupping one hand over her mouth. "Okay, see you soon."

"I overheard. Help is on the way?" asked Connor.

"Your car's going to get towed."

Connor managed a weak smile as he looked away. It was too soon to leave. Everything had been perfect this morning. Breakfast was barely over, and now this—his hopes were dashed again just as he was working up the nerve to tell her how he felt. Would he get another chance?

He was expecting the knock on the door. Still, he jumped at the sound.

Mary Ann opened the door. The sound of her voice, clear and welcoming, as if she was greeting an old friend.

He heard a murmur, a masculine voice. Long arms reaching out to embrace Mary Ann, large, lean, strong hands protruding from the sleeves clasped around her back.

A sinking feeling grabbed Connor, seeing the man's arms wrapped around her. A coldness seized his heart, seeping into it. The embrace—was there a possessiveness, a familiarity? The warm blood pumping in his arteries turned to an iciness, slowing his heart, spreading throughout his body with each heartbeat. The pumping sound of his heart dimmed to a slow beat, crawling, almost frozen in space. Was he too late?

She pulled back and glanced at Connor standing in the living room, his jacket already on. "He's here. Let's go."

Connor gripped the pull on the zipper, tugging it as he pulled it closed, and strode across the living room, keys in one hand, expecting to meet the tow-truck guy or someone from the repair shop. But the guy *wasn't* a stranger.

"Ron," said Connor, stopped in his tracks.

Ron flinched, doing a double take. Recovering quickly, he let go of Mary Ann and grabbed Connor's shoulders, then shook his hand. "Didn't expect to see you here."

Thoughts whirled in Connor's mind as muscles tightened around his throat. What was he doing here? But most of all, he wanted to know why Ron had his arms wrapped around Mary Ann.

"You're back?" asked Ron.

"Yup."

"For good?"

"I left the city and moved back."

Ron squinted and took a step back. "I thought you'd take up my offer to partner with me on my hardware store."

"Your offer was generous, and I wrestled with the decision. But, like I said to you, thank you, but I can't accept."

"You had months to think about it," Ron persisted, irritation coming across in his voice.

"I'm sorry for taking so long to respond." Pulling his head back, Connor gave a slight shake. "I came back, but it wasn't for that."

Chapter 20

TUGGING OFF HIS gloves, Connor glanced at Ron sitting beside him, driving the tow truck with his SUV in the back. The crunch of tires in the snow was the only sound. The silence stretched as Connor looked out the frost-coated passenger side window, his breathing fogging the glass. The snowy landscape whirled by in a mass of white, broken by the contrasting stark darkness of trees, partially coated with thick layers of snow. Icicles hung from the exposed branches like icy daggers.

A cold stillness replaced the fury of yesterday's blowing wind. He could see the frozen beauty of the wintry day. In the silence of the truck's cab, Connor reflected on his friendship with Ron. He remembered, as kids, the silly pranks they had played, the scrapes and troubles they had gotten into, and out of, together. The fun times they'd had. He took a deep breath and broke the silence.

"Hey Ron, thanks for the tow. How's Clay?"

"Clay worked so hard yesterday he wore himself out. He called me this morning and asked me to help."

"Last night I talked to him, it sounded like he was swamped," said Connor.

"You stayed overnight at Mary Ann's house?" Ron asked, changing the subject.

"Yep, my car wouldn't start."

"How did you two meet?"

"I met her at the flower shop when I came back to town. She made the floral arrangements for my mother's funeral." Connor bristled at the questions. But he kept his tone even.

"Are the two of you just friends?" asked Ron, casually. His hands tightened their grip on the wheel.

"She's the best florist I know," said Connor. "After the funeral, I got to know her better, so yes, I'd say we are friends. Why are you asking?" This line of questioning was getting personal. He threw his question back at Ron.

Ron didn't answer right away. He clenched his teeth and pressed his lips, staring straight ahead at the road. "We've been dating."

Dating? Connor's thoughts came to a full stop. He didn't see this coming. He choked back a gasp, touching his throat. Was this the reason Mary Ann didn't accept his invitation for Christmas supper? He opened his mouth to say something, but all he managed was a raspy repeat of the word, "Dating—"

Hiding a cocky half-smile, Ron kept his eyes on the road and nodded.

Connor's shoulders sagged as he looked down, twisting the gloves in his hands. *Was he too late?* The thought of losing Mary Ann brought a heaviness he couldn't shake off. Hope had sustained him in the months of grief after his mother's death—in moments of dark despair when his heart ached in deep places it had never sunk to before, when the loss and pain was unbearable, when he came face-to-face with the stark loneliness of being all alone in this world.

He shivered, tightening the scarf around his neck.

Chapter 21

A SINKING SENSATION descended in Mary Ann's stomach when the tow truck pulled away.

She had listened to the exchange between the two men. How could she have been so wrong? She had incorrectly assumed Ron's offer of partnership was the *real* reason Connor had come back into town—a business deal. But he had turned Ron down. Connor said he didn't come back for that … so why did he? She had surmised he wasn't interested in her.

Mary Ann's mouth suddenly felt dry. She pictured the two of them riding in the tow truck. Would Ron mention they had dated, that she spent Christmas with him instead? How would Connor react when he found out about it? How was she to know Connor would come back to stay? If it wasn't for a business partnership with Ron, then Connor moved back to his hometown for another reason. It had been a surprise to her too.

Connor had often appeared in her thoughts out of the blue. It didn't matter what she was doing. He'd pop up at odd times and places: when Mary Ann was taking a shower, doing the dishes, reading, walking. Out of nowhere. It put a smile to her lips.

She had felt renewed as she flipped the new calendar to January. What would this new year bring? Although Mary Ann hadn't made resolutions in recent years, she had felt inspired to make one this year.

Hope had seeped into her heart—new thoughts and feelings put a spring in her steps and a song in her heart. She wasn't a mushy kind of girl, but always the sensible, calm one. It was unlike her to live her life this way. She kept this newness within her, not telling anyone, giving it time to grow, like a seed newly sprouted.

Once, years ago, she had been the object of a crush. A boy in school had followed her all year, leaving her little notes but never signing them. However, it wasn't hard to figure out who it was. She felt pleased at first, but then it got irritating, like a buzzing gnat circling around her, not leaving her alone. She tried to be polite to the boy, throwing him an occasional smile out of pity, which only seemed to encourage him. He got bolder, writing longer notes, leaving them on her desk or slipping them through the cracks in her locker. Once he even bumped into her in the hallway. When she dropped her books, he picked them up. As he handed them to her, his hands touched hers. She was sure he did it on purpose. When they touched, she felt nothing. No sparks, no tingling, nothing.

Eventually, he tired of it. But it took months.

This thing, with Ron, was nothing like that. He was a grown man, tall, muscular, and smart. She liked that combination. Her equal. Oh, and did she forget handsome? A list-topper. At first glance, he had the most wonderful qualities and other talents. She told herself there was a reason why tall, dark, and handsome fit the bill.

Ron had called her every day between Christmas and New Year's Eve. They talked, quickly if it was during the day, longer in the evening. They had dinner together two times that week. The first time in a restaurant she had picked. Ron was hopeless in the kitchen, and he'd only get in the way. Mary Ann tried to teach him how to make spaghetti once, and he even messed that up. She didn't mind cooking, since it was fun for her. But cooking for one was certainly not as much fun as for two. Not counting her cat, Isabella, that is. Besides, Isabella's taste buds resided strictly within cat food, and she had the most discriminating tastes for certain particularly tasty, and expensive, brands.

Mary Ann had built up this thing with Ron in her mind, fitting him into a desired slot, filling an empty void made even more pressing because of the holidays. He checked most of her boxes. *Most, but not all.* The kiss on New Year's Eve betrayed what was, or rather, what *wasn't* in her heart of hearts. Boosted by the desire for love and a connection in the holiday season, Mary Ann had lost herself before coming face-to-face with the truth. There was no depth, no spark. The superficial connection fizzled.

Mary Ann closed the door to her home. Alone with Isabella.

Chapter 22

CONNOR WENT STRAIGHT to Mrs. Rainer's home after Ron dropped him off, leaving his towed car at Clay's garage.

"You're here," said Alana as she opened the door, a wide grin splashed across her face as she greeted him warmly.

"I came by to let you guys know and pick up Tom," said Connor. He averted his eyes, looking downward.

"How's your car? Come in and tell me what happened."

Connor didn't look like his usual self. Alana kept the worry out of her voice. He was her friend, and she was determined to find out what went wrong, if it was his car or if it was something else.

Alana tugged his arm, pulling him inside. "You look like you need a warm cup of coffee. I've got a fresh pot, and I'm not taking 'no' for an answer."

As the door closed behind him, Connor heard the crackles from the fireplace and saw the bright flames dancing. Tom was curled up on a rug on the floor in front of the fire, sleeping.

"Let me hang this up," said Alana, as Connor shrugged

off his jacket. "You can sit on the sofa and get warmed up while I get the coffee. Mom's in her room taking a nap, but I'm sure she'll be delighted to see you when she wakes up."

The faint odor of fresh paint lingered in the air, and Connor noticed the drop cloth flung on top of the closed paint bucket lid in the hallway. Alana had replaced the dull gray somber–looking walls with new colors in the living room, livening it up and bringing warmth and comfort to the home she now shared with her mother. This was her labor of love when she returned home on Christmas Eve.

"It looks amazing—you've given it a face-lift," said Connor.

"When I finished the living room after Christmas, Mom loved it so much she wanted me to paint the rest of the rooms," said Alana. She handed Connor a mug of steaming coffee and sat down beside him.

"You got yourself a big project."

"We went together to pick out the paint color at the hardware store. You should've seen Mom, how excited she was. The dull gray in her room needed to go."

"What color did she pick?"

"It's a toss between the white or another shade of gray. I told her to try beige and pick the shade she wanted for paint color."

Connor raised his eyebrows. "And?"

"I was half-joking, expecting her to pick the pale gray that was closer to the gray in her room now, but she's considering the other one I suggested."

"At least she didn't go for bright red," Connor said.

Alana rolled her eyes, laughing. "It'll be pretty. I'll pick up more paint tomorrow. It keeps me busy."

"Are you going to change the color in your bedroom?"

"I've got mine picked out. It's a light, airy shade of blue-green. I think Mom may go with a classic beige, which goes well with her rustic wood furniture and the wooden floors."

"If you need help, just holler. I'm next door." Connor chuckled.

"I may take you up on that."

Connor sat back on the comfy sofa. It was old, the fabric faded, and his body slid into the concave depression in the cushioned seat. Connor's tense muscles relaxed as he sipped the coffee, the warm liquid making its way to his belly. The heat from the fireplace warmed his fingers and toes. Dottie's place felt more like a home now, but it hadn't been that way for years.

After her husband had died and Alana left, Dottie's heart was broken. She had let this place go, and her home fell into disrepair. No longer inviting, it became cold and dark. Dottie would visit Connor's mom next door. When Connor came home during the holidays, Dottie would be there. She was like family—she had no one, and they were the only family she had.

He felt a gentle touch on his arm. Alana leaned in, peering intently into his eyes.

Connor took a deep breath, reminded once more of his troubles.

"How's your car?" asked Alana.

"It got towed to the service station."

"You're not hurt or anything?"

Connor shook his head.

"What's wrong?" A frown furrowed Alana's smooth face. "Look, I'm here if you want to talk about it."

"I—"

"We've both gone through so much pain." Alana squeezed Connor's arm gently.

Connor bowed his head, feeling the sadness in his heart.

She said, "I'm sorry about your mom. I miss my dad, too. It's been years, but I still cry."

"I'm sorry about your dad, too."

"I have a hard time on anniversaries, especially the day he died, and on holidays—Father's Day and Christmas."

"I miss my mom … just talking about her." Connor wiped away a tear as he choked up.

"You know what I do when I'm feeling that way?"

Connor looked up.

"I keep memories of my dad—of us together. Happy memories," said Alana. She touched her chest. "My birthdays, the fun times we had together. The time I found an inchworm crawling on the ground." Her voice cracked as her eyes stared into space, remembering. "It was this thin, green thing. It crawled, arching in the middle. I had never seen an inchworm before. It fascinated me. My dad used it to encourage learning. We made a trip to the library and looked up interesting facts about the inchworm, its life cycle and its habitat."

"I'm glad you shared that story with me," said Connor. "You're not kidding with me, right? About the inchworm."

"No, I'll never look at an inchworm the same way again," said Alana, her eyes crinkling as a smile crept up.

"I've been thinking of doing something to honor my mother," said Connor.

Alana sat up, alert. "She'd like that. What do you have in mind?"

"You know she had a lot of recipes. I'm going through them and creating new ones inspired by her. I'd like to publish a cookbook and dedicate it to the memory of my mother."

"Ooh," squealed Alana, clapping. "I can help you with that, and I think my mom would like to take part too."

Connor hadn't thought of asking for help, but it seemed like a great idea.

Chapter 23

THEY REMINISCED FOR a good while, trading happy memories with each other. Somehow it lessened the pain.

Connor was on his second cup of coffee and more relaxed. He felt content to just sit there, at ease and leaning back on the sofa—listening to the crackling in the fireplace, soaking in the warmth in the cozy room, while looking at the pretty, freshly painted walls.

"Is something else bothering you? You looked worried when you walked in," said Alana.

"And you're perceptive," Connor quipped.

"Care to talk about it? I'm a good listener."

"Well …" Connor glanced at Tom curled in front of the fireplace. He was the scrawny, stray cat his mother loved so dearly, giving him food, nourishing his body until it became strong and healthy. The ferocious cat had preyed on mice, pouncing on the unsuspecting critters, laying them as presents on their doorstep. Tom wasn't content to stay indoors. He was not a bored, fat cat, but a sleek, lean one.

In the last years of his mother's life, it was Tom that

provided companionship for his mother, and it was his adventures and antics that amused her. At night, she took comfort in his presence, always curled next to her in bed. Tom was so much more to her than just a cat. He was family, a companion to his mother. It had been just the two of them. Connor had wrestled with his guilt for not being there, for putting his work ahead of everything else. He would always regret that. His private pain, one he'd live with for the rest of his life. Would he live his life alone—with just Tom?

"Earth to Connor." Alana interrupted his thoughts.

"I messed up," said Connor.

Alana frowned.

"Mary Ann … she did Mother's funeral arrangements. She has a florist shop. That's where I met her." Connor wrung his hands. "I fell in love with her, but I didn't tell her. I went back to the city with Tom and resumed my life there—my job, my condo. I fell into a funk, grieving and in pain. I didn't contact Mary Ann for four months until I came back to see her on Christmas Eve."

"How did she react when she saw you?"

"She was still angry, and hurt. I don't blame her."

"Did you apologize?"

"I tried to, but words seemed futile at that point. It was my actions that hurt her." Connor paused. "I made a mistake, and I regretted it."

"But you never got to tell her how you felt?"

"No," said Connor, his voice cracking. "I was at Mary Ann's house yesterday when my car wouldn't start. I stayed there until this morning. I … I was working up the nerve to tell her, but I didn't get a chance. The tow truck showed up just as I was about to tell her."

Alana sighed. "So that's why the sad look, my friend."

"I haven't gotten to that part yet," said Connor. "On the way back here, I sat in the front of the tow truck and rode back with the driver. Clay couldn't come, so he had someone else help. It was Ron. I know him. We grew up together, and we went to the same school."

"Do you mean Ron, the guy from the hardware store?"

Connor nodded. "He and I … well, we had a talk." Connor fidgeted, then stared into her eyes. "He went out with Mary Ann. They dated."

Alana's eyes were wide now. "I'm sorry, Connor," she said, patting his arm.

"Have I lost her?" An anguished cry escaped from Connor's lips.

Silence filled the room, broken by a few crackles from the burning logs.

Chapter 24

THE NEXT MORNING, Connor squinted his eyes to zoom in on Tom: his body tensed, focused on a bird, out of his reach as he crouched on the sill, peering out the living room window. Almost a month after the visit to Doc Carlson, the spry tomcat's energy had returned, and he sported his old fearless attitude. Coming back home to the small town where he'd lived, to his familiar home, away from the city, Tom had regained weight, and he had gotten his groove back. The vet was right. The only medicine the grieving tabby cat needed was a big dose of love and attention.

Connor had stocked up on cat food, filling two shelves of the pantry with bags of dry food, cans of wet food, and some tasty treats. Digging through the selection of natural cat foods, he located Tom's favorite—salmon and shrimp. He carried it into the kitchen and set it on the counter. Hearing a loud meow, he reached down to scratch behind Tom's ears as the orange tabby greeted him, rubbing his body between Connor's legs.

"Miss me, old man?" said Connor, as he washed Tom's

bowl and dried it with a paper towel.

He popped the lid on the canned cat food. The popping sound and the sudden release of the pungent smell brought out another "Meow," this time louder and throatier.

"Okay, your food is coming," said Connor. He chuckled and grabbed a spoon to scoop it into Tom's bowl.

He watched as Tom licked and nibbled, imagining how he must have looked the first time the cat appeared at the front door, a scraggly stray.

He grinned to nobody in particular. Connor couldn't help it, thinking about her. He recalled the fresh-faced Mary Ann at the breakfast table. Making slow scrambled eggs for her.

His lips parted. Not a timid tilt of his lips, but a broad one that spread across his face, crinkling the corners of his eyes. A smile of pure joy. He held on to the slimmest of hope. Dare he hope again?

Connor replayed the images and clips of Mary Ann and their times together.

He remembered the bead store where she twirled in delight, wearing the new necklace, the hues of her dress and eyes, the colorful gems glittering in the light.

He remembered the flickering candlelight framing her face at Manini's as they lingered and talked over coffee, long after their meal.

He remembered the blush on her cheeks when she ran into him, their shopping carts clashing as they bumped into each other in the grocery store.

He remembered her take-charge attitude as she designed

floral bouquets for his mother's funeral, when he was overwhelmed with grief and was barely able to say the words to describe what he wanted; but she knew, and her fingers communicated his wishes through the beautiful flowers.

He remembered the alarm on her face when their cats went missing as the last guests left Connor's house where he'd hosted a dinner after his mom's funeral. How they frantically searched for Isabella and his Tom.

He added the newer memories, burnt fresh in his mind. Running into Mary Ann at the market, where she picked her soup then forgot it. Bringing it to her home. Sharing a bowl of vegetarian chili while the storm raged outside. Teaching her to play Go Fish, Mary Ann's childlike curiosity, and her delight when she won. Making slow scrambled eggs for her, the best she'd ever had.

Is this what it's like to be in love? Connor wondered. Experiencing the sweet beginnings, the quiet longings, the wisps of hope and yearning. Unspoken, yet always there. Protected and tender. He had never been in love like this before. It'd always been his job that came first—the drive, the energy; it had taken over his life. Until now. At thirty-eight years old, soon to be thirty-nine.

As announcements of marriages and births came and went over the years, Connor never felt rushed. Sure, he had been on dates here and there, and in a couple of semi-serious relationships. He wasn't a eunuch. However, Connor had never experienced feelings like these before. This was different. Special. It wasn't pure lust, the rush of desire that's fleeting or impulsive, over before he knew it with no strings attached, no promises offered or expected.

He'd never brought a girl home to his parents' house. Connor swallowed, keeping the bitterness down. His mother had died, and before that his stepfather. The house was empty. Now, there was no one *to* bring home, and no one here except for him and Tom.

A knock on the door interrupted his thoughts.

Alana stood at the stoop. With her short-cropped hair and natural, no-makeup face, she looked younger than her twenty-five years.

"You've been baking," said Connor, noticing a smudge of flour on her cheek.

"You got that right." She laughed as she walked in, carrying a baking pan wrapped in foil. "Mom and I made pound cake today. You know how she loves to bake. She's been experimenting with the classic pound cake."

"I can't wait to try it." Connor grabbed two plates from the cupboard and cut big slices.

"You have fresh coffee?"

At his nod, Alana grabbed two mugs and poured. She carried them to the dining room table where Connor sat, waiting.

"You're the guinea pig." Alana watched impatiently, waiting for him to take the first bite.

Connor took his sweet time, making a big deal of the test.

Fidgeting in her seat, Alana could hardly contain herself. "Well, what's your verdict?"

"I'm afraid this isn't up to snuff." said Connor solemnly. He dabbed his lips with a napkin.

Alana's jaw dropped.

"Just kidding," said Connor, enjoying her look of amazement. He quickly took another, larger bite and stuffed his mouth full. He savored the taste of the delicious moist cake, rich and creamy, full of flavor. Not dry, heavy and bland. Smacking his lips, he pronounced, "Now that's first-place-ribbon worthy."

"Whew, you had me worried."

"Yum. What's in it?"

"It's amazing what cream cheese and a dollop of sour cream will do."

"I'll be Dottie's guinea pig anytime." Connor washed it down with a gulp of coffee, before leaning back in his chair.

The Alana he saw before him now was more relaxed: her thin, angular face softened. Dottie made up for lost time in the reconciliation with her long-estranged daughter when Alana came home for Christmas. No longer the rebellious waif of seventeen, Alana had grown into a self-assured woman.

Connor had seen the toll exacted on Dottie in the last eight years, magnified by the death of her husband and the abrupt departure of her only child soon after that. Dottie had turned to her neighbor, Connor's mom. They had grown closer; both having lost their husbands. But later, with the passing of his mom, Dottie had faced her grief alone. Last Christmas, Alana had come back, and mother and daughter reunited over tears of forgiveness and joy.

A sense of guilt had swept over Connor. Although he'd come home for the holidays, his visits had become less frequent as time went by. With each passing year, he rationalized his guilt away, convincing himself his mom would be proud of his achievements. It was of little solace to him now, and the decision he made to quit his job and sell his condo was too late. His life in the city had already become a distant memory. Connor had thought he was irreplaceable at work, that they valued his contributions. How wrong he had been. No doubt he had been replaced by another ambitious young man, much like the one he was years ago.

What did he have to show for his life now? In a few months, he'd be thirty-nine. So close to forty. It was depressing to think he'd passed the halfway mark of his life, or perhaps more than that. Had the best years of his life gone, having slaved them away within the steel confines of a cold corporate building? The death of his mother had been a wake-up call. There *had* to be more to life. Connor was not a quitter, and he'd fight for his life, for what was left of it.

"Earth to Connor, hello—"

Alana waved, snapping her fingers to catch his attention.

Chapter 25

CONNOR FELT HER warm breath on his cheek as she leaned in to check on him. He blinked, adjusting his gaze on her face, momentarily fixed on her thick curvy eyelashes.

"You okay?" said Alana.

"I'm fine," he said, shaking his head.

"You lost? Looked like you'd gone somewhere else."

He cleared his throat, glancing around the room. His fingers glided over the smooth laminate of his mother's favorite table. Alana was right. He *was* lost. He'd lost count of the times he sat at the dining room table. Lost sight of his life, his family, what it really meant. Lost the girl. Would he get a second chance?

He'd been a fighter. Quitting hadn't been in his vocabulary, and it would not be. "No." Connor said. He looked her squarely in the eye with a new surge of vitality and determination. "I'm getting my life back, new year and all."

Alana smiled and threw up her arms. "Well, I've been up to my arms in paint! You know, once I finished the living room, Mom wanted me to do the bedrooms."

"You started a big project you'll have to finish." Connor picked up on her enthusiasm, and he saw the flash in her eyes and realized she was enjoying this task, which was bringing mother and daughter closer together. "I'm glad you found this project to your liking." His thoughts turned to Ron, who had bought the hardware store from Connor's dad, and later offered Connor a joint partnership to expand the store. "You've met Ron?"

"Oh yes," nodded Alana. "He's helpful and courteous. We met when I went to pick up paint and supplies. When I told him about my project, he made sure I had everything I needed. Plus, he threw in some tips and said if I ever got in a pickle, to call him."

"I went to school with him. Ron used to work for my dad when he owned the hardware store."

"He's come a long way since. I don't remember him 'cause he's much older than me, and our paths didn't really cross. Not that I'd recognize him though, since I've been gone for eight years," said Alana.

She brushed away the faraway wistful look on her face, and stood up. "Fight for her," said Alana.

Connor stared at Alana, this toughness coming from such a young girl. Leaving home at seventeen, almost homeless on the street, doing what she had to do to survive the eight years on her own.

"You fought for that office with the window."

"This ... isn't the same."

"So, you're just going to give up on Mary Ann?"

"No, I don't mean that."

"Look at me, Connor. Tell me you're not a quitter."

"It's not that. If I didn't get that office with the window, I'd try again. I could go out the next day and find work in another company." He paused. "Do you know how many corporate offices are in the city?"

"So that's your excuse?"

"Alana, I *want* a second chance with Mary Ann now. More than anything. I don't want to blow it."

"You won't know until you try."

"Every time I get this close, and I mean *this close*—" Connor leaned in, pinching his thumb and index finger closer, leaving a sliver of a gap. "And I'm almost there, but something gets in the way. Like the other day during the storm … we had breakfast, and I'm getting ready to tell her. So you know what happened?"

"You got tongue-tied?"

"Nope, the tow truck shows up. And it's Ron."

"So, the great Connor is afraid of competition, huh?"

"Bad timing."

Alana shook her head. "I once knew this guy, and he wasn't a macho, super-hunk. Quite the opposite. You wouldn't think of him as the guy who gets the girl. But he had us all fooled."

Connor raised his eyebrow. "How so?"

"We knew he was married. He wore a gold band around his finger. But we didn't know how he got the girl."

"Go on—"

"Well, come to find out, she was already engaged to

another man when they met. But she ended up marrying *this* guy. You've got to hand it to him," said Alana, tilting her head to the side.

"You made your point."

"We were scratching our heads. Go figure."

"Are they happy together?"

"Heck, yes."

"Thanks, my friend." Connor said.

"Win her back," Alana said, as she turned to go.

"You're leaving so soon?"

"I'm going to finish baking with Mother, then do some prep work before tackling the paint job tomorrow," said Alana. She slid the rest of the pound cake onto a plate and gathered her baking pan. "I'll leave the cake with you."

It was a good day, and Connor wouldn't say no to a sweet dessert.

Chapter 26

IT WAS MONDAY morning when Mary Ann reopened her flower shop. She was glad the storm was milder than predicted. The townspeople had prepared for it just in case. They were used to it. The last days of winter, before the spring equinox, were sometimes the worst, as if old man winter huffed and puffed to leave his mark before retreating.

The flower shop was her baby. She loved the smell of fresh flowers, and this was her dream come true. Norma would be here any minute. Mary Ann couldn't sleep, so she got there early. She'd have time to make a quick round and check on everything. She had saved money to buy the walk-in cooler for the flowers she kept in stock. Mary Ann had gotten used to the familiar sound of the refrigeration motors in the back, next to where she created the floral arrangements. Her mind was lost in thought, busy with plans for Valentine's Day and the order for a large shipment of flowers.

Absentmindedly, Mary Ann reached out to open the cooler door, not registering the fact that the blast of air that met her wasn't cold at all. It took a moment before she realized something was wrong. It was quiet. Too quiet. The humming motors were silent.

The power had gone out. The cooler shut down. She took a step toward the first bunch of flowers and her heart sank. The flowers had gotten too hot and wilted. Bending down, her fingers touched the drooping petals. Her knees shook as she took a swift assessment, glancing across the space. "Oh no, how can this be?"

Mary Ann stumbled to the cooler entrance, barely hearing the click as she closed the door. She had put all the flowers in the floral cooler for safekeeping. The storm must have knocked out the electricity. She flicked on the light switches. The lights were out too.

The bell on the door chimed as Norma stepped in. She took one look at Mary Ann's face and knew something was wrong. "You're as pale as a ghost."

"We lost power. The flowers in the cooler are all wilted." Mary Ann's shoulders slumped, her voice trailing.

"Oh no," said Norma, rushing over to Mary Ann to comfort her. "What are we going to do?"

"I don't have orders for today yet. Let's hope the phone won't ring anytime soon before someone calls in an order." Mary Ann looked up, her face animated as an idea popped up. "It's still early. I could go pick up flowers in the city. It'll take me all day, but if I leave now, I may be back late tonight."

"You can make it in one day. But it'll take you longer, with the snow on the road."

"Okay, then please stay here. Call the power company," said Mary Ann, the words rushing out now. "Oh, and can you get a repair guy to come and check the cooler when the electricity is back on? I want to be sure the motor is working fine." Mary Ann switched to action mode, making decisions, finding solutions to take care of the problem.

Norma nodded. "What if the power isn't back on and the cooler isn't working by the time you get back with the flowers?"

"That's a good point," said Mary Ann. She paused, mulling over this with her arms crossed.

"I'll keep you posted while you're on the road."

Mary Ann grabbed her purse and gathered the scarf around her neck as she rushed out the door. "Plan B."

Chapter 27

WALKING CAREFULLY ON the sidewalk, stepping around slippery areas, occasionally crunching snow on the edges of the pavement, Mary Ann made her way to the market a few doors down farther on the street. She breathed a sigh of relief when she saw the lights were on. *Good!* This store had large walk-in coolers in the kitchen and a tall, glass dairy cooler in the front. She quickly sketched out a Plan B as she made her way inside, looking for the manager's office.

"Mary Ann," a voice shouted.

She looked around and saw Connor, waving his arms. Jerking her head up, she slowed down, while her heartbeat speeded up.

"You look like you're in a hurry. Can I help you?"

"I'm looking for the manager."

"Oh, you mean Mrs. Steele," Connor said. "She's the owner and manager. You've met her."

Mary Ann squinted, tilting her head.

"The old lady in your flower shop on Christmas Eve— the one that said to us 'You kids should catch up. No time's better than now.'"

She nodded, putting the name to the face. "I know her."

Connor was grinning, looking over Mary Ann's shoulder. "Here she comes now."

Mary Ann turned around to face her. "Connor was just telling me about you."

"*Good* things?" Mrs. Steele turned to wink at Connor.

Mary Ann chuckled.

"What brings you here?" asked Mrs. Steele as she hugged her in a warm greeting.

Mary Ann touched Mrs. Steele's hand and pointed down the street. "The power is out in my flower shop." She paused, frowning. "This morning when I checked on the flowers in the cooler, they were all wilted."

"My dear, what can I do to help?" Mrs. Steele asked, leaning closer.

"We're contacting the electric company, but there's no telling how long it'll take before the power is back on. We'll need a cooler."

"For your wilted flowers?"

"No, I must order fresh flowers and pick them up in person. That's the quickest way."

"Where?"

"In the city."

"When will you be back?"

"I need to leave now and drive to the city to get back tonight. But with this weather, it'll take longer, and I'll have to drive slower."

"So, you'll need the cooler if you return this evening?"

"Yes, if the power doesn't come back on."

"How much room do you need? I can let you have the dairy cooler in front. I'm afraid we can't put flowers in the kitchen walk-in coolers."

"Thank you, Mrs. Steele. This is a backup plan, just in case. The sooner I leave for the city, the sooner I can come back. I'm not thrilled about driving at night in the dark, especially when I'm not familiar with the road," said Mary Ann.

"I'll go with you. I know the way like the back of my hand," Connor suddenly offered.

Mary Ann's cheeks flushed red. When she found her voice, it was soft. "It's sweet of you to offer, but I can't ask you to do that."

Connor's eyes sparkled. "I've driven that way many times, going back and forth. You helped me with my car; let me at least do this one thing."

Mary Ann felt Mrs. Steele nudge her.

"You kids should *really* catch up. No time's better than now." Mrs. Steele gave them a wink—*again*.

Chapter 28

MARY ANN WASTED no time walking to her car, Connor by her side. She was eager to get started, now that he was going. She hoped Connor didn't see her blush. Had she blushed because of him? Was the quick walk making her breathless, or was it because of Connor?

He seemed different somehow, quieter, after Ron showed up at her house yesterday. She didn't have time to talk to Connor as he'd dashed to get his car ready, scraping the snow off, and helping Ron get it hitched to the tow truck.

Seeing Ron again was unexpected. They remained friends after New Year's Eve, although it was awkward at first. She talked to him about what had happened between them and drew the line to stay in the friend-zone. She tried to be gentle and kind, but firm. He wasn't happy to hear that and called her a few times to convince her otherwise. He stopped by to see her again, but she kept her voice polite and proper, repeating it until he got the message, for good.

"Here we are," said Mary Ann, as they walked up to her car.

Connor reached out for the keys. "I'll drive."

As she handed over her keys, he opened the passenger door for her.

He slid in the driver's side and pushed back the seat, adjusting it to allow for his long legs. The car was roomier on the inside than it appeared at first glance. "You want anything before we get started?"

"Oh, I'm good," said Mary Ann, buckling up. "I want to get on the road."

"We can get something to drink when I stop for gas," said Connor, looking at the needle to see how much gas they had.

Connor had made this trip many times. He knew the roads and was used to driving in the snow.

"I'm glad you came," said Mary Ann.

He smiled, flicking a quick look at her. Connor's heart flipped, beating faster. He concentrated on driving, quickly leaving the small town behind. The highway had been plowed, white mounds piled on the sides turned to dirty gray. He watched for slippery patches, slick areas where the snow was packed down.

"We should make good time with this early start. I'll check the weather before we head back."

They rode in silence for a while, Mary Ann staring at the snowy scenery. It was still cold, but the sunlight shined on the snow, bringing glitter and sparkle. Eyeing the wintery landscape, the beauty of nature took her attention. She could feel her stress and tension drop as the mountain scenery streamed by. Her hands stopped twitching. Her muscles relaxed. Eventually she closed her eyes and rested her head on the seat.

Mary Ann turned her body sideways, tucking her legs in. Her eyelids drooped heavier, strands of hair slipped from her ponytail, a dreamy look drifting on her face. She looked so childlike, fragile, and vulnerable. The Mary Ann the world saw was an independent, smart, self-sufficient businesswoman. She didn't wear her heart on her sleeve. She kept her feelings close to her. Yet underneath throbbed the beating heart of a mature woman capable of and filled with love—love ready to gush out, love that couldn't be measured or contained—for a deserving man, for the right man.

Chapter 29

GAS STATIONS WERE few and far between. Connor had calculated the amount of fuel in the tank and how far it was to the gas station. He passed on the first that came into view. It looked derelict—mounds of snow piled up, trash cans overflowing, litter spilling on the ground, and yellow tape wrapped around a pump.

A road sign indicated the next gas station would be in forty-five miles. A glance at the tank monitor, a third full, assured Connor they would make it there in good shape.

Connor's thoughts turned to Mary Ann. The other day would have been his chance to tell her—or so he'd thought, until Ron turned up. He mulled over his options. Was she Ron's girl now? Had he lost her?

It had been an emotional time for Connor. His grieving heart filled with pain, regret, and guilt. He hadn't been able to forgive himself for a past that he could not change.

This Christmas, unexpectedly, Connor witnessed love, hope, and the power of forgiveness as Mrs. Rainer and Alana reconciled, their lives changing forever. It hadn't come easy;

nothing worthwhile was easy. Dottie and Alana had crossed the dark gulf of pain and heartbreak—swallowed their pride and overcome the anger that pushed them apart—and allowed forgiveness to bring them together, opening their hearts to love again.

This magical Christmas, Connor changed, too. What he witnessed stirred something deep inside him, reaching to the depth of his heart and touching his soul. He moved away from the darkness he had dwelled in, and the thoughtless pain he caused others. He finally forgave himself. He chose a new path, a bright path, one of love—for himself—and the love he would give to others.

Chapter 30

CONNOR DROVE UP to the next gas station. It was bustling with customers, vehicles lined up at the pumps, and more cars parked in front of a small café beside it.

Mary Ann stirred, then arched her back and stretched before sitting up to look out the window.

"Enjoy your nap?"

"Oh, *yeah*." She threw Connor a sheepish grin. "Thanks for letting me sleep so long."

"I'm stopping for gas," said Connor. He gestured to the café sporting a crooked sign tacked on the porch railing, "Wild Horses Roadside Café." "If you want to get us a table, I'll meet you in there."

"Okay, I need to make some calls. Check with Norma," said Mary Ann.

It took a few minutes for Connor to fill up the gas and pay. He hopped back in the car and parked in front of the café.

Walking up the steps, Connor opened the door to the smell of strong coffee, sizzling food on the grill, and the distinct odor of frying onions. The clinking of utensils on plates, the hollering of orders, and the chatter of talk melted into the amorphous noise of a busy café. Somebody coughed. Laughter drifted. He scanned the room, looking for Mary Ann. She was sitting at a table by the far wall and waved him over, keeping an eye on him as she talked on her cell phone.

Connor pulled out a chair, noticing the cheap padding had split, the stuffing exposed. As he sat down, she finished her call. "Good news?"

"The power company is working on it. They will try to get it fixed as soon as possible."

"Can you salvage the flowers?"

"I'm afraid not. Norma is throwing them out. But I have some good news. I just called the flower shop in the city to place an order. It'll be on the delivery truck headed our way. We can meet them here."

"When?"

"About three hours. It'll save us from driving the six-hour round trip there and back. They deliver to shops in this area anyway. When I explained the situation, the lady on the phone was so nice. She said it'll be no trouble at all to make an extra stop at the café."

"I'm glad that worked out."

"Perfectly."

"Have you ordered?"

"Just coffee for us, the waitress will be back to take our food order."

Connor relaxed, leaning back in his chair, toying with his

napkin. What a stroke of luck to be here with Mary Ann. Different from Manini's, this greasy spoon had its own charm. Scratched wood tabletops, worn-out chairs, scuffed flooring trodden by countless feet—the café had welcomed many travelers over the years. On the wall hung a framed black-and-white photo of The Rolling Stones. He felt at ease, being here. Was this the right place … and time? Would Connor have the courage—here and now—to tell Mary Ann that he loved her?

The waitress brought two mugs of coffee, sloshing and spilling some as she set them on the table in her haste, clutching a pad.

"Ready to order?"

Connor nodded at Mary Ann, waiting for her to go first.

"How's your grilled cheese sandwich?"

"Ma'am, it's good. The cook piles on lots of cheese so it's thick and gooey."

"I'll take it. And a small cup of your vegetable soup, please," said Mary Ann, as she handed back the sticky menu with brown stains and bent corners.

"And you sir, what'll you have?"

"I'll have the biscuits and gravy with hash browns and fried eggs."

The waitress nodded and picked up his menu. "Coming right up."

Chapter 31

THE FOOD WAS every bit as good as he hoped. Connor ate quickly, finishing before Mary Ann did. "How was your grilled cheese sandwich?"

"It was perfect—crisp and crunchy on the outside, soft and gooey on the inside." Mary Ann grinned as she wiped her greasy fingers on the paper napkin before cutting into the thick slices of red tomatoes on her plate, the juice and seeds spilling out.

He watched as Mary Ann dipped her spoon into the soup, scooping up the liquid, tipping the bowl slightly to get the last drops at the bottom. He was a fast eater and finished first; he liked to watch her, observing her good table manners.

She dabbed the napkin on her lips and pushed back the bowl.

"Don't tell me you like this better than mine," said Connor, making a face, pretending to look hurt.

"If I did, I wouldn't tell you," Mary Ann retorted, giving a wink as she said, "But you got serious competition."

Connor sat up in his chair. "I'm a big boy, I can take it." He enjoyed seeing her light, playful side. Giggles had replaced the frowns from earlier this morning.

The ringing of his cell phone interrupted Connor's thoughts. He answered it.

"Hey, Clay here. Looked at your SUV."

"What's wrong?"

"It's your battery. I can order you a new one, but it may take two or three days to get here."

Connor sighed with relief as he ended the call. "Okay, thanks, man."

The waitress came by to refill their coffees. "Anything else I can get you?" She paused. "We have homemade brownies, thick double chocolate. Topped with vanilla ice cream."

Connor was not one to pass up dessert, especially *double* chocolate brownies—his favorite chocolaty dessert. "Sure, I'll have one. Mary Ann?"

She nodded. "Make it two."

The waitress reappeared as they finished their dessert, clearing their plates, and bringing more coffee.

"Thank you. It was delicious," said Connor.

Mary Ann echoed her "thanks" as the waitress refilled their coffee mugs and left.

Connor cleared his throat. "Mrs. Steele said we should catch up. You know … have a little chat." He looked up at her. Connor thought he saw a twinkle in Mary Ann's eyes. He relaxed, breathing easier now, and leaned back in his chair. So far so good.

"Well, I also heard her say 'No time's better than now,' and she's darn right," said Mary Ann. "So, you're back. What are your plans?"

"Take it easy for now. I've got enough money to do that for a while."

"How do you feel about coming back?"

"Honestly? I feel great. I have more freedom to sleep in, to make my schedule or not have one at all. I'll never put my nose to the grindstone again for anyone other than myself."

"Be your own boss."

"Exactly. I have to take care of myself. Eat healthy food, exercise, and reduce stress. All the stuff I know I need to do. You know I'm almost thirty-nine and older than you."

"By six years … yeah." Mary Ann giggled.

"Your time will come, young lady," Connor teased.

"Do you have hopes and dreams?"

"I've been thinking about my mother. You remember that wooden recipe box of hers?"

Mary Ann nodded, recalling the time they cooked together in his kitchen.

"I've been experimenting with new recipes, cooking with different foods, textures, and flavors—inspired by her recipes. I'd like to put together a cookbook and dedicate it to her."

"What a wonderful tribute to your mother," said Mary Ann, clapping softly.

Connor gulped his coffee. His mother and father were both gone, but the throbbing pain remained, still a fresh wound. There were days when it hurt so much he almost couldn't bear it. "I remember one time, when my mother had an injury and couldn't walk, my father carried her. In the morning when she woke up, he'd help her go to the bathroom, get dressed, and carry her to the living room. He did everything for her, including bathing her."

"Did he complain?"

"Not to her. But the effort and the exertion took its toll on him from the way he walked, the dark shadows under his eyes, and how tired he looked." Connor's lips quivered. "Mom referred to him as her 'big teddy,' usually when she didn't think I was around. He was a tall, big guy, and she loved it when he gave her a bear hug." He smiled, recalling the fond memory. "They acted quite proper around me, no kissing, nothing like that. But they gave each other hugs. There was no shortage of hugs."

"So sweet."

"Even after all those years." Connor nodded. "He loved her. Adored her so much he'd do anything for her."

"Anything?"

"Yes, he raised me—like a father." Connor paused, his glance steady as his voice quivered. "Even though I wasn't *his*."

Chapter 32

"I RODE WITH Ron in the tow truck. He told me you've been dating. But I want to hear it from you." Connor spoke quietly.

"After you left, I went out with Ron. We had a few dates … and we spent the Christmas holidays together."

"Are you still seeing him?"

"I … well, *no*."

"You ended it?" Connor's heart skipped a beat, as he reminded himself not to celebrate prematurely.

"On our last date … we kissed—"

He had clenched his teeth so hard, grinding the molars. Jealousy sprang and caught him in its claws. Connor had a sudden urge to lash out. A kiss? He didn't want to go there. He closed his eyes, but he could still see them in his mind. Was it a shy, furtive kiss? Was it demanding and seeking? Did she kiss him back? Did she enjoy it?

He'd dreamt of the moment their lips touched. It would begin with a sweet, slow kiss that weakened his knees and sent a surge of warmth spreading through his body. A tender kiss. A firm kiss.

"—but I knew then it wasn't what I wanted," said Mary Ann, finishing her sentence.

He wanted to step in and take her, swoop her into his arms. In his mind she had been his, always his. Connor knew what *he* wanted, but his attempts to tell Mary Ann had failed each time, slipping through his fingertips.

Chapter 33

THE CROWD HAD thinned at the café, but to the couple with heads bent forward, eyes focused on each other, lost in conversation—it seemed like it was just the two of them. Nearby, music played softly from the coin-operated jukebox.

"What *do* you want, Mary Ann?"

"You know those old couples walking and holding hands?" She smiled with her lips and her eyes, meeting his in a shy gaze.

"Like they're still sweethearts," said Connor.

"I see their wizened hands and gnarled fingers, their thin, lined faces, and their weary feet, dragging and moving slowly, with an effort," said Mary Ann, almost in a whisper. "But they touch each other, not letting go. It's as if they exist together. Isn't that real love?"

"Some people aren't so demonstrative," said Connor with a shrug, thinking of his own parents. "There are other ways. Small acts of love showing how they care for each other. Thoughtful things. It doesn't have to be dramatic, or showy, or expensive."

"I want the love that lasts forever. I believe it exists, long after our physical bodies turn to dust. A love so strong it joins our souls together."

"I apologize for hurting you," said Connor. He held up his hand. "Please hear me out. I've been selfish. I was in a dark place since my mother died, and I didn't want to bring you into my world. But I also hurt you. I realize it now—that in keeping the distance and pushing you away, I increased your pain. I'm so sorry."

Mary Ann was quiet.

"In the end, when I look back on my life, I don't want to have regrets," said Connor. His chin quivered as he spoke. "I can't go back and change the past and agonizing over it won't help."

Mary Ann saw the intensity in his eyes. She heard the sincerity in his voice and the rawness of his emotions.

"Can you find it in your heart to forgive me?"

The bitterness that Mary Ann had carried tore her up like a sharp thorn, pricking and drawing blood as long as she held the grudge. Connor had asked for her forgiveness before, but she had hardened her heart—holding herself above him, as if she was the righteous one and he, the sinner. But it gave her no pleasure. She dropped her head in shame.

"I'm sorry," whispered Connor. He would ask her for forgiveness a thousand times rather than hurt her again.

A tear trickled down her cheeks. Connor's heart sank at the thought that he'd caused her to cry. He felt helpless, afraid he'd made it worse. He lifted her chin and wiped away the drops gently with his thumb.

Mary Ann struggled to find her voice. "Can you forgive *me?*"

Connor reached across the table and sought Mary Ann's hand, his fingertips curling around hers.

Mary Ann didn't pull away—through the warmth of his hands flowed the strength of Connor's love. She saw the confirmation in his eyes.

Connor swallowed. "I want you beside me—*always.*"

She turned her hand around reaching for his, her palm facing Connor's, bending her fingers to clasp around his fingers.

"I love you," Connor croaked, his voice raw and raspy, as he scooted his chair next to Mary Ann and put his arm around her shoulder, drawing her closer. They stayed that way, without speaking, for a long while. Tenderness and love welled up inside him and filled his heart. He had let her in his heart—and he'd never let her go.

Chapter 34

A SONG PLAYED on the jukebox—soulful and heart-wrenching, yet infused with sweetness and hope.

Mary Ann's eyes misted over, as she turned to Connor and whispered softly, "I love you."

"I love you, too." He reached for her fingers and kissed the back of her hand.

She smiled and glanced at the couple dancing near the jukebox: their bodies melded together, moving as one to the music.

"Dance with me," Connor breathed in her ear, as his lips brushed against Mary Ann's hair, inhaling her fresh citrus scent. He stood up, holding her hand, not letting go, and led her to a cleared area in front of the jukebox.

Mary Ann felt the touch of Connor's hands, and then his body, as she leaned in—yielding to him, letting him take the lead.

Their movements became smoother as their feet, awkward at first, stepped in sync to the music.

Mary Ann closed her eyes, secure in Connor's arms,

swaying to the hauntingly beautiful melody. Happiness engulfed her, swelling from deep inside, transporting her home to a place she had longed to go, where her heart throbbed, beating strong and steady.

She rested her head on his shoulder.

He tucked a wisp of loose hair behind Mary Ann's ears.

Connor held her in a tender grip, spilling his love into her and feeling the love returned as she hugged back, embracing him. It was just the two of them now—arms wrapped around each other—slow dancing.

When the song ended, he didn't let go. They stayed in the small cleared area in front of the brightly lit jukebox.

Connor raised his head, hearing coins dropping in the coin slot on the jukebox. Displayed on the screen was "Compact Disc" in big letters on the first line, and underneath it, three lines in smaller lettering: "3 plays for $1.00, 7 plays for $2.00, 18 plays for $5.00."

The waitress made a selection, pushing the first button, "Press for Most Popular Selection." She walked by them as "Wild Horses" played again, smiling as she said in passing, "We like to keep the music going."

Epilogue
THREE MONTHS LATER

Chapter 35

IT WAS A beautiful April morning. Connor watched Tom frolic outside as he felt the warmth of the sun and smelled the freshness sprinkled by a spring shower, awakening the earth from the long cold months of hibernation. He inhaled deeply, taking in the fresh, after-rain smell.

He almost envied Tom and his carefree life. Yesterday he had taken the tabby cat to see Doc Carlson. This time, Connor knew that he didn't need to worry. Over the last few months, Tom had gradually returned to his old self—chasing butterflies, watching birds, catching mice, nibbling on blades of grass, stopping to investigate a new nook or cranny, and napping outside.

It hadn't been easy, and the two of them had struggled together. It was a hard journey—especially early on, in the dark days when he felt too depressed to come out of his shell and take care of Tom. Some days, he'd rather stay in bed, and not face the world. Tom's spirit had a lightening effect on Connor, and he returned it with affection and as much love as you can give to a cat—a member of the family.

Friday nights became date night. Connor would pick up Mary Ann, and they'd go out to dinner. More often than not, it was at Manini's.

He paid more attention to his appearance. He showered, meticulously groomed, and splashed on his favorite aftershave. A sharp dresser from years in a corporate environment, Connor had donated his expensive suits, ties, and buffed, shiny leather dress shoes before he left the city. Still sharply dressed, his new wardrobe of stylish, casual clothing accentuated the trim, muscular build underneath.

They'd check out what movies were playing in the town's only theater, which had two small screens. Connor would let Mary Ann pick the movie. He preferred action or thrillers. Although Connor wasn't into the mushy movies, he went along with her—that was what Mary Ann wanted to see. Seated, he'd take her small hand in his, his arm reaching across Mary Ann's seat to find it resting in her lap.

For years, Connor rarely went to the movies when he lived in the city. The theaters there were monstrous caverns with high ceilings and long, sloped aisles. When he had a hankering to see a first-run action blockbuster that was playing, he'd slip in the back of the theater and watch it alone. He felt swallowed up in the darkness among strangers—as if he didn't belong.

Now he couldn't wait for Friday nights. With Mary Ann by his side, Connor no longer felt alone. They belonged there, in a theater full of lovers in the dark—hands clasping, fingers entwined, shoulders touching, and the excited giggles—like they were experiencing the magic of the big screen for the first time.

Bridget Jones's Diary was one of Mary Ann's favorites. And so, when the latest film in the series came out, they went to see the movie the first night it was showing. Connor was there as Mary Ann laughed and cried her way through the romantic comedy. He glimpsed her face, lit by bright flashes of images flickering on the screen, heard her sniffles, and saw the wetness on her cheeks when she teared up. Although Connor wouldn't admit it, he found himself silently cheering for Mark Darcy.

Connor was a man used to taking charge. He had excelled in his job in the city, rising to the corporate management levels. He was still that guy—and letting Mary Ann choose movies was an act of love. Connor could no longer be selfish and insist on having his way. Nor did he want to.

They were standing in line to get the movie tickets, a few weeks later on another Friday night, when Mary Ann made a suggestion as they moved up to the ticket window. She spoke up when they reached the teller. Connor thought he had heard wrong, asking her to repeat it, but her voice was firm. The movie she chose was an action thriller, an international blockbuster with his favorite actor in the leading role.

Chapter 36

PLAYING CARDS WITH Mary Ann also became a favorite pastime, chasing away the gloom of the wintry evenings. After that first time, it became a weekly event. A tradition that started by chance and turned into a fixture in their routine. Every Sunday night. Quick to catch on, Mary Ann proved a worthy adversary. At first, he'd chalked it up to beginner's luck, but that streak kept going. More often than not, she'd beat him.

A few weeks in, one day Mary Ann casually asked him to come earlier so they could cook dinner together before the card games. Connor was pleased at this unexpected invite, and he shopped at the market to pick out the freshest fruits and vegetables. During the week, he experimented with new recipes or practiced making dishes from old ones his mother had kept in the wooden recipe box in the kitchen.

Sunday dinners became special as Connor looked forward to seeing Mary Ann. Eventually he even brought Tom, who quickly became reacquainted with Isabella. At first, there was a bit of hissing and loud meows. Isabella wasn't used to sharing her space. She held her nose in the air and acted like a prissy princess, but Tom would have none of it. He made himself at home.

The day Isabella first met Tom, Mary Ann had been invited to dinner at Connor's home and had carried her cat in her arms. Isabella had caught sight of Tom sprawled on Connor's couch in the living room. Then Tom gave a low growl, short and throaty, as Isabella slipped out of Mary Ann's grasp and leapt on the couch, landing close to his orange-striped tail as he flicked it in the air. She swiped at it, a few hairs brushing the tips of her claws. Isabella sniffed such delectable new smells—a faint masculine scent, dirt, and a bit of the wild. A strong, heady smell of someone who traveled off the beaten path.

Isabella had been an indoor cat most of her life. Used to the confines of her home, she remained content to prowl familiar territory—her paws sinking in the plush carpeting in the bedroom cushioned by countless acrylic fibers underneath; the click of her toenails as she padded her way across the cold smooth tiles of the kitchen and the hardwoods in the living room.

She was never one to get her paws dirty. After all, she was a beautiful white cat, her fur impeccably groomed.

One day, while playing cards, Mary Ann pointed toward the couch. Both of the cats were lounging on it, each taking up their space, yet a part of their bodies touched, almost overlapping like a Venn diagram. The cats were quiet, not fighting. Connor stifled a grunt and winked.

Connor stepped outside, kicking his shoes off. His feet sank into the wet blades of grass. He ran after Tom, feeling the freedom and the odd sensation of bare feet on the lawn. He skipped, turning around as he spread his arms. Connor closed his eyes and lifted his face toward the sun, seeking its warmth and energy.

If he lived in another era, Connor would be riding a horse bareback, hair blowing in the wind. Or he'd be drumming, the rhythmic pounding on the rawhide-stretched drum pulsating with the wild beating of his heart. He felt savagely free, connected with life around him—the flowers, plants, trees, wild critters, even the insects that fly or the bugs that crawl. The drops of spring rain nourished him, lifting his spirits. Raising his eyes toward the sky, he looked up to the heavens, sending a silent message to his mother. A message of love, strength, and raw desire to survive, to live.

Connor had stifled the feelings of hopelessness and despair. Fear too, of being left alone in this world, with no one to call family except for the cat. The long nights of sleeplessness as he tossed and turned in his childhood bed, watching the gentle rise and fall of Tom's chest. He felt tenderness wash over him, listening to the soft breathing of this cat curled and nestled next to him, its pink nose half-buried in the comforter. Connor's heart filled with wonder—this precious, living being, this scruffy orange tabby cat, had managed to show him what love is without uttering a single word.

It had been almost a month of April showers, bringing forth life in the world around them. May was around the corner. The stirring outside awakened Connor's dormant heart. Opening his heart to feel, to love, baring it to emotions he had clamped down. Two sides of a coin. Love and pain. Baring his heart and soul would mean risking it all, opening it to loss, hurt, and pain.

Time hadn't erased the pain and grief he felt after the death of his mother. It had eased, but it had never gone.

He turned and walked slowly back home, pausing in the doorway. Sunlight beamed on the bare wooden floors and brightened the living room. In the distance, he heard the birds singing. Their caws belting loudly, wings flapping fearless and high over the treetops. As if they were calling him, urging him to join them in living.

Chapter 37

THEY HAD DINNER with family and friends last night. Mary Ann had made it clear to her mother that her stepfather wasn't invited. Her mother had made the trip alone. Connor had invited his best friend, Mark, from the city to spend the weekend. They had met at the community college, shortly after Connor moved to the city, and kept in touch after they graduated and found jobs. Mark had brought his younger sister, Deb. Mary Ann took an instant liking to her. They quickly became friends, chatting away as if they'd known each other forever.

Mary Ann glanced at the alarm clock next to her bed, before jumping in the shower and getting dressed. Connor would be here soon to pick her up for the short drive to the cemetery to pay their respects to his parents. She had made two bouquets of spring flowers to place at their graves. Mary Ann quickly applied a dash of eyeshadow, using a new shade of violet she'd just bought. She didn't fiddle with her hair, leaving it down to be styled later.

Chapter 38

THE GARDEN WAS transformed into a magical place of beauty for the late-afternoon event. Sparkling lights were strung among the trees. The patio area was decorated with lights and lanterns, and dotted with tables covered with white tablecloths with a strip of burlap running down the middle. Glass vases of colorful spring wildflowers, hand-picked and fresh, decorated each table, each floral centerpiece a beautiful creation of nature's art that rested next to scented candles.

An area was cleared in the middle for the dance. Speakers had been erected overlooking the patio, with a table for the DJ.

Alongside the patio, a row of tables was lined up for the food and drinks. Manini's catered the food—*Calamari Fritti*, *Eggplant Parmigiana*, *Linguini Clams*, and salads. Wild Horses Roadside Café catered the dessert. Homemade brownies, thick double chocolate with vanilla ice cream.

The wedding cake was a special creation inspired by a recipe from Connor's mom: layered with berries inside, a luscious buttercream icing wrapped the round cake, topped with fresh fruit and sprigs of green leaves.

Ice-filled tall glassware held drinks: a Shirley Temple with lemon-lime soda and a splash of grenadine, or a Mojito with fresh lime juice, garnished with mint leaves and lime wedges.

A walkway connected the patio to a grassy area, surrounded by trees and flowers. An arch stood erected at the beginning of the path. Its latticed wood intertwined with beautiful blossoms and green vines. Pink rose petals were scattered along the pathway from the arch to the patio. The scent of flowers fragranced the air.

Connor stood by the arch as he waited with Pastor Maller, facing the seated guests as the flute and violin music played. In the front row sat Mary Ann's mom, Eva Maller, Mrs. Dottie Rainer and Alana. Behind them sat Norma and Stan and their kids, Mrs. Steele, Doc Carlson, and Mark and Deb. Mikey and Sally and their two boys and even Dale Williams, Mr. Monroe and Ron were also present, sitting among other invited guests.

Connor looked sharp in a tux, his slim body fit and lean. A boutonniere was pinned on the lapel. His heart beat faster in anticipation of seeing Mary Ann any minute now, as the music changed to the *Wedding March*.

She looked radiant, wearing a flower crown in her long, flowing hair and dressed in a white lace, floral print dress. Mary Ann walked slowly down the path, carrying a beautiful bridal bouquet.

Mary Ann and Connor were united on a gorgeous day, favored by a warm, bright sun, a clear blue sky, the caress of a gentle spring breeze, and the chirping of songbirds. As the beaming Pastor Maller pronounced them husband and wife, he said, "You may kiss."

Champagne glasses were raised in toast as the wedding party moved to the reception in the garden. As the happy couple, Mr. and Mrs. Connor Norton, mingled among the guests celebrating and laughing, Tom and Isabella frisked and frolicked together in the garden.

Author's note

I hope you've enjoyed the *Flowers in December Trilogy.*

Thanks for sharing Connor and Mary Ann's journey to find their happily ever after!

Entering her second season in the North American Hockey League, Sophie Fournier sets her expectations high. The Concord Condors will make the playoffs for the first time in franchise history. They have the veteran core to do it and the new talent to give them the extra push.

From the beginning, things don't go according to plan. The season begins without one of their best players, and they lose others to injury and trades as the season progresses. Hockey is a team sport, and Sophie can't drag them to the playoffs on her own. Is her voice loud enough to convince her team to believe the way she does?